PENGUIN CLASSICS

PENGUIN SELECTED ENGLISH POETS
GENERAL EDITOR: CHRISTOPHER RICKS

JONATHAN SWIFT: SELECTED POEMS

Jonathan Swift was born in Dublin in 1667 after his father's death. He was educated at Kilkenny Grammar School and at Trinity College, Dublin, where he was censured for offences against discipline and had to obtain his degree by 'special grace'. Throughout his life, his ferocity was to alienate many people, but at the same time he counted among his close friends several distinguished men, notably Bolingbroke and Pope. Swift was ordained in Ireland in 1695 and was given a prebend at St Patrick's, Dublin, where he was later made Dean. An ardent pacifist who loathed cruelty, imperialism and war, he wrote many pamphlets on religion and war and during the course of frequent visits to London did much to try and improve the political situation in Ireland. His loyalties were initially with the Whigs, but he was disgusted at their alliance with dissent in 1710 and went over to the Tories, attacking Whig ministers in *The Examiner*, which he edited. The details of his daily life in London are recounted in a series of intimate letters to Esther Johnson, published as *Journal to Stella*. He was also very close to Esther Vanhomrigh, whom he met in 1708, and his final rupture with her in about 1723 may have hastened her death. The story of their love affair is related in Swift's poem 'Cadenus and Vanessa'. Swift's masterpiece, *Gulliver's Travels*, appeared in 1726. It was an overnight success, but soon triggered heated debate, and to this day it has remained extremely controversial. *Gulliver's Travels* was the only one of his publications for which Swift received any payment (£200) and, like much of his work, it was published anonymously. Throughout his life Swift suffered from a form of vertigo, and his illness became very marked in about 1738. As a result of his increasing dementia, he was declared 'of unsound mind' in 1742 and guardians were appointed to manage his affairs. He died in 1745.

Pat Rogers is DeBartolo Professor in the Liberal Arts at the University of South Florida. He was educated at Cambridge, where he gained a double first in English and went on to obtain a Ph.D. and Litt.D. He has held teaching posts at the universities of Cambridge, London, Wales and Bristol. His books include *Grub Street* (1972), *The Augustan Vision* (1974), *Eighteenth-Century Encounters* (1985) and *Literature and Popular Culture in Eighteenth-Century England* (1985), as well as works on Swift, Pope, Defoe, Fielding and Johnson. He is editor of *The Oxford Illustrated History of English Literature* (1987) and advisory editor of *The Blackwell Companion to the Enlightenment* (1992). He has also edited Swift's *Complete Poems*, Joshua Reynolds's *Discourses* and Daniel Defoe's *A Tour through the Whole Island of Great Britain* for Penguin Classics.

Jonathan Swift

Selected Poems

**EDITED WITH AN INTRODUCTION
BY PAT ROGERS**

PENGUIN BOOKS

PENGUIN BOOKS

Published by the Penguin Group
Penguin Books Ltd, 27 Wrights Lane, London w8 5TZ, England
Penguin Books USA Inc., 375 Hudson Street, New York, New York 10014, USA
Penguin Books Australia Ltd, Ringwood, Victoria, Australia
Penguin Books Canada Ltd, 10 Alcorn Avenue, Toronto, Ontario, Canada M4V 3B2
Penguin Books (NZ) Ltd, 182–190 Wairau Road, Auckland 10, New Zealand

Penguin Books Ltd, Registered Offices: Harmondsworth, Middlesex, England

First published 1993
10 9 8 7 6 5 4 3 2 1

Typeset by DatIX International Ltd, Bungay, Suffolk
Set in 10/11½ pt Monophoto Ehrhardt
Printed in England by Clays Ltd, St Ives plc

To the people of Woodland Road

Contents

Contents

Introduction ix
Table of Dates xiii
Further Reading xvii

Verses Wrote in a Lady's Ivory Table-book 1
The Humble Petition of Frances Harris 2
The Description of a Salamander 5
Baucis and Philemon 7
A Description of the Morning 12
The Virtues of Sid Hamet the Magician's Rod 13
A Description of a City Shower 15
An Excellent New Song 17
Cadenus and Vanessa 19
Horace, Epistle VII, Book I: Imitated and Addressed to the Earl
    of Oxford 43
The Author upon Himself 47
Horace, Lib. 2, Sat. 6 49
Mary the Cook-maid's Letter to Dr Sheridan 52
Stella's Birthday [1719] 54
The Progress of Beauty 54
To Stella, Who Collected and Transcribed His Poems 58
Upon the South Sea Project 62
Stella's Birthday [1721] 69
The Part of a Summer 70
The Progress of Marriage 74
A Satirical Elegy on the Death of a Late Famous General 78
Upon the Horrid Plot Discovered by Harlequin the Bishop of
    Rochester's French Dog 79
Stella's Birthday [1723] 82
To Charles Ford, Esq. on His Birthday 84
Pethox the Great 87
To Stella. Written on the Day of Her Birth 90

Prometheus 91
Stella's Birthday [1725] 93
A Receipt to Restore Stella's Youth 95
To Quilca 97
A Pastoral Dialogue between Richmond Lodge and Marble
    Hill 97
The Furniture of a Woman's Mind 101
Holyhead. September 25, 1727 103
The Journal of a Modern Lady 104
The Grand Question Debated 112
A Libel on the Reverend Dr Delany and His Excellency John,
    Lord Carteret 118
Death and Daphne 123
An Excellent New Ballad 126
The Lady's Dressing Room 129
A Beautiful Young Nymph Going to Bed 133
Strephon and Chloe 135
Cassinus and Peter 143
To Mr Gay 147
Verses on the Death of Dr Swift, D.S.P.D. 152
On the Day of Judgement 165
On Poetry: a Rhapsody 166
To a Lady 181
A Character, Panegyric, and Description of the Legion Club 189

Notes 197
Index of Titles 219
Index of First Lines 221

Introduction

Most of what Swift said about himself as a writer, in prose or in verse, was wilfully misleading. It could be flippant or disingenuous, teasing or prevaricating – but it never told the whole truth. Once or twice, however, almost (it seems) in spite of himself or (more likely) to spite the world, he deviates into an honest claim:

> Had he but spared his tongue and pen,
> He might have rose like other men . . .
> (*Verses on the Death of Dr Swift*, 359–60)

Assuredly, Swift made more enemies than friends through his poetry. It is nearly all in a deep sense oppositional: it unsettles our stock ideas, it affronts established values, it carries round its own canister of salt looking for open wounds. A primary aim of this selection is to present what has been called 'the refractory Swift', because that is the condition to which most of his best writing aspires.

This leads us to a second principle of selection. I have not tried to show all of Swift's moods and phases, but Swift at his strongest as a poet. By the most rigorous statistical tests, this must produce a case of skewed samples; but statistics is a pretty dismal science for establishing literary merit, and readers who wish for an equal scan of the entire career can always read every third item in the complete works. The judgements underlying my own inclusions can be defined by looking at the categories of poem excluded.

Few of the early poems are to be found in this selection. Swift wrote a number of ambitious Pindaric odes in the 1690s, and these included some of the longest poems he ever wrote. They do not constitute juvenilia in the ordinary sense, for Swift was well into his middle twenties when he composed them. If he had died at the same age as Keats or even Shelley, he would have left not a single line to survive in the collective memory. These works touch on significant issues of the day, and they embody a painfully intense effort to find a voice; but they are forced and overworked, like the teenage effusions of others. Beside the amazingly powerful and controlled wit of *A Tale of a Tub*, written around the same date, they are slender achievements.

Another category of omissions includes almost everything that Swift wrote by the way of riddle, rebus and word-game. Although linguistic play was a lifelong diversion for Swift, and made its contribution to the absurd names in *Gulliver's Travels*, it cannot be said that the laborious versions of the conundrums so much enjoyed by Swift and his friends travel well into the twentieth century. One exception (therefore included here) is 'Pethox the Great', an extended riddle which shows invention and *brio*. Many of the other poems in this category take the form of brief personal messages between Swift and his punning allies, notably Thomas Sheridan. They bear some resemblance to the facetious interoffice memoranda sometimes shuttled around large corporations today. A student of Swift's mental pathology may need to peruse them, but for a lover of literature there are many better choices.

Swift wrote a large number of occasional poems and, with the exception of the birthday poems to Stella, they seldom rise much above the occasion. Their omission here leads to an under-representation of short poems, but Swift needed space to produce his best effects, particularly in the later part of his career. I have retained a few political broadsides which are kept fresh by the sharpness of Swift's venom and the irresistible energy with which he secretes his bile; one poem, the 'satirical elegy' on the death of the Duke of Marlborough, escapes from the category of occasional verse. It follows once more that this selection gives a less than faithful picture of Swift's poetic activity in that it contains a smaller proportion of verses on short-lived Irish quarrels than does the full poetic *œuvre*. Most of the poems surrounding the affair of Wood's coinage are omitted, since Swift found a far more suitable vehicle in the prose of his *Drapier's Letters*. Again this apparent imbalance is an inevitable consequence of seeking out the poems which display Swift at his most trenchant and least parochial.

Other categories, though covered to some degree, have less than their strict numerical due. These include the relaxed and amusing poems in the Market Hill series, written to one of Swift's most agreeable patrons, Lady Acheson. Their quality can be properly weighed by considering 'The Grand Question Debated', which is included here. About the same time Swift was writing some coarse and abrasive satires on his enemies, notably those attacking the Irish politician Richard Tighe; whatever credit these may do to Swift's patriotic concern for the welfare of the Irish people, they do not advance his reputation as a poet.

To sum up, this selection concentrates on the most substantial poems, and those which are least tied up in personal animosities or private diversions. This means an emphasis on longer works; on the later poetry, especially that written in the years surrounding 1730; on items with a marked literary heritage, as opposed to the relatively unmediated idiom of praise and abuse found in the occasional poems; and on pieces which outdo their prose equivalents, where there is such an equivalent. This has allowed ample space for major poems, not just the famous *Verses on the Death of Dr Swift* and the scandalous or scatological group, but also the demotic energy of 'Mrs Harris's Petition', the terse drama of 'On the Day of Judgement' and the elegant travesties and transformations, such as 'Baucis and Philemon'. When all the retrenchments have been made, there is an abundance of considerable poetry left to charm, provoke and tease us.

This is a modernized text, and the process has been carried out in a thoroughgoing manner. Spelling, punctuation and typography are all brought into the modern conventional form; thus, italics are preserved only where we should use them today, for the sake of emphasis (rather than signalizing a proper noun or indicating a quotation, as often in the original). In those cases where a given item was included in the edition of Swift's *Works* produced by George Faulkner in 1735, this has been the basis of the text, since all round it is the most reliable version we have. Another edition with some claim to authority is the volume of *Miscellanies* issued by Benjamin Tooke (working through the 'trade publisher' John Morphew) in 1711; I have taken note of its readings in appropriate cases, but the 1735 text is usually more authoritative. The most important modern edition is that of Harold Williams (1937 and 1958), which supplies a wealth of information on textual matters. Williams was perhaps slightly less successful in his annotations, and the notes to each poem at the end of this selection have been able to profit from considerable advances in Swiftian scholarship since Williams prepared his edition. The aim of the notes is to provide basic facts in a short space, firstly on the composition and publication of the poem, and secondly on its themes, ideas, rhetorical workings and patterns of allusion. Swift is a highly referential poet, and to get the most from him we must be ready to follow the tracks of his mind across literature, history, mythology and the life of his time.

The poems are printed in order of composition, so far as this can be established. Fuller discussion of dating problems and publishing history will be found in *Jonathan Swift: The Complete Poems* (Penguin, 1983).

An accent is marked on the stressed syllable where it is different from that found today, e.g. stágnate.

Table of Dates

1667   March or April: Swift's father dies.
        30 November: Swift born in Dublin.
1673   Enters Kilkenny School.
1682   April: Admitted to Trinity College, Dublin.
1686   Graduates BA 'by special grace', with moderate aca-
        demic record.
1689   Leaves Trinity College and moves to Moor Park,
        Surrey, as secretary to Sir William Temple;
        there meets the eight-year-old Esther Johnson
        ('Stella').
1690   First symptoms of Ménière's disease, causing lifelong
        fits of giddiness, deafness and other discomforts.
1690–91 First surviving poem, 'Ode to the King', written.
1692   Proceeds to Oxford MA as step to ordination.
1695   13 January: Ordained priest in Dublin.
        28 January: Presented to prebend of Kilroot, on the
        shore of Belfast Lough. Spends an unhappy year at
        Kilroot before returning to Moor Park.
1697–8 At work on *A Tale of a Tub*.
1699   27 January: Death of Temple.
        August: Travels to Dublin as chaplain to the Earl of
        Berkeley, Lord Justice of Ireland.
1700   20 February: Presented to living of Laracor, near Trim
        (Co. Meath).
        22 October: Installed as prebend of St Patrick's
        Cathedral, Dublin.
1701   April: Berkeley, dismissed as Lord Justice, returns to
        England; Swift goes with him.
        August: Esther Johnson emigrates to Dublin; Swift
        follows with the new Lord Lieutenant a month
        later.
1702   16 February: DD, Trinity College, Dublin.

1704   10 May: At the end of another period in England, publishes *A Tale of a Tub*.

1707–9   Back in England as emissary of the Irish clergy; in contact with Addison, Steele and other literary men.

1708   *Bickerstaff Papers*.

1709   Inception of *The Tatler* by Steele (runs 271 numbers to 1711); Swift contributes several items.

1710   August: Whig ministry forced out of office and Tories, led by Harley and Bolingbroke, replace them.

            September: Swift comes to England and begins *Journal to Stella*. Writes on behalf of the Tory ministry (33 numbers of *The Examiner* from 2 November to 14 June 1711).

1711   27 February: Publication of first authorized collection, *Miscellanies in Prose and Verse*.

            27 November: First edition of the hugely successful pamphlet, *The Conduct of the Allies*.

1712   Friendship with Addison and Steele cooling fast, for political reasons.

1713   13 June: Installed as Dean of St Patrick's in the course of a rapid visit to Ireland.

            Probable first meeting of Swift and Pope, who form the Scriblerus group with Gay, Arbuthnot and Parnell. Swift enjoys close relations with the leading Tory ministers.

1714   1 August: Death of Queen Anne, and ministerial crisis which sees fall of the Tories; Swift leaves immediately for Dublin and takes up permanent residence in Ireland.

            November: Esther Vanhomrigh ('Vanessa'), who had made Swift's acquaintance in London, moves to Ireland.

1720   April or May: Publication of *A Proposal for the Universal Use of Irish Manufacture*, declared seditious for its criticism of English economic policy towards Ireland.

1721   Working on *Gulliver's Travels*.

1723   June: Death of Vanessa. Atterbury affair comes to a head.

1724–5   Publication of *The Drapier's Letters* (first letter in March).

1726   March–August: Visits England, spends much time in company with Pope, and prepares for publication of *Gulliver's Travels* (28 October).

1727   April–September: Final visit to England, again staying with Pope at Twickenham. The joint *Miscellanies* begin to appear (24 June).

1728   28 January: Death of Stella.

         7 March: The 'last' volume of *Miscellanies* containing many poems by Swift.

1729   October: Publication of *A Modest Proposal*.

1731   November: Probable composition of *Verses on the Death of Dr Swift*, published in 1739.

1732   October: Another volume of Pope–Swift *Miscellanies*.

         4 December: Death of Gay.

1734–5   Publication of four volumes of collected works in Dublin, issued by George Faulkner under the supervision of Swift.

1738   Spring: Publication of *Polite Conversation*.

1742   August: Found 'of unsound mind and memory', and guardians appointed to manage his affairs; his condition was caused by Ménière's disease and senility.

1744   30 May: Death of Pope.

1745   19 October: Death of Swift; buried in St Patrick's alongside Stella; bequeathed money to found hospital for the insane.

Further Reading

EDITIONS

The Poems of Jonathan Swift, ed. Harold Williams (Oxford, 2nd edn, 1958), 3 vols. The standard edition.

Jonathan Swift: The Complete Poems, ed. Pat Rogers (Harmondsworth and New Haven, 1983).

OTHER WORKS

The Prose Works of Jonathan Swift, ed. Herbert Davis et al. (Oxford, 1939–68), 14 vols.

The Correspondence of Jonathan Swift, ed. Harold Williams (Oxford, 1963–5), 5 vols.

Journal to Stella, ed. Harold Williams (Oxford, 1948), 2 vols. Throws light on Swift's activity as a poet, 1710–13.

BIOGRAPHY

Irvin Ehrenpreis, *Swift: The Man, His Works, and the Age* (London, 1962–83), 3 vols. The fullest and critically most incisive biography.

David Nokes, *Jonathan Swift: A Hypocrite Reversed* (Oxford, 1985). One of the best one-volume lives.

CRITICISM

Jonathan Swift: A Critical Anthology, ed. Denis Donoghue (Harmondsworth, 1971).

Ellen Pollak, *The Poetics of Sexual Myth: Gender and Ideology in the Verse of Swift and Pope* (Chicago, 1985).

Essential Articles for the Study of Jonathan Swift's Poetry, ed. David M. Vieth (Hamden, Connecticut, 1985).

Swift: The Critical Heritage, ed. Kathleen Williams (London, 1970).

Verses Wrote in a Lady's Ivory Table-book

Peruse my leaves through every part,
And think thou seest my owner's heart;
Scrawled o'er with trifles thus; and quite
As hard, as senseless, and as light:
Exposed to every coxcomb's eyes,
But hid with caution from the wise.
Here may you read, 'Dear charming saint',
Beneath 'A new receipt for paint'.
Here, in beau-spelling, 'tru tel death'.
There, in her own, 'far an el breath'.
Here, 'lovely nymph pronounce my doom'.
There, 'a safe way to use perfume'.
Here, a page filled with billet-doux;
On t'other side, 'laid out for shoes.
(Madam, I die without your Grace.)
Item, for half a yard of lace.'
Who that had wit would place it here,
For every peeping fop to jeer?
In power of spittle and a clout,
Whene'er he please, to blot it out;
And then to heighten the disgrace,
Clap his own nonsense in the place.
Who'er expects to hold his part
In such a book, and such a heart,
If he be wealthy, and a fool,
Is in all points the fittest tool;
Of whom it may be justly said,
He's a *gold* pencil tipped with *lead*.

The Humble Petition of Frances Harris

To their Excellencies the Lords Justices of Ireland.
The humble petition of Frances Harris,
Who must starve, and die a maid if it miscarries.

Humbly showeth

That I went to warm myself in Lady Betty's chamber,
    because I was cold,
And I had in a purse seven pound, four shillings and
    sixpence (besides farthings) in money and gold;
So because I had been buying things for my Lady last night,
I was resolved to tell my money, to see if it was right.
Now you must know, because my trunk has a very bad lock,
Therefore all the money I have (which, God knows, is a
    very small stock)
I keep in my pocket tied about my middle, next my smock.
So, when I went to put up my purse, as God would have it,
    my smock was unripped;
And, instead of putting it into my pocket, down it slipped:
10 Then the bell rung, and I went down to put my Lady to bed;
And, God knows, I thought my money was as safe as my
    maidenhead.
So, when I came up again, I found my pocket feel very light,
But when I searched, and missed my purse, Lord! I thought
    I should have sunk outright:
Lord! 'Madam,' says Mary, 'how d'ye do?' 'Indeed,' said I,
    'never worse;
But pray, Mary, can you tell what I have done with my
    purse?'
'Lord help me,' said Mary, 'I never stirred out of this place!'
'Nay,' said I, 'I had it in Lady Betty's chamber, that's a
    plain case.'
So Mary got me to bed, and covered me up warm,
However, she stole away my garters, that I might do myself
    no harm.

20   So I tumbled and tossed all night, as you may very well think;
      But hardly ever set my eyes together, or slept a wink.
      So I was a-dreamed, methought, that we went and searched
          the folks round;
      And in a corner of Mrs Dukes's box, tied in a rag, the
          money was found.
      So next morning we told Whittle, and he fell a-swearing;
      Then my Dame Wadgar came, and she, you know, is thick
          of hearing:
      'Dame,' said I, as loud as I could bawl, 'do you know what
          a loss I have had?'
      'Nay,' said she, 'my Lord Collway's folks are all very sad,
      For my Lord Dromedary comes a Tuesday without fail';
      'Pugh,' said I, 'but that's not the business that I ail.'
30   Says Cary, says he, 'I have been a servant this five and
          twenty years, come spring,
      And in all the places I lived, I never heard of such a thing.'
      'Yes,' says the steward, 'I remember when I was at my
          Lady Shrewsbury's,
      Such a thing as this happened, just about the time of
          gooseberries.'
      So I went to the party suspected, and I found her full of grief;
      (Now you must know, of all things in the world, I hate a
          thief.)
      However, I was resolved to bring the discourse slily about,
      'Mrs Dukes,' said I, 'here's an ugly accident has happened
          out;
      'Tis not that I value the money three skips of a louse;
      But the thing I stand upon, is the credit of the house;
40   'Tis true, seven pound, four shillings, and six pence, makes
          a great hole in my wages;
      Besides, as they say, service is no inheritance in these ages.
      Now, Mrs Dukes, you know, and everybody understands,
      That though 'tis hard to judge, yet money can't go without
          hands.'
      'The Devil take me,' said she (blessing herself), 'if ever I
          saw't!'
      So she roared like a Bedlam, as though I had called her all
          to naught;

So you know, what could I say to her any more:
I e'en left her, and came away as wise as I was before.
Well: but then they would have had me gone to the
    cunning-man;
'No,' said I, ''tis the same thing, the chaplain will be here
    anon.'
50   So the chaplain came in. Now the servants say he is my
    sweetheart,
Because he's always in my chamber, and I always take his
    part;
So, as the Devil would have it, before I was aware, out I
    blundered,
'Parson,' said I, 'can you cast a nativity, when a body's
    plundered?'
(Now you must know, he hates to be called 'Parson' like the
    devil.)
'Truly,' says he, 'Mrs Nab, it might become you to be more
    civil:
If your money be gone, as a learned divine says, d'ye see,
You are no text for my handling, so take that from me;
I was never taken for a conjuror before, I'd have you to
    know.'
'Lord,' said I, 'don't be angry, I am sure I never thought
    you so;
60   You know, I honour the cloth, I design to be a parson's wife,
I never took one in your coat for a conjuror in all my life.'
With that, he twisted his girdle at me like a rope, as who
    should say,
Now you may go hang yourself for me, and so went away.
Well; I thought I should have swooned: 'Lord,' said I,
    'what shall I do?
I have lost my money; and I shall lose my true-love too.'
So, my Lord called me; 'Harry,' said my Lord, 'don't cry,
I'll give something towards thy loss;' and says my Lady, 'so
    will I.'
'Oh but,' said I, 'what if after all, the chaplain won't
    come to?'
For that, he said (an't please your Excellencies) I must
    petition you.

70   The premises tenderly considered, I desire your Excel-
         lencies' protection,
And that I may have a share in next Sunday's collection:
And over and above, that I may have your Excellencies' letter,
With an order for the chaplain aforesaid; or instead of him,
     a better.
And then your poor petitioner, both night and day,
Or the chaplain (for 'tis his trade) as in duty bound, shall
     ever pray.

The Description of a Salamander

OUT OF PLINY'S NAT. HIST. LIB. 10 C. 67 AND LIB. 29 C. 4

As mastiff dogs in modern phrase are
Called Pompey, Scipio, and Caesar;
As pies and daws are often styled
With Christian nicknames like a child;
As we say 'Monsieur' to an ape
Without offence to human shape:
So men have got from bird and brute
Names that would best their natures suit:
The lion, eagle, fox and boar
10   Were heroes' titles heretofore,
Bestowed as hieroglyphics fit
To show their valour, strength or wit.
For what is understood by fame
Besides the getting of a name?
But e'er since men invented guns,
A different way their fancy runs:
To paint a hero, we inquire
For something that will conquer fire.
Would you describe Turenne or Trump,
20   Think of a bucket or a pump.
Are these too low? Then find out grander,
Call my Lord Cutts a salamander.
'Tis well: but since we live among
Detractors with an evil tongue,

Who may object against the term,
Pliny shall prove what we affirm:
Pliny shall prove, and we'll apply,
And I'll be judged by standers-by.

First then, our author has defined
30   This reptile, of the serpent kind,
With gaudy coat, and shining train,
But loathsome spots his body stain:
Out from some hole obscure he flies
When rains descend, and tempests rise,
Till the sun clears the air; and then
Crawls back, neglected, to his den.

So when the war has raised a storm
I've seen a snake in human form,
All stained with infamy and vice,
40   Leap from the dunghill in a trice;
Burnish and make a gaudy show,
Become a general, peer and beau,
Till peace hath made the sky serene,
Then shrink into its hole again.

All this we grant – why, then look yonder,
Sure that must be a salamander!

Farther we are by Pliny told,
This serpent is extremely cold;
So cold, that put it in the fire,
50   'Twill make the very flames expire:
Besides, it spews a filthy froth,
(Whether through rage, or lust, or both)
Of matter purulent and white,
Which happening on the skin to light,
And there corrupting to a wound,
Spreads leprosy and baldness round.

So have I seen a battered beau
By age and claps grown cold as snow,
Whose breath or touch, where'er he came,
60   Blew out love's torch, or chilled the flame:

And should some nymph who ne'er was cruel,
Like Carleton cheap, or famed Du Ruel,
Receive the filth which he ejects;
She soon would find the same effects,
Her tainted carcass to pursue,
As from the salamander's spew:
A dismal shedding of her locks
And, if no leprosy, a pox.

    Then I'll appeal to each bystander,
70   If this be not a salamander?

Baucis and Philemon

IMITATED FROM THE EIGHTH BOOK OF OVID

In ancient times, as story tells,
The saints would often leave their cells,
And stroll about, but hide their quality,
To try good people's hospitality.

    It happened on a winter night,
(As authors of the legend write)
Two brother hermits, saints by trade,
Taking their tour in masquerade,
Disguised in tattered habits, went
10   To a small village down in Kent;
Where, in the stroller's canting strain,
They begged from door to door in vain;
Tried every tone might pity win,
But not a soul would let them in.

    Our wandering saints in woeful state,
Treated at this ungodly rate,
Having through all the village passed,
To a small cottage came at last;
Where dwelt a good old honest yeoman,
20   Called in the neighbourhood, Philemon.

Who kindly did the saints invite
In his poor hut to pass the night;
And then the hospitable sire
Bid Goody Baucis mend the fire;
While he from out the chimney took
A flitch of bacon off the hook;
And freely from the fattest side,
Cut out large slices to be fried:
Then stepped aside to fetch 'em drink,
30 Filled a large jug up to the brink;
And saw it fairly twice go round;
Yet (what was wonderful) they found
'Twas still replenished to the top,
As if they ne'er had touched a drop.
The good old couple was amazed,
And often on each other gazed:
For both were frighted to the heart,
And just began to cry, 'What art!'
Then softly turned aside to view,
40 Whether the lights were burning blue.
The gentle pilgrims soon aware on't,
Told them their calling, and their errand:
'Good folks, you need not be afraid,
We are but saints,' the hermits said;
'No hurt shall come to you, or yours;
But, for that pack of churlish boors,
Not fit to live on Christian ground,
They and their houses shall be drowned:
Whilst you shall see your cottage rise,
50 And grow a church before your eyes.'

They scarce had spoke; when fair and soft
The roof began to mount aloft;
Aloft rose every beam and rafter;
The heavy wall climbed slowly after.

The chimney widened, and grew higher,
Became a steeple with a spire.

The kettle to the top was hoist,
And there stood fastened to a joist:
But with the upside down, to show
60   Its inclination for below;
In vain; for some superior force
Applied at bottom, stops its course,
Doomed ever in suspense to dwell,
'Tis now no kettle, but a bell.

A wooden jack, which had almost
Lost, by disuse, the art to roast,
A sudden alteration feels,
Increased by new intestine wheels:
And what exalts the wonder more,
70   The number made the motion slower,
The flier, which though't had leaden feet,
Turned round so quick you scarce could see't;
Now slackened by some secret power,
Can hardly move an inch an hour.
The jack and chimney, near allied,
Had never left each other's side;
The chimney to a steeple grown,
The jack would not be left alone;
But up against the steeple reared,
80   Became a clock, and still adhered:
And still its love to household cares
By a shrill voice at noon declares,
Warning the cook-maid not to burn
That roast meat which it cannot turn.

The groaning chair was seen to crawl,
Like an huge snail half up the wall;
There stuck aloft, in public view;
And with small change, a pulpit grew.

The porringers, that in a row
90   Hung high, and made a glittering show,
To a less noble substance changed,
Were now but leathern buckets, ranged.

The ballads pasted on the wall,
Of Joan of France, and English Moll,
Fair Rosamund, and Robin Hood,
'The little children in the wood':
Now seemed to look abundance better,
Improved in picture, size, and letter;
And high in order placed describe
100   The heraldry of every tribe.

A bedstead of the antique mode,
Compact of timber many a load;
Such as our grandsires wont to use,
Was metamorphosed into pews;
Which still their ancient nature keep,
By lodging folks disposed to sleep.

The cottage by such feats as these,
Grown to a church by just degrees;
The hermits then desire their host
110   To ask for what he fancied most.
Philemon having paused a while,
Returned 'em thanks in homely style;
Then said, 'My house is grown so fine,
Methinks I still would call it mine:
I'm old, and fain would live at ease,
Make me the parson, if you please.'

He spoke, and presently he feels
His grazier's coat fall down his heels;
He sees, yet hardly can believe,
120   About each arm a pudding-sleeve:
His waistcoat to a cassock grew,
And both assumed a sable hue;
But being old, continued just
As threadbare, and as full of dust.
His talk was now of tithes and dues:
Could smoke his pipe, and read the news;
Knew how to preach old sermons next,
Vamped in the preface and the text;

At christening well could act his part,
130 And had the service all by heart:
Wished women might have children fast,
And thought whose sow had farrowed last:
Against dissenters would repine,
And stood up firm for right divine:
Found his head filled with many a system,
But classic authors – he ne'er missed 'em.

Thus having furbished up a parson,
Dame Baucis next they played their farce on:
Instead of homespun coifs were seen
140 Good pinners edged with colbertine:
Her petticoat transformed apace,
Became black satin, flounced with lace.
Plain Goody would no longer down;
'Twas Madam, in her grogram gown.
Philemon was in great surprise,
And hardly could believe his eyes;
Amazed to see her look so prim:
And she admired as much at him.

Thus, happy in their change of life,
150 Were several years the man and wife:
When on a day, which proved their last,
Discoursing o'er old stories past,
They went by chance, amidst their talk,
To the churchyard, to fetch a walk;
When Baucis hastily cried out,
'My dear, I see your forehead sprout!'
'Sprout,' quoth the man, 'what's this you tell us?
I hope you don't believe me jealous:
But yet, methinks, I feel it true;
160 And really yours is budding too –
Nay – now I cannot stir my foot:
It feels as if 'twere taking root.'

Description would but tire my muse:
In short, they both were turned to yews.

Old Goodman Dobson, of the Green,
Remembers he the trees has seen;
He'll talk of them from noon to night,
And goes with folks to show the sight;
On Sundays, after evening prayer,
170   He gathers all the parish there;
Points out the place of either yew;
Here Baucis, there Philemon grew:
Till once, a parson of our town,
To mend his barn, cut Baucis down;
At which, 'tis hard to be believed,
How much the other tree was grieved:
Grew scrubby, died a-top, was stunted:
So, the next parson stubbed and burnt it.

A Description of the Morning

Now hardly here and there a hackney coach
Appearing, showed the ruddy morn's approach.
Now Betty from her master's bed has flown,
And softly stole to discompose her own.
The slipshod prentice from his master's door
Had pared the dirt, and sprinkled round the floor.
Now Moll had whirled her mop with dexterous airs,
Prepared to scrub the entry and the stairs.
The youth with broomy stumps began to trace
10   The kennel-edge, where wheels had worn the place.
The smallcoal man was heard with cadence deep;
Till drowned in shriller notes of chimney-sweep.
Duns at his Lordship's gate began to meet;
And Brickdust Moll had screamed through half a street.
The turnkey now his flock returning sees,
Duly let out a-nights to steal for fees.
The watchful bailiffs take their silent stands;
And schoolboys lag with satchels in their hands.

The Virtues of Sid Hamet the Magician's Rod

The rod was but a harmless wand,
While Moses held it in his hand;
But soon as e'er he laid it down,
'Twas a devouring serpent grown.

Our great magician, Hamet Sid,
Reverses what the prophet did:
His rod was honest English wood,
That senseless in a corner stood,
Till metamorphosed by his grasp,
It grew an all-devouring asp;
Would hiss and sting, and roll, and twist,
By the mere virtue of his fist:
But when he laid it down, as quick
Resumed the figure of a stick.

So to her midnight feasts the hag
Rides on a broomstick for a nag,
That raised by magic of her breech,
O'er land and sea conveys the witch:
But with the morning dawn resumes
The peaceful state of common brooms.

They tell us something strange and odd,
About a certain magic rod,
That bending down its top divines
Whene'er the soil has golden mines:
Where there are none, it stands erect,
Scorning to show the least respect.
As ready was the wand of Sid
To bend where golden mines were hid;
In Scottish hills found precious ore,
Where none e'er looked for it before:
And by a gentle bow divined
How well a cully's purse was lined:
To a forlorn and broken rake,
Stood without motion, like a stake.

The rod of Hermes was renowned
For charms above and under ground;
To sleep could mortal eyelids fix,
And drive departed souls to Styx.
That rod was just a type of Sid's,
40   Which o'er a British senate's lids
Could scatter opium full as well,
And drive as many souls to hell.

Sid's rod was slender, white, and tall,
Which oft he used to fish withal:
A *place* was fastened to the hook,
And many a score of gudgeons took;
Yet, still so happy was his fate,
He caught his fish, and saved his bait.

Sid's brethren of the conjuring tribe
50   A circle with their rod describe,
Which proves a magical redoubt,
To keep mischievous spirits out:
Sid's rod was of a larger stride,
And made a circle thrice as wide;
Where spirits thronged with hideous din,
And he stood there to take them in.
But, when the enchanted rod was broke,
They vanished in a stinking smoke.

Achilles' sceptre was of wood,
60   Like Sid's, but nothing near so good:
Though down from ancestors divine,
Transmitted to the hero's line,
Thence, through a long descent of kings,
Came an heirloom, as Homer sings,
Though this description looks so big,
That sceptre was a sapless twig;
Which, from the fatal day when first
It left the forest where 'twas nursed,
As Homer tells us o'er and o'er,
70   Nor leaf, nor fruit, nor blossom bore.

Sid's sceptre, full of juice, did shoot
In golden boughs, and golden fruit;
And he, the dragon never sleeping,
Guarded each fair Hesperian pippin.
No hobbyhorse, with gorgeous top,
The dearest in Charles Mather's shop,
Or glittering tinsel of May Fair,
Could with this rod of Sid's compare.

 Dear Sid, then why wert thou so mad
80 To break thy rod like naughty lad?
You should have kissed it in your distress,
And then returned it to your mistress;
Or made it a Newmarket switch,
And not a rod for thy own breech.
But since old Sid has broken this,
His next may be a rod in piss.

A Description of a City Shower

Careful observers may foretell the hour
(By sure prognostics) when to dread a shower.
While rain depends, the pensive cat gives o'er
Her frolics, and pursues her tail no more.
Returning home at night you find the sink
Strike your offended sense with double stink.
If you be wise, then go not far to dine,
You spend in coach-hire more than save in wine.
A coming shower your shooting corns presage,
10 Old aches throb, your hollow tooth will rage:
Sauntering in coffee-house is Dulman seen;
He damns the climate, and complains of spleen.

 Meanwhile the south, rising with dabbled wings,
A sable cloud athwart the welkin flings;
That swilled more liquor than it could contain,
And like a drunkard gives it up again.

Brisk Susan whips her linen from the rope,
While the first drizzling shower is born aslope:
Such is that sprinkling which some careless quean
20   Flirts on you from her mop, but not so clean:
You fly, invoke the gods; then turning, stop
To rail; she singing, still whirls on her mop.
Nor yet the dust had shunned the unequal strife,
But aided by the wind, fought still for life;
And wafted with its foe by violent gust,
'Twas doubtful which was rain, and which was dust.
Ah! where must needy poet seek for aid,
When dust and rain at once his coat invade?
Sole coat, where dust cemented by the rain
30   Erects the nap, and leaves a cloudy stain.

   Now in contiguous drops the flood comes down,
Threatening with deluge this devoted town.
To shops in crowds the daggled females fly,
Pretend to cheapen goods, but nothing buy.
The templar spruce, while every spout's abroach,
Stays till 'tis fair, yet seems to call a coach.
The tucked-up seamstress walks with hasty strides,
While streams run down her oiled umbrella's sides.
Here various kinds by various fortunes led,
40   Commence acquaintance underneath a shed.
Triumphant Tories, and desponding Whigs,
Forget their feuds, and join to save their wigs.
Boxed in a chair the beau impatient sits,
While spouts run clattering o'er the roof by fits;
And ever and anon with frightful din
The leather sounds; he trembles from within.
So when Troy chairmen bore the wooden steed,
Pregnant with Greeks, impatient to be freed;
(Those bully Greeks, who, as the moderns do,
50   Instead of paying chairmen, run them through)
Laocoon struck the outside with his spear,
And each imprisoned hero quaked for fear.

Now from all parts the swelling kennels flow,
And bear their trophies with them as they go:
Filths of all hues and odours, seem to tell
What streets they sailed from, by the sight and smell.
They, as each torrent drives with rapid force
From Smithfield, or St Pulchre's shape their course;
And in huge confluent join at Snow Hill ridge,
60   Fall from the conduit prone to Holborn Bridge.
Sweepings from butchers' stalls, dung, guts, and blood,
Drowned puppies, stinking sprats, all drenched in mud,
Dead cats and turnip-tops come tumbling down the flood.

An Excellent New Song

BEING THE INTENDED SPEECH OF A FAMOUS
ORATOR AGAINST PEACE

An orator dismal of Nottinghamshire,
Who has forty years let out his conscience to hire,
Out of zeal for his country, and want of a place,
Is come up, *vi et armis*, to break the Queen's peace.
He has vamped up an old speech, and the court to their
    sorrow,
Shall hear him harangue against Prior tomorrow.
When once he begins, he never will flinch,
But repeats the same note a whole day, like a finch.
I have heard all the speech repeated by Hoppy,
10   And, mistakes to prevent, I have obtained a copy.

THE SPEECH

Whereas, notwithstanding, I am in great pain,
To hear we are making a peace without Spain;
But, most noble senators, 'tis a great shame
There should be a peace, while I'm not in game.
The Duke showed me all his fine house; and the Duchess
From her closet brought out a full purse in her clutches:

I talked of a peace, and they both gave a start,
His Grace swore by God, and her Grace let a fart:
My long old-fashioned pocket was presently crammed;
20   And sooner than vote for a peace I'll be damned.
But some will cry, 'Turncoat!', and rip up old stories,
How I always pretended to be for the Tories:
I answer; the Tories were in my good graces,
Till all my relations were put into places.
But still I'm in principle ever the same,
And will quit my best friends, while I'm not in game.

When I and some others subscribed our names
To a plot for expelling my master King James;
I withdrew my subscription by help of a blot,
30   And so might discover, or gain by the plot:
I had my advantage, and stood at defiance,
For Daniel was got from the den of the lions:
I came in without danger; and was I to blame?
For rather than hang, I would be not in game.

I swore to the Queen that the Prince of Hanover
During her sacred life, should never come over:
I made use of a trope; that 'an heir to invite,
Was like keeping her monument always in sight.'
But when I thought proper, I altered my note;
40   And in her own hearing I boldly did vote,
That her Majesty stood in great need of a tutor,
And must have an old, or a young coadjútor:
For why; I would fain have put all in a flame,
Because, for some reasons, I was not in game.

Now my new benefactors have brought me about,
And I'll vote against peace, with Spain, or without:
Though the court gives my nephews, and brothers, and
      cousins,
And all my whole family, places by dozens;
Yet since I know where a full purse may be found,
50   And hardly pay eighteen pence tax in the pound:
Since the Tories have thus disappointed my hopes,
And will neither regard my figures nor tropes;

I'll speech against peace while Dismal's my name,
And be a true Whig, while I am not in game.

Cadenus and Vanessa

The shepherds and the nymphs were seen
Pleading before the Cyprian queen.
The counsel for the fair began,
Accusing that false creature, man:
The brief with weighty crimes was charged,
On which the pleader much enlarged;
That 'Cupid now has lost his art,
Or blunts the point of every dart;
His altar now no longer smokes,
His mother's aid no youth invokes:
This tempts freethinkers to refine,
And brings in doubt their power divine.
Now love is dwindled to intrigue,
And marriage grown a money-league.
Which crimes aforesaid' (with her leave)
'Were' (as he humbly did conceive)
'Against our sovereign lady's peace,
Against the statute in that case,
Against her dignity and crown.'
Then prayed an answer, and sat down.

The nymphs with scorn beheld their foes:
When the defendant's counsel rose;
And, what no lawyer ever lacked,
With impudence owned all the fact:
But, what the gentlest heart would vex,
Laid all the fault on t'other sex.
That 'Modern love is no such thing
As what those ancient poets sing;
A fire celestial, chaste, refined,
Conceived and kindled in the mind.
Which having found an equal flame,
Unites, and both become the same,

In different breasts together burn,
Together both to ashes turn.
But women now feel no such fire;
And only know the gross desire:
Their passions move in lower spheres,
Where'er caprice or folly steers:
A dog, a parrot, or an ape,
40 Or some worse brute in human shape,
Engross the fancies of the fair,
The few soft moments they can spare,
From visits to receive and pay;
From scandal, politics, and play,
From fans and flounces, and brocades,
From equipage and park-parades;
From all the thousand female toys,
From every trifle that employs
The out or inside of their heads,
50 Between their toilets and their beds.

'In a dull stream, which moving slow
You hardly see the current flow;
If a small breeze obstructs the course,
It whirls about for want of force,
And in its narrow circle gathers
Nothing but chaff, and straws, and feathers:
The current of a female mind
Stops thus, and turns with every wind;
Thus whirling round, together draws
60 Fools, fops, and rakes, for chaff and straws.
Hence we conclude, no women's hearts
Are won by virtue, wit, and parts;
Nor are the men of sense to blame,
For breasts incapable of flame;
The fault must on the nymphs be placed,
Grown so corrupted in their taste.'

The pleader having spoke his best,
Had witness ready to attest,
Who fairly could on oath depose,
70 When questions on the fact arose,

That every article was true;
'Nor further those deponents knew':
Therefore he humbly would insist,
The bill might be with costs dismissed.

The cause appeared of so much weight,
That Venus, from her judgement-seat,
Desired them not to talk so loud,
Else she must interpose a cloud:
For if the heavenly folks should know
80   These pleadings in the courts below,
That mortals here disdain to love;
She ne'er could show her face above.
For gods, their betters, are too wise
To value that which men despise:
'And then,' said she, 'my son and I
Must stroll in air 'twixt land and sky;
Or else, shut out from heaven and earth,
Fly to the sea, my place of birth;
There live with daggled mermaids pent,
90   And keep on fish perpetual Lent.'

But since the case appeared so nice,
She thought it best to take advice.
The muses, by their king's permission,
Though foes to love, attend the session;
And on the right hand took their places
In order; on the left, the Graces:
To whom she might her doubts propose
On all emergencies that rose.
The muses oft were seen to frown;
100   The Graces half ashamed looked down;
And 'twas observed, there were but few
Of either sex, among the crew,
Whom she or her assessors knew.
The goddess soon began to see
Things were not ripe for a decree:
And said, she must consult her books,
The lovers' *Fleta*'s, Bractons, Cokes.

First to a dapper clerk she beckoned,
To turn to Ovid, book the second;
110   She then referred them to a place
In Virgil (*vide* Dido's case):
As for Tibullus's reports,
They never passed for laws in courts;
For Cowley's briefs, and pleas of Waller,
Still their authority was smaller.

There was on both sides much to say:
She'd hear the cause another day;
And so she did, and then a third:
She heard it – there she kept her word;
120   But with rejoinders and replies,
Long bills and answers, stuffed with lies;
Demur, imparlance, and essoign,
The parties ne'er could issue join:
For sixteen years the cause was spun,
And then stood where it first begun.

Now, gentle Clio, sing or say,
What Venus meant by this delay.
The goddess much perplexed in mind,
To see her empire thus declined,
130   When first this grand debate arose
Above her wisdom to compose,
Conceived a project in her head,
To work her ends; which if it sped,
Would show the merits of the cause,
Far better than consulting laws.

In a glad hour Lucina's aid
Produced on earth a wondrous maid,
On whom the Queen of Love was bent
To try a new experiment:
140   She threw her law-books on the shelf,
And thus debated with herself.

'Since men allege, they ne'er can find
Those beauties in a female mind,

Which raise a flame that will endure
For ever, uncorrupt and pure;
If 'tis with reason they complain,
This infant shall restore my reign.
I'll search where every virtue dwells,
From courts inclusive, down to cells,
150　What preachers talk, or sages write,
These I will gather and unite,
And represent them to mankind
Collected in the infant's mind.'

　　This said, she plucks in heaven's high bowers
A sprig of amaranthine flowers,
In nectar thrice infuses bays,
Three times refined in Titan's rays:
Then calls the Graces to her aid,
And sprinkles thrice the new-born maid:
160　From whence the tender skin assumes
A sweetness above all perfumes;
From whence a cleanliness remains,
Incapable of outward stains;
From whence that decency of mind,
So lovely in the female kind;
Where not one careless thought intrudes,
Less modest than the speech of prudes;
Where never blush was called in aid;
That spurious virtue in a maid;
170　A virtue but at second hand;
They blush because they understand.

　　The Graces next would act their part,
And showed but little of their art;
Their work was half already done,
The child with native beauty shone;
The outward form no help required:
Each breathing on her thrice, inspired
That gentle, soft, engaging air,
Which, in old times, adorned the fair;
180　And said, 'Vanessa be the name,
By which thou shalt be known to fame:

Vanessa, by the gods enrolled:
Her name on earth – shall not be told.'

But still the work was not complete;
When Venus thought on a deceit:
Drawn by her doves, away she flies,
And finds out Pallas in the skies:
'Dear Pallas, I have been this morn
To see a lovely infant born:
190   A boy in yonder isle below,
So like my own, without his bow:
By beauty could your heart be won,
You'd swear it is Apollo's son;
But it shall ne'er be said, a child
So hopeful, has by me been spoiled;
I have enough besides to spare,
And give him wholly to your care.'

Wisdom's above suspecting wiles:
The Queen of Learning gravely smiles;
200   Down from Olympus comes with joy,
Mistakes Vanessa for a boy;
Then sows within her tender mind
Seeds long unknown to womankind,
For manly bosoms chiefly fit,
The seeds of knowledge, judgement, wit.
Her soul was suddenly endued
With justice, truth and fortitude;
With honour, which no breath can stain,
Which malice must attack in vain;
210   With open heart and bounteous hand:
But Pallas here was at a stand;
She knew in our degenerate days
Bare virtue could not live on praise,
That meat must be with money bought;
She therefore, upon second thought,
Infused, yet as it were by stealth,
Some small regard for state and wealth:
Of which, as she grew up, there stayed
A tincture in the prudent maid:

220 She managed her estate with care,
Yet liked three footmen to her chair.
But lest he should neglect his studies
Like a young heir, the thrifty goddess
(For fear young master should be spoiled)
Would use him like a younger child;
And, after long computing, found
'Twould come to just five thousand pound.

The Queen of Love was pleased, and proud,
To see Vanessa thus endowed;
230 She doubted not but such a dame
Through every breast would dart a flame;
That every rich and lordly swain
With pride would drag about her chain;
That scholars would forsake their books
To study bright Vanessa's looks:
As she advanced, that womankind
Would by her model form their mind,
And all their conduct would be tried
By her, as an unerring guide.
240 Offending daughters oft would hear
Vanessa's praise rung in their ear:
Miss Betty, when she does a fault,
Lets fall a knife, or spills the salt,
Will thus be by her mother chid,
' 'Tis what Vanessa never did.'
'Thus by the nymphs and swains adored,
My power shall be again restored,
And happy lovers bless my reign –'
So Venus hoped, but hoped in vain.

250 For when in time the martial maid
Found out the trick that Venus played,
She shakes her helm, she knits her brows,
And fired with indignation vows,
Tomorrow, ere the setting sun,
She'd all undo, that she had done.

But in the poets we may find,
A wholesome law, time out of mind,
Had been confirmed by fate's decree;
That gods, of whatsoe'er degree,
260   Resume not what themselves have given,
Or any brother god in heaven:
Which keeps the peace among the gods,
Or they must always be at odds.
And Pallas, if she broke the laws,
Must yield her foe the stronger cause;
A shame to one so much adored
For wisdom, at Jove's council-board.
Besides, she feared, the Queen of Love
Would meet with better friends above.
270   And though she must with grief reflect,
To see a mortal virgin decked
With graces, hitherto unknown
To female breasts, except her own;
Yet she would act as best became
A goddess of unspotted fame:
She knew, by augury divine,
Venus would fail in her design:
She studied well the point, and found
Her foe's conclusions were not sound,
280   From premises erroneous brought,
And therefore the deductions naught;
And must have contrary effects
To what her treacherous foe expects.

In proper season Pallas meets
The Queen of Love, whom thus she greets
(For gods, we are by Homer told,
Can in celestial language scold),
'Perfidious goddess! but in vain
You formed this project in your brain,
290   A project for thy talents fit,
With much deceit and little wit;
Thou hast, as thou shalt quickly see,
Deceived thyself, instead of me;

For how can heavenly wisdom prove
An instrument to earthly love?
Knowst thou not yet that men commence
Thy votaries, for want of sense?
Nor shall Vanessa be the theme
To manage thy abortive scheme;
300   She'll prove the greatest of thy foes:
And yet I scorn to interpose,
But using neither skill, nor force,
Leave all things to their natural course.'

   The goddess thus pronounced her doom:
When, lo! Vanessa in her bloom,
Advanced like Atalanta's star
But rarely seen, and seen from far:
In a new world with caution stepped,
Watched all the company she kept,
310   Well knowing from the books she read
What dangerous paths young virgins tread;
Would seldom at the park appear,
Nor saw the playhouse twice a year;
Yet not incurious, was inclined
To know the converse of mankind.

   First issued from perfumers' shops
A crowd of fashionable fops;
They asked her, how she liked the play,
Then told the tattle of the day,
320   A duel fought last night at two;
About a Lady – you know who;
Mentioned a new Italian, come
Either from Muscovy or Rome;
Gave hints of who and who's together;
Then fell to talking of the weather:
'Last night was so extremely fine,
The ladies walked till after nine.'
Then in soft voice and speech absurd,
With nonsense every second word,
330   With fustian from exploded plays,
They celebrate her beauty's praise,

Run o'er their cant of stupid lies,
And tell the murders of her eyes.

　　With silent scorn Vanessa sat,
Scarce listening to their idle chat;
Further than sometimes by a frown,
When they grew pert, to pull them down.
At last she spitefully was bent
To try their wisdom's full extent;
340　And said, she valued nothing less
Than titles, figure, shape, and dress;
That, merit should be chiefly placed
In judgement, knowledge, wit, and taste;
And these, she offered to dispute,
Alone distinguished man from brute:
That, present times have no pretence
To virtue, in the noblest sense,
By Greeks and Romans understood,
To perish for our country's good.
350　She named the ancient heroes round,
Explained for what they were renowned;
Then spoke with censure, or applause,
Of foreign customs, rites, and laws;
Through nature, and through art she ranged,
And gracefully her subjects changed:
In vain: her hearers had no share
In all she spoke, except to stare.
Their judgement was upon the whole,
'That lady is the dullest soul' –
360　Then tipped their forehead in a jeer,
As who should say – 'she wants it here;
She may be handsome, young and rich,
But none will burn her for a witch.'

　　A party next of glittering dames,
From round the purlieus of St James,
Came early, out of pure good will,
To catch the girl in dishabille.
Their clamour lighting from their chairs,
Grew louder, all the way upstairs;

370 At entrance loudest, where they found
    The room with volumes littered round.
    Vanessa held Montaigne, and read,
    Whilst Mrs Susan combed her head:
    They called for tea and chocolate,
    And fell into their usual chat,
    Discoursing with important face,
    On ribbons, fans, and gloves and lace;
    Showed patterns just from India brought,
    And gravely asked her what she thought,
380 Whether the red or green were best,
    And what they cost? Vanessa guessed,
    As came into her fancy first,
    Named half the rates, and liked the worst.
    To scandal next – 'What awkward thing
    Was that, last Sunday in the Ring?'
    – 'I'm sorry Mopsa breaks so fast;
    I said her face would never last.'
    'Corinna with that youthful air,
    Is thirty, and a bit to spare.
390 Her fondness for a certain earl
    Began when I was but a girl.'
    'Phyllis, who but a month ago
    Was married to the Tunbridge beau,
    I saw coquetting t'other night
    In public with that odious knight.'

    They rallied next Vanessa's dress;
    'That gown was made for old Queen Bess.'
    'Dear madam, let me set your head:
    Don't you intend to put on red?'
400 'A petticoat without a hoop!
    Sure, you are not ashamed to stoop;
    With handsome garters at your knees,
    No matter what a fellow sees.'

    Filled with disdain, with rage inflamed,
    Both of her self and sex ashamed,
    The nymph stood silent out of spite,
    Nor would vouchsafe to set them right.

Away the fair detractors went,
And gave, by turns, their censures vent.
410   'She's not so handsome, in my eyes:
For wit, I wonder where it lies.'
'She's fair and clean, and that's the most;
But why proclaim her for a toast?'
'A babyface, no life, no airs,
But what she learnt at country fairs;
Scarce knows what difference is between
Rich Flanders lace, and colbertine.'
'I'll undertake my little Nancy
In flounces has a better fancy.'
420   'With all her wit, I would not ask
Her judgement, how to buy a mask.'
'We begged her but to patch her face,
She never hit one proper place;
Which every girl at five years old
Can do as soon as she is told.'
'I own, that out-of-fashion stuff
Becomes the creature well enough.'
'The girl might pass, if we could get her
To know the world a little better.'
430   (*To know the world*, a modern phrase,
For visits, ombre, balls and plays.)

Thus, to the world's perpetual shame,
The Queen of Beauty lost her aim.
Too late with grief she understood,
Pallas had done more harm than good;
For great examples are but vain,
Where ignorance begets disdain.
Both sexes armed with guilt and spite,
Against Vanessa's power unite;
440   To copy her, few nymphs aspired;
Her virtues fewer swains admired:
So stars beyond a certain height
Give mortals neither heat nor light.

Yet some of either sex, endowed
With gifts superior to the crowd,
With virtue, knowledge, taste and wit,
She condescended to admit:
With pleasing arts she could reduce
Men's talents to their proper use;
450 And with address each genius held
To that wherein it most excelled;
Thus making other wisdom known,
Could please them, and improve her own.
A modest youth said something new,
She placed it in the strongest view.
All humble worth she strove to raise;
Would not be praised, yet loved to praise.
The learned met with free approach,
Although they came not in a coach.
460 Some clergy too she would allow,
Nor quarrelled at their awkward bow.
But this was for Cadenus' sake;
A gownman of a different make;
Whom Pallas, once Vanessa's tutor,
Had fixed on for her coadjútor.

But Cupid, full of mischief, longs
To vindicate his mother's wrongs.
On Pallas all attempts are vain;
One way he knows to give her pain:
470 Vows, on Vanessa's heart to take
Due vengeance, for her patron's sake.
Those early seeds by Venus sown,
In spite of Pallas, now were grown;
And Cupid hoped they would improve
By time, and ripen into love.
The boy made use of all his craft,
In vain discharging many a shaft,
Pointed at colonels, lords, and beaux;
Cadenus warded off the blows:
480 For placing still some book betwixt,
The darts were in the cover fixed,

Or often blunted and recoiled,
On Plutarch's *Morals* struck, were spoiled.

The Queen of Wisdom could foresee,
But not prevent the fates' decree;
And human caution tries in vain
To break that adamantine chain.
Vanessa, though by Pallas taught,
By love invulnerable thought,
490 Searching in books for wisdom's aid,
Was, in the very search, betrayed.

Cupid, though all his darts were lost,
Yet still resolved to spare no cost;
He could not answer to his fame
The triumphs of that stubborn dame;
And nymph so hard to be subdued,
Who neither was coquette nor prude.
'I find,' says he, 'she wants a doctor,
Both to adore her and instruct her;
500 I'll give her what she most admires,
Among those venerable sires.
Cadenus is a subject fit,
Grown old in politics and wit;
Caressed by ministers of state,
Of half mankind the dread and hate.
Whate'er vexations love attend,
She need no rivals apprehend.
Her sex, with universal voice,
Must laugh at her capricious choice.'

510 Cadenus many things had writ;
Vanessa much esteemed his wit;
And called for his poetic works;
Meantime the boy in secret lurks,
And while the book was in her hand,
The urchin from his private stand
Took aim, and shot with all his strength
A dart of such prodigious length,

It pierced the feeble volume through,
And deep transfixed her bosom too.
520 Some lines more moving than the rest,
Stuck to the point that pierced her breast;
And born directly to the heart,
With pains unknown increased her smart.

Vanessa, not in years a score,
Dreams of a gown of forty-four;
Imaginary charms can find,
In eyes with reading almost blind;
Cadenus now no more appears
Declined in health, advanced in years.
530 She fancies music in his tongue,
Nor further looks, but thinks him young.
What mariner is not afraid,
To venture in a ship decayed?
What planter will attempt to yoke
A sapling with a fallen oak?
As years increase, she brighter shines,
Cadenus with each day declines,
And he must fall a prey to time,
While she continues in her prime.

540 Cadenus, common forms apart,
In every scene had kept his heart;
Had sighed and languished, vowed and writ,
For pastime, or to show his wit;
But time, and books, and state affairs,
Had spoiled his fashionable airs;
He now could praise, esteem, approve,
But understood not what was love:
His conduct might have made him styled
A father, and the nymph his child.
550 That innocent delight he took
To see the virgin mind her book,
Was but the master's secret joy
In school to hear the finest boy.
Her knowledge with her fancy grew;
She hourly pressed for something new:

Ideas came into her mind
So fast, his lessons lagged behind:
She reasoned, without plodding long,
Nor ever gave her judgement wrong.
560 But now a sudden change was wrought,
She minds no longer what he taught.
She wished her tutor were her lover;
Resolved she would her flame discover:
And when Cadenus would expound
Some notion subtle or profound,
The nymph would gently press his hand,
As if she seemed to understand;
Or dextrously dissembling chance,
Would sigh, and steal a secret glance.
570 Cadenus was amazed to find
Such marks of a distracted mind;
For though she seemed to listen more
To all he spoke, than e'er before;
He found her thoughts would absent range,
Yet guessed not whence could spring the change.
And first he modestly conjectures
His pupil might be tired with lectures;
Which helped to mortify his pride,
Yet gave him not the heart to chide;
580 But in a mild dejected strain,
At last he ventured to complain:
Said, she should be no longer teased;
Might have her freedom when she pleased:
Was now convinced he acted wrong,
To hide her from the world so long;
And in dull studies to engage,
One of her tender sex and age.
That every nymph with envy owned,
How she might shine in the *grand monde*,
590 And every shepherd was undone
To see her cloistered like a nun.
This was a visionary scheme,
He waked, and found it but a dream;

A project far above his skill,
For nature must be nature still.
If he was bolder than became
A scholar to a courtly dame,
She might excuse a man of letters;
Thus tutors often treat their betters.
600 And since his talk offensive grew,
He came to take his last adieu.

Vanessa, filled with just disdain,
Would still her dignity maintain,
Instructed from her early years
To scorn the art of female tears.

Had he employed his time so long,
To teach her what was right or wrong,
Yet could such notions entertain,
That all his lectures were in vain?
610 She owned the wandering of her thoughts,
But he must answer for her faults.
She well remembered to her cost,
That all his lessons were not lost.
Two maxims she could still produce,
And sad experience taught their use:
That virtue, pleased by being shown,
Knows nothing which it dare not own;
Can make us without fear disclose
Our inmost secrets to our foes:
620 That common forms were not designed
Directors to a noble mind.
'Now,' said the nymph, 'to let you see
My actions with your rules agree,
That I can vulgar forms despise,
And have no secrets to disguise:
I knew by what you said and writ,
How dangerous things were men of wit,
You cautioned me against their charms,
But never gave me equal arms:
630 Your lessons found the weakest part,
Aimed at the head, but reached the heart.'

Cadenus felt within him rise
Shame, disappointment, guilt, surprise.
He knew not how to reconcile
Such language, with her usual style:
And yet her words were so expressed
He could not hope she spoke in jest.
His thoughts had wholly been confined
To form and cultivate her mind.
640 He hardly knew, till he was told,
Whether the nymph were young or old;
Had met her in a public place,
Without distinguishing her face.
Much less could his declining age
Vanessa's earliest thoughts engage.
And if her youth indifference met,
His person must contempt beget.
Or grant her passion be sincere,
How shall his innocence be clear?
650 Appearances were all so strong,
The world must think him in the wrong;
Would say, he made a treacherous use
Of wit, to flatter and seduce:
The town would swear he had betrayed,
By magic spells, the harmless maid;
And every beau would have his jokes,
That scholars were like other folks:
That when platonic flights were over,
The tutor turned a mortal lover.
660 So tender of the young and fair?
It showed a true paternal care –
'Five thousand guineas in her purse:
The doctor might have fancied worse . . .'

Hardly at length he silence broke,
And faltered every word he spoke;
Interpreting her complaisance,
Just as a man *sans conséquence*.
She rallied well, he always knew,
Her manner now was something new;

670 And what she spoke was in an air,
    As serious as a tragic player.
    But those who aim at ridicule
    Should fix upon some certain rule,
    Which fairly hints they are in jest,
    Else he must enter his protest:
    For, let a man be ne'er so wise,
    He may be caught with sober lies;
    A science, which he never taught,
    And, to be free, was dearly bought:
680 For, take it in its proper light,
    'Tis just what coxcombs call, a 'bite'.

    But not to dwell on things minute;
    Vanessa finished the dispute,
    Brought weighty arguments to prove
    That reason was her guide in love.
    She thought he had himself described,
    His doctrines when she first imbibed;
    What he had planted, now was grown;
    His virtues she might call her own;
690 As he approves, as he dislikes,
    Love or contempt, her fancy strikes.
    Self-love, in nature rooted fast,
    Attends us first, and leaves us last:
    Why she likes him, admire not at her,
    She loves herself, and that's the matter.
    How was her tutor wont to praise
    The geniuses of ancient days!
    (Those authors he so oft had named
    For learning, wit, and wisdom famed);
700 Was struck with love, esteem and awe,
    For persons whom he never saw.
    Suppose Cadenus flourished then,
    He must adore such godlike men.
    If one short volume could comprise
    All that was witty, learned, and wise,
    How would it be esteemed, and read,
    Although the writer long were dead?

If such an author were alive,
How would all for his friendship strive;
710 And come in crowds to see his face:
And this she takes to be her case:
Cadenus answers every end,
The book, the author, and the friend.
The utmost her desires will reach,
Is but to learn what he can teach;
His converse is a system, fit
Alone to fill up all her wit;
While every passion of her mind
In him is centred and confined.

720   Love can with speech inspire a mute,
And taught Vanessa to dispute.
This topic, never touched before,
Displayed her eloquence the more:
Her knowledge, with such pains acquired,
By this new passion grew inspired:
Through this she made all objects pass,
Which gave a tincture o'er the mass:
As rivers, though they bend and twine,
Still to the sea their course incline:
730 Or, as philosophers, who find
Some favourite system to their mind,
In every point to make it fit,
Will force all nature to submit.

     Cadenus, who would ne'er suspect
His lessons would have such effect,
Or be so artfully applied,
Insensibly came on her side;
It was an unforeseen event,
Things took a turn he never meant.
740 Whoe'er excels in what we prize,
Appears a hero to our eyes;
Each girl when pleased with what is taught,
Will have the teacher in her thought:
When Miss delights in her spinnet,
A fiddler may a fortune get;

A blockhead with melodious voice
In boarding schools can have his choice;
And oft the dancing-master's art
Climbs from the toe to touch the heart.
750 In learning let a nymph delight,
The pedant gets a mistress by't.
Cadenus, to his grief and shame,
Could scarce oppose Vanessa's flame;
But though her arguments were strong,
At least could hardly wish them wrong.
Howe'er it came, he could not tell,
But sure she never talked so well.
His pride began to interpose,
Preferred before a crowd of beaux:
760 So bright a nymph to come unsought,
Such wonder by his merit wrought:
'Tis merit must with her prevail,
He never knew her judgement fail;
She noted all she ever read,
And had a most discerning head.

'Tis an old maxim in the schools,
That vanity's the food of fools;
Yet now and then your men of wit
Will condescend to take a bit.
770 So when Cadenus could not hide,
He chose to justify his pride;
Construing the passion she had shown,
Much to her praise, more to his own.
Nature in him had merit placed,
In her, a most judicious taste.
Love, hitherto a transient guest,
Ne'er held possession of his breast;
So, long attending at the gate,
Disdained to enter in so late.
780 Love, why do we one passion call?
When 'tis a compound of them all;
Where hot and cold, where sharp and sweet,
In all their equipages meet;

Where pleasures mixed with pains appear,
Sorrow with joy, and hope with fear;
Wherein his dignity and age
Forbid Cadenus to engage.
But friendship in its greatest height,
A constant, rational delight,
On virtue's basis fixed to last,
When love's allurements long are past;
Which gently warms, but cannot burn;
He gladly offers in return:
His want of passion will redeem,
With gratitude, respect, esteem:
With that devotion we bestow,
When goddesses appear below.

    While thus Cadenus entertains
Vanessa in exalted strains,
The nymph in sober word entreats
A truce with all sublime conceits.
For why such raptures, flights, and fancies,
To her, who durst not read romances;
In lofty style to make replies,
Which he had taught her to despise?
But when her tutor will affect
Devotion, duty, and respect,
He fairly abdicates his throne,
The government is now her own;
He has a forfeiture incurred:
She vows to take him at his word,
And hopes he will not think it strange
If both should now their stations change.
The nymph will have her turn, to be
The tutor; and the pupil, he:
Though she already can discern,
Her scholar is not apt to learn;
Or wants capacity to reach
The science she designs to teach:
Wherein his genius was below
The skill of every common beau;

Who, though he cannot spell, is wise
Enough to read a lady's eyes;
And will each accidental glance
Interpret for a kind advance.

But what success Vanessa met,
Is to the world a secret yet:
Whether the nymph, to please her swain,
Talks in a high romantic strain;
830   Or whether he at last descends
To like with less seraphic ends;
Or, to compound the business, whether
They temper love and books together;
Must never to mankind be told,
Nor shall the conscious muse unfold.

Meantime the mournful Queen of Love
Led but a weary life above.
She ventures now to leave the skies,
Grown by Vanessa's conduct wise:
840   For though by one perverse event
Pallas had crossed her first intent;
Though her design was not obtained,
Yet had she much experience gained;
And, by the project vainly tried,
Could better now the cause decide.

She gave due notice, that both parties,
Coram Regina prox' die Martis,
Should at their peril without fail,
'Come and appear, and save their bail.'
850   All met, and silence thrice proclaimed,
One lawyer to each side was named.
The judge discovered in her face
Resentments for her late disgrace;
And, full of anger, shame and grief,
Directed them to mind their brief;
Nor spend their time to show their reading;
She'd have a summary proceeding.

She gathered, under every head,
The sum of what each lawyer said;
860 Gave her own reasons last; and then
Decreed the cause against the men.

But in a weighty cause like this,
To show she did not judge amiss,
Which evil tongues might else report,
She made a speech in open court;
Wherein she grievously complains,
'How she was cheated by the swains:
On whose petition (humbly showing
That women were not worth the wooing;
870 And that unless the sex would mend,
The race of lovers soon must end)
She was at Lord knows what expense
To form a nymph of wit and sense;
A model for her sex designed,
Who never could one lover find.
She saw her favour was misplaced;
The fellows had a wretched taste;
She needs must tell them to their face,
They were a stupid, senseless race:
880 And were she to begin again,
She'd study to reform the men;
Or add some grain of folly more
To women than they had before,
To put them on an equal foot;
And this, or nothing else, would do't.
This might their mutual fancy strike,
Since every being loves its like.

'But now, repenting what was done,
She left all business to her son:
890 She puts the world in his possession,
And let him use it at discretion.'

The crier was ordered to dismiss
The court, so made his last 'Oyez!'
The goddess would no longer wait;
But rising from her chair of state,

Left all below at six and seven,
Harnessed her doves, and flew to heaven.

Horace, Epistle VII, Book I: Imitated and Addressed to the Earl of Oxford

Harley, the nation's great support,
Returning home one day from court
(His mind with public cares possessed,
All Europe's business in his breast)
Observed a parson near Whitehall,
Cheapening old authors on a stall.
The priest was pretty well in case,
And showed some humour in his face;
Looked with an easy, careless mien,
A perfect stranger to the spleen;
Of size that might a pulpit fill,
But more inclining to sit still.
My Lord, who (if a man may say't)
Loves mischief better than his meat,
Was now disposed to crack a jest;
And bid friend Lewis go in quest
(This Lewis is an arrant shaver,
And very much in Harley's favour);
In quest, who might this parson be,
What was his name, of what degree:
If possible, to learn his story,
And whether he were Whig or Tory?

Lewis his patron's humour knows;
Away upon his errand goes;
And quickly did the matter sift,
Found out that it was Dr Swift:
A clergyman of special note,
For shunning those of his own coat;
Which made his brethren of the gown,
Take care betimes to run him down:

No libertine, nor over-nice,
Addicted to no sort of vice;
Went where he pleased, said what he thought;
Not rich, but owed no man a groat.
In state opinions *à la mode*,
He hated Wharton like a toad;
Had given the faction many a wound,
And libelled all the Junta round;
Kept company with men of wit,
40   Who often fathered what he writ;
His works were hawked in every street,
But seldom rose above a sheet:
Of late indeed the paper-stamp
Did very much his genius cramp;
And since he could not spend his fire,
He now intended to retire.

    Said Harley, 'I desire to know
From his own mouth, if this be so?
Step to the Doctor straight, and say,
50   I'd have him dine with me today.'
Swift seemed to wonder what he meant,
Nor would believe my Lord had sent;
So never offered once to stir,
But coldly said, 'Your servant, sir.'
'Does he refuse me?' Harley cried.
'He does, with insolence and pride.'

    Some few days after, Harley spies
The Doctor fastened by the eyes,
At Charing Cross, among the rout,
60   Where painted monsters dangle out.
He pulled the string, and stopped his coach,
Beckoning the Doctor to approach.

    Swift, who could neither fly nor hide,
Came sneaking to the chariot-side,
And offered many a lame excuse:
He never meant the least abuse –

'My Lord – the honour you designed –
Extremely proud – but I had dined –
I'm sure I never should neglect –
70 No man alive has more respect . . .'
'Well, I shall think of that no more,
If you'll be sure to come at four.'

    The Doctor now obeys the summons,
Likes both his company and commons;
Displays his talent, sits till ten;
Next day invited, comes again:
Soon grows domestic, seldom fails
Either at morning, or at meals;
Comes early, and departeth late:
80 In short, the gudgeon took the bait.
My Lord would carry on the jest,
And down to Windsor takes his guest.
Swift much admires the place and air,
And longs to be a canon there;
In summer, round the park to ride,
In winter – never to reside.
'A canon! that's a place too mean:
No, Doctor, you shall be a dean;
Two dozen canons round your stall,
90 And you the tyrant o'er them all:
You need but cross the Irish seas,
To live in plenty, power and ease.'
Poor Swift departs, and, what is worse,
With borrowed money in his purse;
Travels at least a hundred leagues,
And suffers numberless fatigues.

    Suppose him, now, a dean complete,
Demurely lolling in his seat;
The silver verge, with decent pride,
100 Stuck underneath his cushion-side:
Suppose him gone through all vexations,
Patents, instalments, abjurations,
First-fruits and tenths, and chapter-treats,
Dues, payments, fees, demands and – cheats

(The wicked laity's contriving,
To hinder clergymen from thriving),
Now all the Doctor's money's spent,
His tenants wrong him in his rent;
The farmers, spitefully combined,
110   Force him to take his tithes in kind;
And Parvisol discounts arrears,
By bills for taxes and repairs.

Poor Swift, with all his losses vexed,
Not knowing where to turn him next,
Above a thousand pounds in debt;
Takes horse, and in a mighty fret,
Rides day and night at such a rate,
He soon arrives at Harley's gate;
But was so dirty, pale, and thin,
120   Old Read would hardly let him in.

Said Harley, 'Welcome, reverend Dean!
What makes your worship look so lean?
Why sure you won't appear in town,
In that old wig and rusty gown?
I doubt your heart is set on pelf
So much, that you neglect yourself.
What! I suppose now stocks are high,
You've some good purchase in your eye;
Or is your money out at use?' –
130   'Truce, good my Lord, I beg a truce!'
(The Doctor in a passion cried),
'Your raillery is misapplied:
Experience I have dearly bought,
You know I am not worth a groat:
But it's a folly to contest,
When you resolve to have your jest;
And since you now have done your worst,
Pray leave me where you found me first.'

The Author upon Himself

By an old red-pate, murdering hag pursued,
A crazy prelate, and a royal prude.
By dull divines, who look with envious eyes,
On every genius that attempts to rise;
And pausing o'er a pipe, with doubtful nod,
Give hints, that poets ne'er believe in God.
So, clowns on scholars as on wizards look,
And take a folio for a conjuring book.

Swift had the sin of wit, no venial crime;
Nay, 'twas affirmed, he sometimes dealt in rhyme:
Humour, and mirth, had place in all he writ:
He reconciled divinity and wit.
He moved, and bowed, and talked with too much grace;
Nor showed the parson in his gait or face;
Despised luxurious wines, and costly meat;
Yet, still was at the tables of the great.
Frequented lords; saw those that saw the Queen;
At Child's or Truby's never once had been;
Where town and country vicars flock in tribes,
Secured by numbers from the laymen's gibes;
And deal in vices of the graver sort,
Tobacco, censure, coffee, pride, and port.

But, after sage monitions from his friends,
His talents to employ for nobler ends;
To better judgements willing to submit,
He turns to politics his dangerous wit.

And now, the public interest to support,
By Harley Swift invited comes to court.
In favour grows with ministers of state;
Admitted private, when superiors wait:
And, Harley, not ashamed his choice to own,
Takes him to Windsor in his coach, alone.
At Windsor Swift no sooner can appear,
But, St John comes and whispers in his ear;

The waiters stand in ranks; the yeomen cry,
'Make room', as if a duke were passing by.

Now Finch alarms the Lords; he hears for certain,
This dangerous priest is got behind the curtain:
Finch, famed for tedious elocution, proves
40   That Swift oils many a spring which Harley moves.
Walpole and Aislabie, to clear the doubt,
Inform the Commons, that the secret's out:
'A certain Doctor is observed of late,
To haunt a certain minister of state:
From whence, with half an eye we may discover,
The peace is made, and Perkin must come over.'
York is from Lambeth sent, to show the Queen
A dangerous treatise writ against the spleen;
Which by the style, the matter, and the drift,
50   'Tis thought could be the work of none but Swift.
Poor York! The harmless tool of others' hate;
He sues for pardon, and repents too late.

No Madam Königsmark her vengeance vows
On Swift's reproaches for her murdered spouse:
From her red locks her mouth with venom fills;
And thence into the royal ear instils.
The Queen incensed, his services forgot,
Leaves him a victim to the vengeful Scot;
Now, through the realm a proclamation spread,
60   To fix a price on his devoted head.
While innocent, he scorns ignoble flight;
His watchful friends preserve him by a sleight.

By Harley's favour once again he shines;
Is now caressed by candidate divines;
Who change opinions with the changing scene:
Lord! how they were mistaken in the Dean!
Now, Delaware again familiar grows;
And in Swift's ear thrusts half his powdered nose.
The Scottish nation, whom he durst offend,
70   Again apply that Swift would be their friend.

By faction tired, with grief he waits a while,
His great contending friends to reconcile.
Performs what friendship, justice, truth require:
What could he more, but decently retire?

Horace, Lib. 2, Sat. 6

PART OF IT IMITATED

I often wished that I had clear
For life, six hundred pounds a year,
A handsome house to lodge a friend,
A river at my garden's end,
A terrace walk, and half a rood
Of land, set out to plant a wood.

Well: now I have all this and more,
I ask not to increase my store;
And should be perfectly content,
10   Could I but live on this side Trent;
Not cross the Channel twice a year,
To spend six months with statesmen here.

I must by all means come to town,
'Tis for the service of the crown.
'Lewis; the Dean will be of use,
Send for him up, take no excuse.'
The toil, the danger of the seas;
Great ministers ne'er think of these;
Or let it cost five hundred pound,
20   No matter where the money's found;
It is but so much more in debt,
And that they ne'er considered yet.

'Good Mr Dean, go change your gown,
Let my Lord know you're come to town.'
I hurry me in haste away,
Not thinking it is levee day;

And find his honour in a pound,
Hemmed by a triple circle round,
Chequered with ribbons blue and green,
30 How should I thrust myself between?
Some wag observes me thus perplexed,
And smiling, whispers to the next,
'I thought the Dean had been too proud,
To jostle here among a crowd.'
Another in a surly fit,
Tells me I have more zeal than wit,
'So eager to express your love,
You ne'er consider whom you shove,
But rudely press before a duke.'
40 I own, I'm pleased with this rebuke,
And take it kindly meant to show
What I desire the world should know.

I get a whisper, and withdraw,
When twenty fools I never saw
Come with petitions fairly penned,
Desiring I would stand their friend.

This, humbly offers me his case:
That, begs my interest for a place.
A hundred other men's affairs
50 Like bees are humming in my ears.
'Tomorrow my appeal comes on,
Without your help the cause is gone –'
'The Duke expects my Lord and you,
About some great affair, at two –'
'Put my Lord Bolingbroke in mind,
To get my warrant quickly signed:
Consider, 'tis my first request.'
Be satisfied. I'll do my best –
Then presently he falls to tease:
60 'You may for certain, if you please;
I doubt not, if his Lordship knew –
And Mr Dean, one word from you –'

'Tis (let me see) three years and more
(October next, it will be four)
Since Harley bid me first attend,
And chose me for an humble friend;
Would take me in his coach to chat,
And question me of this and that;
As 'What's o-clock?' and 'How's the wind?
70   Whose chariot's that we left behind?'
Or gravely try to read the lines
Writ underneath the country signs;
Or, 'Have you nothing new today
From Pope, from Parnell or from Gay?'
Such tattle often entertains
My Lord and me as far as Staines:
As once a week we travel down
To Windsor and again to town;
Where all that passes, *inter nos*,
80   Might be proclaimed at Charing Cross.

Yet some I know with envy swell,
Because they see me used so well:
'How think you of our friend the Dean?
I wonder what some people mean;
My Lord and he are grown so great,
Always together, *tête à tête*:
What, they admire him for his jokes –
See but the fortune of some folks!'

There flies about a strange report
90   Of some express arrived at court;
I'm stopped by all the fools I meet,
And catechized in every street.
'You, Mr Dean, frequent the great;
Inform us, will the Emperor treat?
Or do the prints and papers lie?'
Faith, Sir, you know as much as I.
'Ah Doctor, how you love to jest!
'Tis now no secret' – I protest
'Tis one to me. 'Then, tell us, pray
100   When are the troops to have their pay?'

And though I solemnly declare
I know no more than my Lord Mayor,
They stand amazed, and think me grown
The closest mortal ever known.

Thus in a sea of folly tossed,
My choicest hours of life are lost;
Yet always wishing to retreat;
Oh, could I see my country seat!
There leaning near a gentle brook,
110 Sleep, or peruse some ancient book;
And there in sweet oblivion drown
Those cares that haunt a court and town.

Mary the Cook-maid's Letter to Dr Sheridan

Well; if ever I saw such another man since my mother
    bound my head,
You a gentleman! marry come up, I wonder where you
    were bred?
I am sure such words does not become a man of your cloth,
I would not give such language to a dog, faith and troth.
Yes; you called my master a knave; fie Mr Sheridan, 'tis a
    shame
For a parson, who should know better things, to come out
    with such a name.
Knave in your teeth, Mr Sheridan, 'tis both a shame and a sin,
And the Dean my master is an honester man than you and
    all your kin:
He has more goodness in his little finger, than you have in
    your whole body,
10 My master is a parsonable man, and not a spindle-shanked
    hoddy-doddy.
And now whereby I find you would fain make an excuse,
Because my master one day, in anger, called you goose.
Which, and I am sure I have been his servant four years
    since October,

And he never called me worse than 'sweetheart', drunk or
    sober:
Not that I know his Reverence was ever concerned to my
    knowledge,
Though you and your come-rogues keep him out so late in
    your wicked college.

You say you will eat grass on his grave: a Christian eat
    grass!
Whereby you now confess yourself to be a goose or an ass:
But that's as much as to say, that my master should die
    before ye;
Well, well, that's as God pleases, and I don't believe that's
    a true story,
And so say I told you so, and you may go tell my master;
    what care I?
And I don't care who knows it, 'tis all one to Mary.
Everybody knows, that I love to tell truth, and shame the
    devil;
I am but a poor servant, but I think gentlefolks should be
    civil.
Besides, you found fault with our victuals one day that you
    was here,
I remember it was upon a Tuesday, of all days in the year.
And Saunders the man says, you are always jesting and
    mocking,
'Mary,' said he (one day, as I was mending my master's
    stocking),
'My master is so fond of that minister that keeps the school;
I thought my master a wise man, but that man makes him a
    fool.'
'Saunders,' said I, 'I would rather than a quart of ale,
He would come into our kitchen, and I would pin a
    dishclout to his tail.'
And now I must go, and get Saunders to direct this letter,
For I write but a sad scrawl, but sister Marget she writes
    better.
Well, but I must run and make the bed before my master
    comes from prayers,

And see now, it strikes ten, and I hear him coming upstairs:
Whereof I could say more to your verses, if I could write
    written hand,
And so I remain in a civil way, your servant to command,
                           MARY

Stella's Birthday

WRITTEN IN THE YEAR 1719

Stella this day is thirty-four,
(We shan't dispute a year or more):
However Stella, be not troubled,
Although thy size and years are doubled,
Since first I saw thee at sixteen,
The brightest virgin on the green.
So little is thy form declined;
Made up so largely in thy mind.

Oh, would it please the gods to *split*
10   Thy beauty, size, and years, and wit,
No age could furnish out a pair
Of nymphs so graceful, wise and fair:
With half the lustre of your eyes,
With half your wit, your years, and size:
And then before it grew too late,
How should I beg of gentle fate,
(That either nymph might have her swain),
To split my worship too in twain.

The Progress of Beauty

When first Diana leaves her bed,
Vapours and steams her looks disgrace,
A frowzy dirty coloured red
Sits on her cloudy wrinkled face;

But, by degrees, when mounted high,
Her artificial face appears
Down from her window in the sky,
Her spots are gone, her visage clears.

'Twixt earthly females and the moon,
10   All parallels exactly run;
      If Celia should appear too soon,
Alas, the nymph would be undone!

To see her from her pillow rise
All reeking in a cloudy steam,
Cracked lips, foul teeth, and gummy eyes;
Poor Strephon, how would he blaspheme!

The soot or powder which was wont
To make her hair look black as jet,
Falls from her tresses on her front
20   A mingled mass of dirt and sweat.

Three colours, black, and red, and white,
So graceful in their proper place,
Remove them to a different light.
They form a frightful hideous face.

For instance, when the lily skips
Into the precincts of the rose,
And takes possession of the lips,
Leaving the purple to the nose.

So, Celia went entire to bed,
30   All her complexions safe and sound;
But when she rose, white, black, and red,
Though still in sight, had changed their ground.

The black, which would not be confined,
A more inferior station seeks,
Leaving the fiery red behind,
And mingles in her muddy cheeks.

The paint by perspiration cracks,
And falls in rivulets of sweat,
On either side you see the tracks,
40   While at her chin the confluents met.

A skilful housewife thus her thumb
With spittle while she spins, anoints,
And thus the brown meanders come
In trickling streams betwixt her joints.

But Celia can with ease reduce,
By help of pencil, paint and brush,
Each colour to its place and use,
And teach her cheeks again to blush.

She knows her early self no more:
50   But filled with admiration stands,
As other painters oft adore
The workmanship of their own hands.

Thus, after four important hours
Celia's the wonder of her sex;
Say, which among the heavenly powers
Could cause such marvellous effects?

Venus, indulgent to her kind,
Gave women all their hearts could wish
When first she taught them where to find
60   White lead and Lusitanian dish.

Love with white lead cements his wings,
White lead was sent us to repair
Two brightest, brittlest, earthly things,
A lady's face, and china-ware.

She ventures now to lift the sash,
The window is her proper sphere:
Ah, lovely nymph! be not too rash,
Nor let the beaux approach too near.

Take pattern by your sister star,
70   Delude at once, and bless our sight,
When you are seen, be seen from far,
And chiefly choose to shine by night.

In the Pall Mall when passing by,
Keep up the glasses of your chair,
Then each transported fop will cry,
'God damn me Jack, she's wondrous fair.'

But, art no longer can prevail
When the materials all are gone,
The best mechanic hand must fail,
80 When nothing's left to work upon.

Matter, as wise logicians say,
Cannot without a form subsist;
And form, say I, as well as they,
Must fail, if matter brings no grist.

And this is fair Diana's case;
For all astrologers maintain,
Each night a bit drops off her face,
While mortals say she's in her wane.

While Partridge wisely shows the cause
90 Efficient of the moon's decay,
That Cancer with his poisonous claws,
Attacks her in the Milky Way:

But Gadbury, in art profound,
From her pale cheeks pretends to show,
That swain Endymion is not sound,
Or else, that Mercury's her foe.

But, let the cause be what it will,
In half a month she looks so thin,
That Flamsteed can, with all his skill
100 See but her forehead and her chin.

Yet, as she wastes, she grows discreet,
Till midnight never shows her head:
So rotting Celia strolls the street,
When sober folks are all abed.

For sure if this be Luna's fate,
Poor Celia, but of mortal race,
In vain expects a longer date
To the materials of her face.

When Mercury her tresses mows
110 To think of black lead combs is vain,
No painting can restore a nose,
Nor will her teeth return again.

Two balls of glass may serve for eyes,
White lead can plaster up a cleft,
But these alas, are poor supplies
If neither cheeks, nor lips be left.

Ye powers, who over love preside,
Since mortal beauties drop so soon,
If you would have us well supplied,
120   Send us new nymphs with each new moon.

To Stella, Who Collected and Transcribed His Poems

As when a lofty pile is raised,
We never hear the workmen praised,
Who bring the lime, or place the stones;
But all admire Inigo Jones:
So if this pile of scattered rhymes
Should be approved in after-times,
If it both pleases and endures,
The merit and the praise are yours.

 Thou, Stella, wert no longer young,
10   When first for thee my harp I strung:
Without one word of Cupid's darts,
Of killing eyes, or bleeding hearts:
With friendship and esteem possessed,
I ne'er admitted love a guest.

 In all the habitudes of life,
The friend, the mistress, and the wife,
Variety we still pursue,
In pleasure seek for something new:
Or else, comparing with the rest,
20   Take comfort, that our own is best:
(The best we value by the worst,
As tradesmen show their trash at first):

But his pursuits are at an end,
Whom Stella chooses for a friend.

A poet, starving in a garret,
Conning old topics like a parrot,
Invokes his mistress and his muse,
And stays at home for want of shoes:
Should but his muse descending drop
30   A slice of bread, and mutton-chop,
Or kindly when his credit's out,
Surprise him with a pint of stout,
Or patch his broken stocking soles,
Or send him in a peck of coals;
Exalted in his mighty mind
He flies, and leaves the stars behind;
Counts all his labours amply paid,
Adores her for her timely aid.

Or should a porter make enquiries
40   For Chloe, Sylvia, Phyllis, Iris;
Be told the lodging, lane, and sign,
The bowers that hold those nymphs divine;
Fair Chloe would perhaps be found
With footmen tippling underground;
The charming Sylvia beating flax,
Her shoulders marked with bloody tracks;
Bright Phyllis mending ragged smocks,
And radiant Iris in the pox.

These are the goddesses enrolled
50   In Curll's collections, new and old,
Whose scoundrel fathers would not know 'em,
If they should meet 'em in a poem.

True poets can depress and raise;
Are lords of infamy and praise:
They are not scurrilous in satire,
Nor will in panegyric flatter.
Unjustly poets we asperse;
Truth shines the brighter, clad in verse;

And all the fictions they pursue,
60 Do but insinuate what is true.

Now, should my praises owe their truth
To beauty, dress, or paint, or youth,
What Stoics call *without our power*,
They could not be insured an hour:
'Twere grafting on an annual stock,
That must our expectation mock,
And making one luxuriant shoot,
Die the next year for want of root:
Before I could my verses bring,
70 Perhaps you're quite another thing.

So Maevius, when he drained his skull
To celebrate some suburb trull;
His similes in order set,
And every crambo he could get;
Had gone through all the commonplaces
Worn out by wits who rhyme on faces;
Before he could his poem close,
The lovely nymph had lost her nose.

Your virtues safely I commend,
80 They on no accidents depend:
Let malice look with all her eyes,
She dare not say the poet lies.

Stella, when you these lines transcribe,
Lest you should take them for a bribe;
Resolved to mortify your pride,
I'll here expose your weaker side.

Your spirits kindle to a flame,
Moved with the lightest touch of blame;
And when a friend in kindness tries
90 To show you where your error lies,
Conviction does but more incense;
Perverseness is your whole defence:
Truth, judgement, wit, give place to spite,
Regardless both of wrong and right.

Your virtues, all suspended, wait
Till time hath opened reason's gate:
And what is worse, your passion bends
Its force against your nearest friends;
Which manners, decency, and pride,
100 Have taught you from the world to hide:
In vain; for see, your friend hath brought
To public light your *only* fault;
And yet a fault we often find
Mixed in a noble generous mind;
And may compare to Etna's fire,
Which, though with trembling, all admire;
The heat that makes the summit glow,
Enriching all the vales below.
Those who in warmer climes complain,
110 From Phoebus' rays they suffer pain;
Must own, that pain is largely paid
By generous wines beneath a shade.

Yet when I find your passions rise,
And anger sparkling in your eyes,
I grieve those spirits should be spent,
For nobler ends by nature meant.
One passion, with a different turn,
Makes wit inflame, or anger burn;
So the sun's heat, by different powers,
120 Ripens the grape, the liquor sours.
Thus Ajax, when with rage possessed,
By Pallas breathed into his breast,
His valour would no more employ;
Which might alone have conquered Troy;
But blinded by resentment, seeks
For vengeance on his friends the Greeks.

You think this turbulence of blood
From stágnating preserves the flood;
Which thus fermenting, by degrees
130 Exalts the spirits, sinks the lees.

Stella, for once you reason wrong;
For should this ferment last too long,
By time subsiding, you may find
Nothing but acid left behind.
From passion you may then be freed,
When peevishness and spleen succeed.

Say Stella, when you copy next,
Will you keep strictly to the text?
Dare you let these reproaches stand,
140 And to your failing set your hand?
Or if these lines your anger fire,
Shall they in baser flames expire?
Whene'er they burn, if burn they must,
They'll prove my accusation just.

Upon the South Sea Project

Ye wise philosophers! explain,
  What magic makes our money rise,
When dropped into the Southern Main;
  Or do these jugglers cheat our eyes?

Put in your money fairly told;
  Presto begone – 'tis here again:
Ladies and gentlemen, behold,
  Here's every piece as big as ten.

Thus in a basin drop a shilling,
10 Then fill the vessel to the brim;
You shall observe, as you are filling,
  The ponderous metal seems to swim.

It rises both in bulk and height,
  Behold it swelling like a sop!
The liquid medium cheats your sight,
  Behold it mounted to the top!

'In stock three hundred thousand pounds;
   I have in view a lord's estate;
My manors all contiguous round;
20   A coach and six, and served in plate!'

Thus the deluded bankrupt raves,
   Puts all upon a desperate bet;
Then plunges in the Southern waves,
   Dipped over head and ears – in debt.

So, by a calenture misled,
   The mariner with rapture sees
On the smooth ocean's azure bed
   Enamelled fields, and verdant trees.

With eager haste he longs to rove
30   In that fantastic scene, and thinks
It must be some enchanted grove;
   And *in* he leaps, and *down* he sinks.

Five hundred chariots just bespoke,
   And sunk in these devouring waves,
The horses drowned, the harness broke,
   And here the owners find their graves.

Like Pharaoh, by directors led,
   They with their spoils went safe before;
His chariots tumbling out the dead,
40   Lay shattered on the Red Sea shore.

Raised up on Hope's aspiring plumes,
   The young adventurer o'er the deep
An eagle's flight and state assumes,
   And scorns the middle way to keep.

On paper wings he takes his flight,
   With wax the father bound them fast;
The wax is melted by the height,
   And down the towering boy is cast.

A moralist might here explain
50   The rashness of the Cretan youth;
Describe his fall into the main,
   And from a fable form a truth.

His wings are his paternal rent,
    He melts his wax at every flame;
His credit sunk, his money spent,
    In Southern Seas he leaves his name.

Inform us, you that best can tell,
    Why in yon dangerous gulf profound,
Where hundreds, and where thousands fell,
60   Fools chiefly float, the wise are drowned?

So have I seen from Severn's brink
    A flock of geese jump down together,
Swim where the bird of Jove would sink,
    And swimming never wet a feather.

But I affirm, 'tis false in fact,
    Directors better know their tools,
We see the nation's credit cracked,
    Each knave hath made a thousand fools.

One fool may from another win,
70   And then get off with money stored;
But if a sharper once comes in,
    He throws at all, and sweeps the board.

As fishes on each other prey
    The great ones swallowing up the small;
So fares it in the Southern Sea;
    But, whale directors eat up all.

When stock is high, they come between,
    Making by second hand their offers,
Then cunningly retire unseen,
80   With each a million in his coffers.

So when upon a moonshine night
    An ass was drinking at a stream;
A cloud arose, and stopped the light,
    By intercepting every beam;

'The day of judgement will be soon'
    (Cries out a sage among the crowd);
An ass hath swallowed up the moon,
    The moon lay safe behind the cloud.

Each poor subscriber to the Sea,
    Sinks down at once, and there he lies;
Directors fall as well as they,
    Their fall is but a trick to rise.

So fishes rising from the main
    Can soar with moistened wings on high;
The moisture dried, they sink again,
    And dip their fins again to fly.

Undone at play, the female troops
    Come here their losses to retrieve;
Ride o'er the waves in spacious hoops,
    Like Lapland witches in a sieve.

Thus Venus to the sea descends
    As poets feign; but where's the moral?
It shows the Queen of Love intends
    To search the deep for pearl and coral.

The sea is richer than the land,
    I heard it from my grannam's mouth,
Which now I clearly understand,
    For by the sea she meant the South.

Thus by directors we are told,
    'Pray gentlemen, believe your eyes,
Our ocean's covered o'er with gold,
    Look round, and see how thick it lies!

We, gentlemen, are your assisters,
    We'll come and hold you by the chin.'
Alas! all is not gold that glisters;
    Ten thousand sunk by leaping in.

Oh! would those patriots be so kind,
    Here in the deep to wash their hands,
Then, like Pactolus, we should find
    The sea indeed had golden sands.

A shilling in the Bath you fling,
    The silver takes a nobler hue,
By magic virtue in the spring,
    And seems a guinea to your view.

But as a guinea will not pass
    At market for a farthing more
Shown through a multiplying glass,
    Than what it always did before.

So cast it in the Southern Seas,
130   And view it through a jobber's bill;
Put on what spectacles you please,
    Your guinea's but a guinea still.

One night a fool into a brook
    Thus from a hillock looking down,
The golden stars for guineas took,
    And silver Cynthia for a crown.

The point he could no longer doubt,
    He ran, he leapt into the flood;
There sprawled awhile, and scarce got out,
140   All covered o'er with slime and mud.

Upon the water cast thy bread
    And after many days thou'lt find it;
But gold upon this ocean spread
    Shall sink, and leave no mark behind it.

There is a gulf where thousands fell,
    Here all the bold adventurers came,
A narrow sound, though deep as hell,
    'Change Alley is the dreadful name.

Nine times a day it ebbs and flows,
150   Yet he that on the surface lies,
Without a pilot seldom knows
    The time it falls, or when 'twill rise.

Subscribers here by thousands float,
    And jostle one another down;
Each paddling in his leaky boat,
    And here they fish for gold and drown:

Now buried in the depth below,
    Now mounted up to heaven again,
They reel and stagger to and fro,
160   *At their wits' end, like drunken men.*

Meantime, secure on Garr'way cliffs,
　　A savage race by shipwrecks fed,
Lie waiting for the foundered skiffs,
　　And strip the bodies of the dead.

But these, you say, are factious lies
　　From some malicious Tory's brain,
For, where directors get a prize,
　　The Swiss and Dutch whole millions drain.

Thus, when by rooks a lord is plied,
170　　Some cully often wins a bet,
By venturing on the cheating side,
　　Though not into the secret let.

While some build castles in the air,
　　Directors build 'em in the seas;
Subscribers plainly see 'em there,
　　For fools will see as wise men please.

Thus oft by mariners are shown,
　　Unless the men of Kent are liars,
Earl Godwin's castles overthrown,
180　　And palace roofs, and steeple spires.

Mark where the sly directors creep,
　　Nor to the shore approach too nigh!
The monsters nestle in the deep,
　　To seize you in your passing by.

Then, like the dogs of Nile, be wise,
　　Who taught by instinct how to shun
The crocodile that lurking lies,
　　Run as they drink, and drink and run.

Antaeus could by magic charms
190　　Recover strength whene'er he fell,
Alcides held him in his arms,
　　And sent him up in air to hell.

Directors thrown into the sea
　　Recover strength and vigour there,
But may be tamed another way,
　　Suspended for a while in air.

Directors! for 'tis you I warn,
      By long experience we have found
What planet ruled when you were born;
200   We see you never can be drowned.

Beware, nor over-bulky grow,
      Nor come within your cully's reach,
For if the sea should sink so low
      To leave you dry upon the beach;

You'll owe your ruin to your bulk:
      Your foes already waiting stand,
To tear you like a foundered hulk
      While you lie helpless on the sand.

Thus when a whale hath lost the tide,
210   The coasters crowd to seize the spoil;
The monster into parts divide,
      And strip the bones, and melt the oil.

Oh, may some Western tempest sweep
      These locusts whom our fruits have fed,
That plague, directors, to the deep,
      Driven from the South Sea to the Red.

May He, whom nature's laws obey,
      Who lifts the poor, and sinks the proud,
Quiet the raging of the sea,
220   And still the madness of the crowd.

But never shall our isle have rest
      Till those devouring swine run down,
(The devil's leaving the possessed),
      And headlong in the waters drown.

The nation then too late will find
      Computing all their cost and trouble,
Directors' promises but wind,
      South Sea at best a mighty *bubble*.

Apparent rari nantes in Gurgite vasto,
Arma virum, tabulaeque, et Troia gaza per undas.
                                             VIRG.

Stella's Birthday

WRITTEN IN THE YEAR 1721

All travellers at first incline
Where'er they see the fairest sign;
And if they find the chamber neat,
And like the liquor, and the meat,
Will call again, and recommend
The Angel Inn to every friend:
What though the painting grows decayed,
The house will never lose its trade;
Nay, though the treacherous tapster Thomas
10 Hangs a new angel two doors from us,
As fine as dauber's hands can make it,
In hopes that strangers may mistake it;
We think it both a shame and sin
To quit the true old Angel Inn.

Now, this is Stella's case in fact,
An angel's face, a little cracked;
(Could poets, or could painters fix
How angels look at thirty-six):
This drew us in at first, to find
20 In such a form an angel's mind:
And every virtue now supplies
The fainting rays of Stella's eyes.
See, at her levee crowding swains,
Whom Stella freely entertains
With breeding, humour, wit, and sense;
And puts them to so small expense:
Their mind so plentifully fills,
And makes such reasonable bills;
So little gets for what she gives,
30 We really wonder how she lives!
And had her stock been less, no doubt
She must have long ago run out.

Then who can think we'll quit the place
When Doll hangs out her newer face;
Nailed to her window full in sight
All Christian people to invite;
Or stop and light at Chloe's head
With scraps and leavings to be fed.

Then Chloe, still go on to prate
40   Of thirty-six, and thirty-eight;
Pursue your trade of scandal-picking,
Your hints that Stella is no chicken;
Your innuendos, when you tell us
That Stella loves to talk with fellows:
But let me warn you to believe
A truth, for which your soul should grieve;
That, should you live to see the day
When Stella's locks must all be grey;
When age must print a furrowed trace
50   On every feature of her face;
Though you and all your senseless tribe,
Could art, or time, or nature bribe,
To make you look like beauty's queen,
And hold forever at fifteen:
No bloom of youth can ever blind
The cracks and wrinkles of your mind,
All men of sense will pass your door,
And crowd to Stella's at fourscore.

The Part of a Summer

AT THE HOUSE OF GEORGE ROCHFORT, ESQ.

Thalia, tell in sober lays,
How George, Nim, Dan, Dean, pass their days.

Begin, my muse, first from our bowers,
We sally forth at different hours;
At seven, the Dean in night-gown dressed,
Goes round the house to wake the rest:

At nine, grave Nim and George facetious,
Go to the Dean to read Lucretius.
At ten, my Lady comes and hectors,
10   And kisses George, and ends our lectures;
And when she has him by the neck fast,
Hauls him, and scolds us down to breakfast.
We squander there an hour or more;
And then all hands, boys, to the oar;
All, heteroclite Dan except,
Who never time nor order kept,
But by peculiar whimsies drawn,
Peeps in the pond to look for spawn;
O'ersees the work, or 'Dragon' rows,
20   Or mars a text, or mends his hose;
Or – but proceed we in our journal –
At two, or after, we return all.
From the four elements assembling,
Warned by the bell, all folks come trembling,
From airy garrets some descend,
Some from the lake's remotest end.
My Lord and Dean, the fire forsake;
Dan leaves the earthly spade and rake:
The loiterers quake, no corner hides them,
30   And Lady Betty soundly chides them.
Now water's brought, and dinner's done,
With Church and King, the lady's gone;
(Not reckoning half an hour we pass
In talking o'er a moderate glass.)
Dan, growing drowsy, like a thief
Steals off to doze away his beef;
And this must pass for reading Hammond –
While George and Dean go to backgammon.
George, Nim and Dean set out at four,
40   And then again, boys, to the oar.
But when the sun goes to the deep
(Not to disturb him in his sleep,
Or make a rumbling o'er his head,
His candle out, and he abed)

We watch his motions to the minute,
And leave the flood when he goes in it:
Now stinted in the shortening day,
We go to prayers, and then to play:
Till supper comes, and after that,
50   We sit an hour to drink and chat.
'Tis late – the old and younger pairs,
By Adam lighted walk upstairs.
The weary Dean goes to his chamber,
And Nim and Dan to garret clamber.
So when this circle we have run,
The curtain falls, and all is done.

    I might have mentioned several facts,
Like episodes between the acts;
And tell who loses, and who wins,
60   Who gets a cold, who breaks his shins.
How Dan caught *nothing* in his net,
And how the boat was overset,
For brevity I have retrenched,
How in the lake the Dean was drenched:
It would be an explóit to brag on,
How valiant George rowed o'er the 'Dragon';
How steady in the storm he sat,
And saved his oar, but lost his hat.
How Nim (no hunter e'er could match him),
70   Still brings us hares, when he can catch them:
How skilfully Dan mends his nets,
How fortune fails him when he sets:
Or how the Dean delights to vex
The ladies, and lampoon the sex.
Or how our neighbour lifts his nose,
To tell what every schoolboy knows:
And, with his finger on his thumb,
Explaining, strikes opposers dumb;
Or how his wife, that female pedant,
80   (But now there need no more be said on't),
Shows all her secrets of housekeeping,
For candles how she trucks her dripping;

Was forced to send three miles for yeast
To brew her ale, and raise her paste:
Tells everything that you can think of,
How she cured Tommy of the chin-cough;
What gave her brats and pigs the measles,
And how her doves were killed by weasels:
How Jowler howled, and what a fright
90   She had with dreams the other night.

But now, since I have gone so far on,
A word or two of Lord Chief Baron;
And tell how little weight he sets
On all Whig papers and gazettes:
But for the politics of Pue,
Thinks every syllable is true;
And since he owns the King of Sweden
Is dead at last without evading;
Now all his hopes are in the Czar;
100   'Why, Muscovy is not so far;
Down the Black Sea, and up the straits,
And in a month he's at your gates:
Perhaps from what the packet brings,
By Christmas we shall see strange things.'

Why should I tell of ponds and drains,
What carps we met with for our pains:
Of sparrows tamed, and nuts innumerable,
To choke the girls, and to consume a rabble?
But you, who are a scholar, know
110   How transient all things are below:
How prone to change is human life;
Last night arrived Clem and his wife –
This grand event hath broke our measures;
Their reign began with cruel seizures:
The Dean must with his quilt supply,
The bed in which these tyrants lie:
Nim lost his wig-block, Dan his jordan;
(My Lady says she can't afford one)
George is half scared out of his wits,
120   For Clem gets all the tiny bits.

Henceforth expect a different survey;
This house will soon turn topsyturvy;
They talk of further alterations,
Which causes many speculations.

The Progress of Marriage

Aetatis suae fifty-two
A rich divine began to woo
A handsome young imperious girl
Nearly related to an Earl.
Her parents and her friends consent,
The couple to the temple went:
They first invite the Cyprian queen,
'Twas answered, she would not be seen.
The Graces next, and all the Muses
10   Were bid in form, but sent excuses:
Juno attended at the porch
With farthing candle for a torch,
While Mistress Iris held her train,
The faded bow distilling rain.
Then Hebe came and took her place
But showed no more than half her face.

Whate'er these dire forebodings meant,
In mirth the wedding-day was spent.
The wedding-day, you take me right,
20   I promise nothing for the night:
The bridegroom dressed, to make a figure,
Assumes an artificial vigour;
A flourished nightcap on, to grace
His ruddy, wrinkled, smirking face,
Like the faint red upon a pippin
Half withered by a winter's keeping.

And, thus set out this happy pair,
The swain is rich, the nymph is fair;

But, which I gladly would forget,
30   The swain is old, the nymph coquette.
Both from the goal together start;
Scarce run a step before they part;
No common ligament that binds
The various textures of their minds,
Their thoughts, and actions, hopes, and fears,
Less corresponding than their years.
Her spouse desires his coffee soon,
She rises to her tea at noon.
While he goes out to cheapen books,
40   She at the glass consults her looks;
While Betty's buzzing at her ear,
Lord, what a dress these parsons wear,
So odd a choice, how could she make,
Wished him a colonel for her sake.
Then on her fingers' ends she counts
Exact to what his age amounts,
The Dean, she heard her uncle say,
Is sixty, if he be a day;
His ruddy cheeks are no disguise;
50   You see the crow's feet round his eyes.

At one she rambles to the shops
To cheapen tea, and talk with fops.
Or calls a council of her maids
And tradesmen, to compare brocades.
Her weighty morning business o'er
Sits down to dinner just at four;
Minds nothing that is done or said,
Her evening work so fills her head;
The Dean, who used to dine at one,
60   Is mawkish, and his stomach gone;
In threadbare gown, would scarce a louse hold,
Looks like the chaplain of the household,
Beholds her from the chaplain's place
In French brocades and Flanders lace;
He wonders what employs her brain;
But never asks, or asks in vain;

His mind is full of other cares,
And in the sneaking parson's airs
Computes, that half a parish dues
70 Will hardly find his wife in shoes.

    Canst thou imagine, dull divine,
'Twill gain her love to make her fine?
Hath she no other wants beside?
You raise desire as well as pride,
Enticing coxcombs to adore,
And teach her to despise thee more.

    If in her coach she'll condescend
To place him at the hinder end
Her hoop is hoist above his nose,
80 His odious gown would soil her clothes,
And drops him at the church, to pray
While she drives on to see the play.
He like an orderly divine
Comes home a quarter after nine,
And meets her hasting to the ball,
Her chairmen push him from the wall:
He enters in, and walks upstairs,
And calls the family to prayers,
Then goes alone to take his rest
90 In bed, where he can spare her best.
At five the footmen make a din,
Her ladyship is just come in,
The masquerade began at two,
She stole away with much ado,
And shall be chid this afternoon
For leaving company so soon;
She'll say, and she may truly say't,
She can't abide to stay out late.

    But now, though scarce a twelve month married,
100 His lady has twelve times miscarried,
The cause, alas, is quickly guessed,
The town has whispered round the jest:
Think on some remedy in time,
You find his Reverence past his prime,

Already dwindled to a lathe;
No other way but try the Bath.

    For Venus rising from the ocean
Infused a strong prolific potion,
That mixed with Achelous' spring,
110   The 'hornéd flood', as poets sing:
Who with an English beauty smitten
Ran underground from Greece to Britain,
The genial virtue with him brought,
And gave the nymph a plenteous draught;
Then fled, and left his horn behind
For husbands past their youth to find;
The nymph who still with passion burned,
Was to a boiling fountain turned,
Where childless wives crowd every morn
120   To drink in Achelous' horn.
And here the father often gains
That title by another's pains.

    Hither, though much against his grain,
The Dean has carried Lady Jane.
He for a while would not consent,
But vowed his money all was spent;
His money spent! a clownish reason!
And must my Lady slip her season?
The doctor with a double fee
130   Was bribed to make the Dean agree.

    Here, all diversions of the place
Are proper in my Lady's case:
With which she patiently complies,
Merely because her friends advise;
His money and her time employs
In music, raffling-rooms, and toys,
Or in the Cross Bath, seeks an heir
Since others oft have found one there;
Where if the Dean by chance appears
140   It shames his cassock and his years.
He keeps his distance in the gallery
Till banished by some coxcomb's raillery;

For, it would his character expose
To bathe among the belles and beaux.

So have I seen within a pen
Young ducklings, fostered by a hen;
But when let out, they run and muddle
As instinct leads them, in a puddle;
The sober hen not born to swim
150   With mournful note clucks round the brim.

The Dean with all his best endeavour
Gets not an heir, but gets a fever;
A victim to the last essays
Of vigour in declining days.
He dies, and leaves his mourning mate
(What could he less?) his whole estate.

The widow goes through all the forms;
New lovers now will come in swarms.
Oh, may I see her soon dispensing
160   Her favours to some broken ensign!
Him let her marry for his face,
And only coat of tarnished lace;
To turn her naked out of doors,
And spend her jointure on his whores:
But for a parting present leave her
A rooted pox to last forever.

A Satirical Elegy on the Death of a Late Famous General

His Grace! impossible! what, dead!
Of old age too, and in his bed!
And could that Mighty Warrior fall?
And so inglorious, after all!
Well, since he's gone, no matter how,
The last loud trump must wake him now:
And, trust me, as the noise grows stronger,
He'd wish to sleep a little longer.

And could he be indeed so old
10   As by the newspapers we're told?
Threescore, I think, is pretty high;
'Twas time in conscience he should die.
This world he cumbered long enough;
He burnt his candle to the snuff;
And that's the reason, some folks think,
He left behind *so great a stink*.
Behold his funeral appears,
Nor widow's sighs, nor orphan's tears,
Wont at such times each heart to pierce,
20   Attend the progress of his hearse.
'But what of that?' his friends may say,
'He had those honours in his day.'
True to his profit and his pride,
He made them weep before he died.

    Come hither, all ye empty things,
Ye bubbles raised by breath of kings;
Who float upon the tide of state,
Come hither, and behold your fate.
Let pride be taught by this rebuke,
30   How very mean a thing's a Duke;
From all his ill-got honours flung,
Turned to that dirt from whence he sprung.

Upon the Horrid Plot Discovered by Harlequin the Bishop of Rochester's French Dog

IN A DIALOGUE BETWEEN A WHIG AND A TORY

I asked a Whig the other night,
How came this wicked plot to light:
He answered, that a dog of late
Informed a minister of state.
Said I, 'From thence I nothing know;
For, are not all informers so?

A villain, who his friend betrays,
We style him by no other phrase;
And so a perjured dog denotes
10   Porter, and Prendergast, and Oates.
And forty others I could name –'

WHIG   But you must know this dog was lame.

TORY   A weighty argument indeed;
Your evidence was lame. Proceed:
Come, help your lame dog o'er the stile.

WHIG   Sir, you mistake me all this while:
I mean a dog, without a joke,
Can howl, and bark, but never spoke.

TORY   I'm still to seek which dog you mean;
20   Whether cur Plunket, or whelp Skean,
An English or an Irish hound;
Or t'other puppy that was drowned,
Or Mason that abandoned bitch:
Then pray be free, and tell me which:
For, every stander-by was marking
That all the noise they made was barking:
You pay them well; the dogs have got
Their dog's-heads in a porridge-pot:
And 'twas but just; for, wise men say,
30   That, 'every dog must have his day'.
Dog Walpole laid a quart of nog on't,
He'd either make a hog or dog on't,
And looked since he has got his wish,
As if he had thrown down a dish.
Yet, this I dare foretell you from it,
He'll soon return to his own vomit.

WHIG   Besides, this horrid plot was found
By Neno after he was drowned.

TORY   Why then the proverb is not right,
40   Since you can teach dead dogs to bite.

WHIG   I proved my proposition full:
But, Jacobites are strangely dull.

Now, let me tell you plainly, sir,
Our witness is a real cur,
A dog of spirit for his years,
Has twice two legs, two hanging ears;
His name is Harlequin, I wot,
And that's a name in every plot:
Resolved to save the British nation,
50 Though French by birth and education:
His correspondence plainly dated,
Was all deciphered, and translated.
His answers were exceeding pretty
Before the secret wise committee;
Confessed as plain as he could bark;
Then with his fore-foot set his mark.

TORY   Then all this while I have been bubbled;
I thought it was a dog in doublet:
The matter now no longer sticks;
60 For statesmen never want dog-tricks.
But, since it was a real cur,
And not a dog in metaphor,
I'll give you joy of the report,
That he's to have a place at court.

WHIG   Yes, and a place he will grow rich in;
A turnspit in the royal kitchen.
Sir, to be plain, I tell you what;
We had occasion for a plot;
And when we found the dog begin it,
70 We guessed the Bishop's foot was in it.

TORY   I own it was a dangerous project;
And you have proved it by dog-logic.
Sure such intelligence between
A dog and bishop ne'er was seen,
Till you began to change the breed;
Your bishops all are dogs indeed.

Stella's Birthday [1723]

A GREAT BOTTLE OF WINE, LONG BURIED, BEING THAT DAY DUG UP

Resolved my annual verse to pay,
By duty bound, on Stella's day;
Furnished with papers, pen, and ink,
I gravely sat me down to think:
I bit my nails, and scratched my head,
But found my wit and fancy fled:
Or, if with more than usual pain,
A thought came slowly from my brain,
It cost me Lord knows how much time
To shape it into sense and rhyme:
And, what was yet a greater curse,
Long-thinking made my fancy worse.

Forsaken by the inspiring nine,
I waited at Apollo's shrine;
I told him what the world would say
If Stella were unsung today;
How I should hide my head for shame,
When both the Jacks and Robin came;
How Ford would frown, how Jim would leer;
How Sheridan the rogue would sneer:
And swear it does not always follow,
That '*Semel'n anno ridet Apollo.*'
I have assured them twenty times,
That Phoebus helped me in my rhymes;
Phoebus inspired me from above,
And he and I were hand in glove.
But finding me so dull and dry since,
They'll call it all poetic licence:
And when I brag of aid divine,
Think Eusden's right as good as mine.

Nor do I ask for Stella's sake;
'Tis my own credit lies at stake
And Stella will be sung, while I
Can only be a stander-by.

Apollo, having thought a little,
Returned this answer to a tittle.

'Though you should live like old Methusalem,
I furnish hints, and you should use all 'em,
You yearly sing as she grows old,
You'd leave her virtues half untold.
But to say truth, such dullness reigns
Through the whole set of Irish deans;
I'm daily stunned with such a medley,
Dean White, Dean Daniel, and Dean Smedley;
That, let what dean soever come,
My orders are, I'm not at home;
And if your voice had not been loud,
You must have passed among the crowd.

'But now, your danger to prevent,
You must apply to Mrs Brent,
For she, as priestess, knows the rites
Wherein the god of Earth delights.
First, nine ways looking, let her stand
With an old poker in her hand;
Let her describe a circle round
In Saunders' cellar on the ground:
A spade let prudent Archy hold,
And with discretion dig the mould:
Let Stella look with watchful eye,
Rebecca, Ford, and Grattans by.

'Behold the bottle, where it lies
With neck elated towards the skies!
The god of winds and god of fire
Did to its wondrous birth conspire;
And Bacchus, for the poet's use,
Poured in a strong inspiring juice:

See! as you raise it from its tomb,
It drags behind a spacious womb,
And in the spacious womb contains
70 A sovereign medicine for the brains.

'You'll find it soon if fate consents;
If not, a thousand Mrs Brents,
Ten thousand Archies armed with spades,
May dig in vain to Pluto's shades.

'From thence a plenteous draught infuse,
And boldly then invoke the muse:
(But first let Robert, on his knees,
With caution drain it from the lees)
The muse will at your call appear,
80 With Stella's praise to crown the year.'

To Charles Ford, Esq. on His Birthday

Come, be content, since out it must,
For, Stella has betrayed her trust,
And, whispering, charged me not to say
That Mr Ford was born today:
Or if at last, I needs must blab it,
According to my usual habit,
She bid me with a serious face
Be sure conceal the time and place,
And not my compliment to spoil
10 By calling this your native soil;
Or vex the ladies, when they knew
That you are turning forty-two.
But if these topics should appear
Strong arguments to keep you here,
We think, though you judge hardly of it,
Good manners must give place to profit.

The nymphs with whom you first began
Are each become a harridan;

And Montagu so far decayed,
20   That now her lovers must be paid;
And every belle that since arose
Has her contemporary beaux.
Your former comrades, once so bright,
With whom you toasted half the night,
Of rheumatism and pox complain,
And bid adieu to dear champagne:
Your great protectors, once in power,
Are now in exile, or the Tower,
Your foes, triumphant o'er the laws,
30   Who hate your person, and your cause,
If once they get you on the spot
You must be guilty of the plot,
For, true or false, they'll ne'er inquire,
But use you ten times worse than Prior.

In London! what would you do there?
Can you, my friend, with patience bear,
Nay, would it not your passion raise,
Worse than a pun, or Irish phrase,
To see a scoundrel strut and hector,
40   A foot-boy to some rogue director?
To look on vice triumphant round,
And virtue trampled on the ground:
Observe where bloody Townshend stands
With informations in his hands,
Hear him blaspheme, and swear, and rail,
Threatening the pillory and gaol.
If this you think a pleasing scene
To London straight return again,
Where you have told us from experience,
50   Are swarms of bugs and Hanoverians.

I thought my very spleen would burst
When fortune drove me hither first;
Was full as hard to please as you,
Nor persons' names, nor places knew;
But now I act as other folk,
Like prisoners when their gall is broke.

If you have London still at heart,
We'll make a small one here by art:
The difference is not much between
60 St James's Park and Stephen's Green;
And, Dawson Street will serve as well
To lead you hither, as Pall Mall,
(Without your passing through the palace
To choke your sight, and raise your malice).
The Deanery house may well be matched
(Under correction) with the Thatched,
Nor shall I, when you hither come,
Demand a crown a quart for stum.
Then, for a middle-agéd charmer,
70 Stella may vie with your Mountharmar:
She's now as handsome every bit,
And has a thousand times her wit.
The Dean and Sheridan, I hope,
Will half supply a Gay and Pope,
Corbet, though yet I know his worth not,
No doubt, will prove a good Arbuthnot:
I throw into the bargain, Jim:
In London can you equal him?
What think you of my favourite clan,
80 Robin and Jack, and Jack and Dan?
Fellows of modest worth and parts,
With cheerful looks, and honest hearts.

Can you on Dublin look with scorn?
Yet here were you and Ormonde born.
Oh, were but you and I so wise
To look with Robin Grattan's eyes:
Robin adores that spot of earth,
That literal spot which gave him birth,
And swears, Cushogue is to his taste,
90 As fine as Hampton Court at least.

When to your friends you would enhance
The praise of Italy or France,
For grandeur, elegance and wit,
We gladly hear you, and submit:

But then, to come and keep a clutter
For this, or that side of a gutter,
To live in this or t'other isle,
We cannot think it worth your while.
For, take it kindly, or amiss,
100 The difference but amounts to this,
We bury, on our side the channel
In linen, and on yours, in flannel.
You, for the news are ne'er to seek,
While we perhaps must wait a week:
You, happy folks, are sure to meet
A hundred whores in every street,
While we may search all Dublin o'er
And hardly hear of half a score.

You see, my arguments are strong;
110 I wonder you held out so long,
But since you are convinced at last
We'll pardon you for what is past.

So – let us now for whisk prepare;
Twelve pence a corner, if you dare.

Pethox the Great

From Venus born, thy beauty shows;
But who thy father, no man knows;
Nor can the skilful herald trace
The founder of thy ancient race.
Whether thy temper, full of fire,
Discovers Vulcan for thy sire;
The god who made Scamander boil,
And round his margin singed the soil;
(From whence philosophers agree,
10 An equal power descends to thee).
Whether from dreadful Mars you claim
The high descent from whence you came,

And, as a proof, show numerous scars
By fierce encounters made in wars;
(Those honourable wounds you bore
From head to foot, and *all before*);
And still the bloody field frequent,
Familiar in each leader's tent.
Or whether, as the learn'd contend,
20   You from your neighbouring Gaul descend;
Or from Parthenope the proud,
Where numberless thy votaries crowd:
Whether thy great forefathers came
From realms that bear Vesputio's name:
For so conjectors would obtrude,
And from thy painted skin conclude.
Whether, as Epicurus shows
The world from jostling seeds arose;
Which mingling with prolific strife
30   In chaos, kindled into life;
So your production was the same,
And from the contending atoms came.

Thy fair indulgent mother crowned
Thy head with sparkling rubies round;
Beneath thy decent steps, the road
Is all with precious jewels strewed.
The bird of Pallas knows his post,
Thee to attend whe'er thou goest.

Byzantians boast, that on the clod
40   Where once their sultan's horse hath trod,
Grows neither grass, nor shrub, nor tree;
The same thy subjects boast of thee.

The greatest lord, when you appear,
Will deign your livery to wear,
In all thy various colours seen,
Of red, and yellow, blue, and green.

With half a word, when you require,
The man of business must retire.

The haughty minister of state
50 With trembling must thy leisure wait;
And while his fate is in thy hands,
The business of the nation stands.

Thou darest the greatest prince attack,
Canst hourly set him on the rack,
And, as an instance of thy power,
Enclose him in a wooden tower,
With pungent pains on every side:
So Regulus in torments died.

From thee our youth all virtues learn,
60 Dangers with prudence to discern;
And well thy scholars are endued
With temperance and with fortitude;
With patience, which all ills supports,
And secrecy, the art of courts.

The glittering beau could hardly tell,
Without your aid, to read or spell;
But, having long conversed with you,
Knows how to scrawl a billet-doux.

With what delight, methinks, I trace
70 Thy blood in every noble race!
In whom thy features, shape, and mien,
Are to the life distinctly seen.

The Britons, once a savage kind,
By you, were brightened and refined:
Descendants of the barbarous Huns,
With limbs robust, and voice that stuns;
But you have moulded them afresh,
Removed the tough superfluous flesh,
Taught them to modulate their tongues,
80 And speak without the help of lungs.

Proteus on you bestowed the boon
To change your visage like the moon;
You sometimes half a face produce,
Keep t'other half for private use.

How famed thy conduct in the fight,
With Hermes, son of Pleias bright:
Outnumbered, half encompassed round,
You strove for every inch of ground;
Then, by a soldierly retreat,
90   Retired to your imperial seat.
The victor, when your steps he traced,
Found all the realms before him waste;
You, o'er the high triumphal arch
Pontific, made your glorious march;
The wondrous arch behind you fell,
And left a chasm profound as hell:
You, in your Capitol secured,
A siege as long as Troy endured.

To Stella

WRITTEN ON THE DAY OF HER BIRTH, BUT NOT ON
THE SUBJECT, WHEN I WAS SICK IN BED

Tormented with incessant pains,
Can I devise poetic strains?
Time was, when I could yearly pay
My verse on Stella's native day:
But now, unable grown to write,
I grieve she ever saw the light.
Ungrateful; since to her I owe
That I these pains can undergo.
She tends me, like a humble slave;
10   And, when indecently I rave,
When out my brutish passions break,
With gall in every word I speak,
She, with soft speech, my anguish cheers,
Or melts my passion down with tears:
Although 'tis easy to descry
She wants assistance more than I;

Yet seems to feel my pains alone,
And is a Stoic in her own.
When, among scholars, can we find
20   So soft, and yet so firm a mind?
All accidents of life conspire
To raise up Stella's virtue higher;
Or else, to introduce the rest
Which had been latent in her breast.
Her firmness who could e'er have known,
Had she not evils of her own?
Her kindness who could ever guess,
Had not her friends been in distress?
Whatever base returns you find
30   From me, dear Stella, still be kind;
In your own heart you'll reap the fruit,
Though I continue still a brute.
But when I once am out of pain,
I promise to be good again:
Meantime your other juster friends
Shall for my follies make amends:
So may we long continue thus,
Admiring you, you pitying us.

Prometheus

ON WOOD THE PATENTEE'S IRISH HALFPENCE

As, when the squire and tinker, Wood,
Gravely consulting Ireland's good,
Together mingled in a mass
Smith's dust, and copper, lead and brass;
The mixture thus by chemic art,
United close in every part,
In fillets rolled, or cut in pieces,
Appeared like one continuous species,
And by the forming engine struck,
10   On all the same *impression* stuck.

So, to confound this hated coin,
All parties and religions join;
Whigs, Tories, trimmers, Hanoverians,
Quakers, conformists, presbyterians,
Scotch, Irish, English, French unite
With equal interest, equal spite,
Together mingled in a lump,
Do all in one opinion jump;
And everyone begins to find
20 The same impression on his *mind*.

A strange event! whom gold incites,
To blood and quarrels, brass unites:
So goldsmiths say, the coarsest stuff
Will serve for solder well enough;
So, by the kettle's loud alarm,
The bees are gathered to a swarm:
So by the brazen trumpet's bluster,
Troops of all tongues and nations muster:
And so the harp of Ireland brings,
30 Whole crowds about its brazen strings.

There is a chain let down from Jove,
But fastened to his throne above;
So strong, that from the lower end,
They say, all human things depend:
This chain, as ancient poets hold,
When Jove was young, was made of gold.
Prometheus once this chain purloined,
Dissolved, and into money coined;
Then whips me on a chain of brass,
40 (Venus was bribed to let it pass).

Now while this brazen chain prevailed,
Jove saw that all devotion failed;
No temple to his godship raised;
No sacrifice on altars blazed;
In short, such dire confusions followed,
Earth must have been in chaos swallowed.

Jove stood amazed, but looking round,
With much ado the cheat he found;
'Twas plain he could no longer hold
50 The world in any chain but gold;
And to the god of wealth his brother,
Sent Mercury to get another.

    Prometheus on a rock was laid,
Tied with the chain himself had made;
On icy Caucasus to shiver,
While vultures eat his growing liver.

    Ye powers of Grub Street, make me able,
Discreetly to apply this fable.
Say, who is to be understood
60 By that old thief Prometheus? Wood.
For Jove, it is not hard to guess him,
I mean His Majesty, God bless him.
This thief and blacksmith was so bold,
He strove to steal that chain of gold,
Which links the subject to the king:
And change it for a brazen string.
But sure, if nothing else must pass
Between the King and us but brass,
Although the chain will never crack,
70 Yet our devotion may grow slack.

    But Jove will soon convert I hope,
This brazen chain into a rope;
With which Prometheus shall be tied,
And high in air for ever ride;
Where, if we find his liver grows,
For want of vultures, we have crows.

Stella's Birthday [1725]

As, when a beauteous nymph decays,
We say, she's past her dancing days;

So, poets lose their feet by time,
And can no longer dance in rhyme.
Your annual bard had rather chose
To celebrate your birth in prose;
Yet, merry folks, who want by chance
A pair to make a country dance,
Call the old housekeeper, and get her
10 To fill a place, for want of better;
While Sheridan is off the hooks,
And friend Delany at his books,
That Stella may avoid disgrace,
Once more the Dean supplies their place.

Beauty and wit, too sad a truth,
Have always been confined to youth;
The god of wit, and beauty's queen,
He twenty-one, and she fifteen:
No poet ever sweetly sung,
20 Unless he were like Phoebus, young;
Nor ever nymph inspired to rhyme,
Unless, like Venus, in her prime.
At fifty-six, if this be true,
Am I a poet fit for you?
Or at the age of forty-three,
Are you a subject fit for me?
Adieu bright wit, and radiant eyes;
You must be grave, and I be wise.
Our fate in vain we would oppose,
30 But I'll be still your friend in prose:
Esteem and friendship to express,
Will not require poetic dress;
And if the muse deny her aid
To have them *sung*, they may be *said*.

But, Stella say, what evil tongue
Reports you are no longer young?
That Time sits with his scythe to mow
Where erst sat Cupid with his bow;
That half your locks are turned to grey;
40 I'll ne'er believe a word they say.

'Tis true, but let it not be known,
My eyes are somewhat dimmish grown;
For nature, always in the right,
To your decays adapts my sight,
And wrinkles undistinguished pass,
For I'm ashamed to use a glass;
And till I see them with these eyes,
Whoever says you have them, lies.

    No length of time can make you quit
50 Honour and virtue, sense and wit,
Thus you may still be young to me,
While I can better *hear* than *see*;
Oh, ne'er may fortune show her spite,
To make me *deaf*, and mend my *sight*.

A Receipt to Restore Stella's Youth

The Scottish hinds, too poor to house
In frosty nights their starving cows,
While not a blade of grass, or hay,
Appears from Michaelmas to May;
Must let their cattle range in vain
For food, along the barren plain;
Meagre and lank with fasting grown,
And nothing left but skin and bone;
Exposed to want, and wind, and weather,
10 They just keep life and soul together,
Till summer showers and evening dew,
Again the verdant glebe renew;
And as the vegetables rise,
The famished cow her wants supplies;
Without an ounce of last year's flesh,
Whate'er she gains is young and fresh;
Grows plump and round, and full of mettle,
As rising from Medea's kettle;

With youth and beauty to enchant
20   Europa's counterfeit gallant.
    Why, Stella, should you knit your brow,
If I compare you to the cow?
'Tis just the case: for you have fasted
So long till all your flesh is wasted,
And must against the warmer days
Be sent to Quilca down to graze;
Where mirth, and exercise, and air,
Will soon your appetite repair.
The nutriment will from within
30   Round all your body, plump your skin;
Will agitate the lazy flood,
And fill your veins with sprightly blood:
Nor flesh nor blood will be the same,
Nor aught of Stella, but the name;
For, what was ever understood
By human kind, but flesh and blood?
And if your flesh and blood be new,
You'll be no more your former *you*;
But for a blooming nymph will pass,
40   Just fifteen, coming summer's grass:
Your jetty locks with garlands crowned,
While all the squires from nine miles round,
Attended by a brace of curs,
With jockey-boots, and silver spurs;
No less than justices o' quorum,
Their cowboys bearing cloaks before 'em,
Shall leave deciding broken pates,
To kiss your steps at Quilca gates;
But, lest you should my skill disgrace,
50   Come back before you're out of case;
For if to Michaelmas you stay,
The new-born flesh will melt away;
The squires in scorn will fly the house
For better game, and look for grouse:
But here, before the frost can mar it,
We'll make it firm with beef and claret.

To Quilca

A COUNTRY HOUSE IN NO GOOD REPAIR, WHERE THE
SUPPOSED AUTHOR, AND SOME OF HIS FRIENDS, SPENT A
SUMMER IN THE YEAR 1725

Let me my properties explain,
A rotten cabin, dropping rain;
Chimneys with scorn rejecting smoke;
Stools, tables, chairs, and bedsteads, broke:
Here elements have lost their uses,
Air ripens not, nor earth produces:
In vain we make poor Sheelah toil,
Fire will not roast, nor waters boil.
Through all the valleys, hills, and plains,
The goddess Want in triumph reigns;
And her chief officers of state,
Sloth, Dirt, and Theft around her wait.

A Pastoral Dialogue between Richmond Lodge and Marble Hill

WRITTEN JUNE 1727, JUST AFTER THE NEWS OF THE
KING'S DEATH

In spite of Pope, in spite of Gay,
And all that he or they can say;
Sing on I must, and sing I will
Of Richmond Lodge, and Marble Hill.

Last Friday night, as neighbours use,
This couple met to talk of news.
For by old proverbs it appears,
That walls have tongues, and hedges, ears.

MARBLE HILL

Quoth Marble Hill, right well I ween,
Your mistress now is grown a queen;
You'll find it soon by woeful proof,
She'll come no more beneath your roof.

RICHMOND LODGE

The kingly prophet well evinces,
That we should put no trust in princes;
My royal master promised me
To raise me to a high degree:
But now he's grown a king, God wot,
I fear I shall be soon forgot.
You see, when folks have got their ends,
How quickly they neglect their friends;
Yet I may say 'twixt me and you,
Pray God they now may find as true.

MARBLE HILL

My house was built but for a show,
My Lady's empty pockets know;
And now she will not have a shilling
To raise the stairs, or build the ceiling;
For, all the courtly madams round,
Now pay four shillings in the pound.
'Tis come to what I always thought;
My dame is hardly worth a groat.
Had you and I been courtiers born,
We should not thus have lain forlorn;
For, those we dexterous courtiers call,
Can *rise* upon their master's *fall*.
But we, unlucky and unwise,
Must *fall*, because our masters *rise*.

RICHMOND LODGE

My master scarce a fortnight since,
Was grown as wealthy as a prince;
But now it will be no such thing,
For he'll be poor as any king:

And, by his crown will nothing get;
But, like a king, to run in debt.

MARBLE HILL
No more the Dean, that grave divine,
Shall keep the key of my (no) wine;
My ice-house rob as heretofore,
And steal my artichokes no more;
Poor Patty Blount no more be seen
Bedraggled in my walks so green;
Plump Johnny Gay will now elope;
50   And here no more will dangle Pope.

RICHMOND LODGE
Here wont the Dean when he's to seek,
To sponge a breakfast once a week;
To cry the bread was stale, and mutter
Complaints against the royal butter.
But, now I fear it will be said,
No butter sticks upon his bread.
We soon shall find him full of spleen,
For want of tattling to the Queen;
Stunning her royal ears with talking,
60   His Reverence and her Highness walking:
Whilst Lady Charlotte, like a stroller,
Sits mounted on the garden roller.
A goodly sight to see her ride,
With ancient Mirmont at her side.
In velvet cap his head lies warm;
His hat for show, beneath his arm.

MARBLE HILL
Some South Sea broker from the city,
Will purchase me, the more's the pity,
Lay all my fine plantations waste,
70   To fit them to his vulgar taste;
Changed for the worse in every part,
My master Pope will break his heart.

RICHMOND LODGE

In my own Thames may I be drownded,
If e'er I stoop beneath a crowned head:
Except her Majesty prevails
To place me with the Prince of Wales.
And then I shall be free from fears,
For, he'll be prince these fifty years.
I then will turn a courtier too,
80   And serve the times as others do.
Plain loyalty not built on hope,
I leave to your contriver, Pope:
None loves his king and country better,
Yet none was ever less their debtor.

MARBLE HILL

Then, let him come and take a nap,
In summer, on my verdant lap:
Prefer our villas where the Thames is,
To Kensington, or hot St James's;
Nor shall I dull in silence sit;
90   For, 'tis to me he owes his wit;
My groves, my echoes, and my birds,
Have taught him his poetic words.
We gardens, and you wildernesses,
Assist all poets in distresses,
Him twice a week I here expect,
To rattle Moody for neglect;
An idle rogue, who spends his quarterage
In tippling at the Dog and Partridge;
And I can hardly get him down
100   Three times a week to brush my gown.

RICHMOND LODGE

I pity you, dear Marble Hill;
But hope to see you flourish still.
All happiness – and so adieu.

MARBLE HILL

Kind Richmond Lodge; the same to you.

The Furniture of a Woman's Mind

A set of phrases learned by rote;
A passion for a scarlet coat;
When at a play to laugh, or cry,
But cannot tell the reason why:
Never to hold her tongue a minute;
While all she prates has nothing in it.
Whole hours can with a coxcomb sit,
And take his nonsense all for wit:
Her learning mounts to read a song,
10   But, half the words pronouncing wrong;
Has every repartee in store,
She spoke ten thousand times before.
Can ready compliments supply
On all occasions, cut and dry.
Such hatred to a parson's gown,
The sight will put her in a swoon.
For conversation well endued;
She calls it witty to be rude;
And, placing raillery in railing,
20   Will tell aloud your greatest failing;
Nor makes a scruple to expose
Your bandy leg, or crooked nose.
Can, at her morning tea, run o'er
The scandal of the day before.
Improving hourly in her skill,
To cheat and wrangle at quadrille.

In choosing lace a critic nice,
Knows to a groat the lowest price;
Can in her female clubs dispute
30   What lining best the silk will suit;
What colours each complexion match:
And where with art to place a patch.
If chance a mouse creeps in her sight,
Can finely counterfeit a fright;

So, sweetly screams if it comes near her,
She ravishes all hearts to hear her.
Can dexterously her husband tease,
By taking fits whene'er she please:
By frequent practice learns the trick
40   At proper seasons to be sick:
Thinks nothing gives one airs so pretty;
At once creating love and pity.
If Molly happens to be careless,
And but neglects to warm her hair-lace,
She gets a cold as sure as death;
And vows she scarce can fetch her breath.
Admires how modest women can
Be so *robustious* like a man.

    In party, furious to her power;
50   A bitter Whig, or Tory sour;
Her arguments directly tend
Against the side she would defend:
Will prove herself a Tory plain,
From principles the Whigs maintain;
And, to defend the Whiggish cause,
Her topics from the Tories draws.

    O yes! If any man can find
More virtues in a woman's mind,
Let them be sent to Mrs Harding;
60   She'll pay the charges to a farthing:
Take notice, she has my commission
To add them in the next edition;
They may outsell a better thing;
So halloo boys! God save the King.

Holyhead. September 25, 1727

Lo here I sit at Holyhead
With muddy ale and mouldy bread:
All Christian victuals stink of fish,
I'm where my enemies would wish.
Convict of lies is every sign,
The inn has not one drop of wine.
I'm fastened both by wind and tide,
I see the ship at anchor ride.
The captain swears the sea's too rough,
He has not passengers enough.
And thus the Dean is forced to stay,
Till others come to help the pay.
In Dublin they'd be glad to see
A packet though it brings in me.
They cannot say the winds are cross;
Your politicians at a loss
For want of matter swears and frets,
Are forced to read the old gazettes.
I never was in haste before
To reach that slavish hateful shore:
Before, I always found the wind
To me was most malicious kind,
But now the danger of a friend
On whom my hopes and fears depend,
Absent from whom all climes are cursed,
With whom I'm happy in the worst,
With rage impatient makes me wait
A passage to the land I hate.
Else, rather on this bleaky shore
Where loudest winds incessant roar,
Where neither herb nor tree will thrive,
Where nature hardly seems alive,
I'd go in freedom to my grave,
Than rule yon isle and be a slave.

The Journal of a Modern Lady

It was a most unfriendly part
In you, who ought to know my heart,
Are well acquainted with my zeal
For all the female commonweal:
How could it come into your mind,
To pitch on me, of all mankind,
Against the sex to write a satire,
And brand me for a woman-hater?
On me, who think them all so fair,
10   They rival Venus to a hair;
Their virtues never ceased to sing,
Since first I learnt to tune a string.
Methinks I hear the ladies cry,
Will he his character belie?
Must never our misfortunes end?
And have we lost our only friend?
Ah lovely nymphs, remove your fears,
No more let fall those precious tears.
Sooner shall . . . &c.

                        [Here several verses are omitted.]

20   The hound be hunted by the hare,
Than I turn rebel to the fair.

    'Twas you engaged me first to write,
Then gave the subject out of spite:
The 'Journal of a Modern Dame'
Is by my promise what you claim:
My word is passed, I must submit;
And yet perhaps you may be bit.
I but transcribe, for not a line
Of all the satire shall be mine.

30   Compelled by you to tag in rhymes
The common slanders of the times,
Of modern times; the guilt is yours,
And me my innocence secures.

Unwilling muse begin thy lay,
The annals of a female day.

By nature turned to play the Rakewell,
(As we shall show you in the sequel)
The modern dame is waked by noon,
Some authors say, not quite so soon;
40   Because, though sore against her will,
She sat all night up at quadrille.
She stretches, gapes, unglues her eyes,
And asks if it be time to rise;
Of headache, and the spleen complains;
And then to cool her heated brains,
(Her nightgown and her slippers brought her),
Takes a large dram of citron-water.
Then to her glass; and 'Betty, pray
Don't I look frightfully today?
50   But was it not confounded hard?
Well, if I ever touch a card:
Four matadors, and lose codille!
Depend upon't, I never will.
But run to Tom, and bid him fix
The ladies here tonight by six.'
'Madam, the goldsmith waits below,
He says, his business is to know
If you'll redeem the silver cup
He keeps in pawn?' – 'Why, show him up.'
60   'Your dressing-plate, he'll be content
To take, for interest *cent percent*.
And, Madam, there's my Lady Spade
Hath sent this letter by her maid.'
'Well, I remember when she won;
And hath she sent so soon to dun?
Here, carry down those ten pistoles
My husband left to pay the coals:
I thank my stars they all are light;
And I may have revenge tonight.'
70   Now, loitering o'er her tea and cream,
She enters on her usual theme;

Her last night's ill success repeats,
Calls Lady Spade a hundred cheats:
She slipped Spadillo in her breast,
Then thought to turn it to a jest.
There's Mrs Cut and she combine,
And to each other give the sign.
Through every game pursues her tale,
Like hunters o'er their evening ale.

80 Now to another scene give place,
Enter the folks with silks and lace:
Fresh matter for a world of chat,
Right Indian this, right Mechlin that.
'Observe this pattern; there's a stuff!
I can have customers enough.
Dear madam, you are grown so hard,
This lace is worth twelve pounds a yard:
Madam, if there be truth in man,
I never sold so cheap a fan.'

90 This business of importance o'er,
And madam almost dressed by four;
The footman, in his usual phrase,
Comes up with, 'Madam, dinner stays';
She answers in her usual style,
'The cook must keep it back awhile;
I never can have time to dress,
No woman breathing takes up less;
I'm hurried so, it makes me sick,
I wish the dinner at Old Nick.'

100 At table now she acts her part,
Has all the dinner-cant by heart:
'I thought we were to dine alone,
My dear, for sure if I had known
This company would come today –
But really 'tis my spouse's way;
He's so unkind, he never sends
To tell, when he invites his friends:
I wish you may but have enough.'
And while with all this paltry stuff,

110 She sits tormenting every guest,
    Nor gives her tongue one moment's rest,
    In phrases battered, stale, and trite,
    Which *modern* ladies call polite;
    You see the booby husband sit
    In admiration at her wit!

    But let me now awhile survey
    Our madam o'er her evening tea;
    Surrounded with her noisy clans
    Of prudes, coquettes, and harridans;
120 When frighted at the clamorous crew,
    Away the god of Silence flew,
    And fair Discretion left the place,
    And Modesty with blushing face:
    Now enters overweening Pride,
    And Scandal ever gaping wide,
    Hypocrisy with frown severe,
    Scurrility with gibing air;
    Rude Laughter seeming like to burst;
    And Malice always judging worst;
130 And Vanity with pocket-glass;
    And Impudence with front of brass;
    And studied Affectation came,
    Each limb, and feature out of frame;
    While Ignorance with brain of lead,
    Flew hovering o'er each female head.

    Why should I ask of thee, my muse,
    An hundred tongues, as poets use,
    When, to give every dame her due,
    An hundred thousand were too few!
140 Or how should I, alas! relate,
    The sum of all their senseless prate,
    Their innuendos, hints, and slanders,
    Their meanings lewd, and *double entendres*.
    Now comes the general scandal-charge,
    What some invent, the rest enlarge;
    And, 'Madam, if it be a lie,
    You have the tale as cheap as I:

I must conceal my author's name,
But now 'tis known to common fame.'

150   Say, foolish females, bold and blind,
Say, by what fatal turn of mind,
Are you on vices most severe
Wherein yourselves have greatest share?
Thus every fool herself deludes;
The prude condemns the absent prudes;
Mopsa, who stinks her spouse to death,
Accuses Chloe's tainted breath;
Hircina, rank with sweat, presumes
To censure Phyllis for perfumes;
160   While crooked Cynthia sneering says,
That Florimel wears iron stays:
Chloe of every coxcomb jealous,
Admires how girls can talk with fellows,
And full of indignation frets
That women could be such coquettes:
Iris, for scandal most notorious,
Cries, 'Lord, the world is so censorious!'
And Rufa with her combs of lead,
Whispers that Sappho's hair is red:
170   Aura, whose tongue you hear a mile hence,
Talks half a day in praise of silence;
And Sylvia full of inward guilt,
Calls Amoret an arrant jilt.

    Now voices over voices rise,
While each to be the loudest vies;
They contradict, affirm, dispute,
No single tongue one moment mute;
All mad to speak, and none to hearken,
They set the very lap-dog barking;
180   Their chattering makes a louder din
Than fishwives o'er a cup of gin:
Not schoolboys at a barring-out,
Raised ever such incessant rout:

The jumbling particles of matter
In chaos made not such a clatter:
Far less the rabble roar and rail,
When drunk with sour election ale.

Nor do they trust their tongue alone,
But speak a language of their own;
Can read a nod, a shrug, a look,
Far better than a printed book;
Convey a libel in a frown,
And wink a reputation down;
Or by the tossing of the fan,
Describe the lady and the man.

But see, the female club disbands,
Each twenty visits on her hands.
Now all alone poor madam sits,
In vapours and hysteric fits:
'And was not Tom this morning sent?
I'll lay my life he never went:
Past six, and not a living soul!
I might by this have won a vole.'
A dreadful interval of spleen!
How shall we pass the time between?
'Here Betty, let me take my drops,
And feel my pulse, I know it stops:
This head of mine, Lord, how it swims!
And such a pain in all my limbs!'
'Dear madam, try to take a nap –'
But now they hear the footman's rap:
'Go run, and light the ladies up:
It must be one before we sup.'

The table, cards and counters set,
And all the gamester ladies met,
Her spleen and fits recovered quite,
Our madam can sit up all night;
'Whoever comes I'm not within –
Quadrille's the word, and so begin.'

220   How can the muse her aid impart,
Unskilled in all the terms of art?
Or in harmonious numbers put
The deal, the shuffle, and the cut?
The superstitious whims relate,
That fill a female gamester's pate?
What agony of soul she feels
To see a knave's inverted heels:
She draws up card by card, to find
Good fortune peeping from behind;

230   With panting heart, and earnest eyes,
In hope to see Spadillo rise;
In vain, alas! her hope is fed;
She draws an ace, and sees it red.
In ready counters never pays,
But pawns her snuff-box, rings, and keys.
Ever with some new fancy struck,
Tries twenty charms to mend her luck.
'This morning when the parson came,
I said I should not win a game.

240   This odious chair how came I stuck in't,
I think I never had good luck in't.
I'm so uneasy in my stays;
Your fan, a moment, if you please.
Stand further, girl, or get you gone,
I always lose when you look on.'
'Lord, madam, you have lost codille,
I never saw you play so ill.'
'Nay, madam, give me leave to say,
'Twas you that threw the game away;

250   When Lady Tricksy played a four,
You took it with a matador;
I saw you touch your wedding-ring
Before my Lady called a king.
You spoke a word began with H,
And I know whom you meant to teach,
Because you held the king of hearts:
Fie, madam, leave these little arts.'

'That's not so bad as one that rubs
Her chair to call the king of clubs,
260 And makes her partner understand
A matador is in her hand.'
'Madam, you have no cause to flounce,
I swear I saw you thrice renounce.'
'And truly, Madam, I know when
Instead of five you scored me ten.
Spadillo here has got a mark,
A child may know it in the dark:
I guess the hand, it seldom fails,
I wish some folk would pare their nails.'

270 While thus they rail, and scold, and storm,
It passes but for common form;
And conscious that they all speak true,
They give each other but their due;
It never interrupts the game,
Or makes 'em sensible of shame.

The time too precious now to waste,
And supper gobbled up in haste,
Again afresh to cards they run,
As if they had but just begun.
280 But I shall not again repeat
How oft they squabble, snarl and cheat.
At last they hear the watchman knock,
'A frosty morn – past four o'clock.'
The chairmen are not to be found,
'Come, let us play another round.'

Now, all in haste they huddle on
Their hoods and cloaks, and get them gone:
But first, the winner must invite
The company tomorrow night.

290 Unlucky madam, left in tears,
(Who now again quadrille forswears),
With empty purse, and aching head,
Steals to her sleeping spouse to bed.

The Grand Question Debated

WHETHER HAMILTON'S BAWN SHOULD BE TURNED INTO
A BARRACKS OR A MALTHOUSE

PREFACE

The author of the following poem, is said to be Dr J.S.D.S.P.D.
who writ it, as well as several other copies of verses of the like
kind, by way of amusement, in the family of an honourable
gentleman in the North of Ireland, where he spent a summer
about two or three years ago.

A certain very great person, then in that kingdom, having
heard much of this poem, obtained a copy from the gentleman,
or, as some say, the lady, in whose house it was written, from
whence, I know not by what accident, several other copies were
transcribed, full of errors. As I have a great respect for the
supposed author, I have procured a true copy of the poem, the
publication whereof can do him less injury than printing any of
those incorrect ones which run about in manuscript, and would
infallibly be soon in the press, if not thus prevented.

Some expressions being peculiar to Ireland, I have prevailed
on a gentleman of that kingdom to explain them, and I have put
the several explanations in their proper places.

> Thus spoke to my Lady, the knight full of care;
> 'Let me have your advice in a weighty affair.
> This Hamilton's Bawn, while it sticks on my hand,
> I lose by the house what I get by the land;
> But how to dispose of it to the best bidder,
> For a barrack or malthouse, we must now consider.
>
> 'First, let me suppose I make it a malthouse:
> Here I have computed the profit will fall t'us.
> There's nine hundred pounds for labour and grain,
> I increase it to twelve, so three hundred remain:
> A handsome addition for wine and good cheer,
> Three dishes a day, and three hogsheads a year.

10

With a dozen large vessels my vault shall be stored,
No little scrub joint shall come on my board:
And you and the Dean no more shall combine,
To stint me at night to one bottle of wine;
Nor shall I for his humour, permit you to purloin
A stone and a quarter of beef from my sirloin.
If I make it a barrack, the crown is my tenant.
20   My dear, I have pondered again and again on't:
In poundage and drawbacks, I lose half my rent,
Whatever they give me I must be content,
Or join with the court in every debate,
And rather than that, I would lose my estate.'

Thus ended the knight: thus began his meek wife:
'It *must*, and it *shall* be a barrack, my life.
I'm grown a mere Mopus; no company comes;
But a rabble of tenants, and rusty dull rums;
With parsons, what lady can keep herself clean?
30   I'm all over daubed when I sit by the Dean.
But, if you will give us a barrack, my dear,
The Captain, I'm sure, will always come here;
I then shall not value his Deanship a straw,
For the Captain, I warrant, will keep him in awe;
Or should he pretend to be brisk and alert,
Will tell him that chaplains should not be so pert;
That men of his coat should be minding their prayers,
And not among ladies to give themselves airs.'

Thus argued my Lady, but argued in vain;
40   The knight his opinion resolved to maintain.

But Hannah, who listened to all that was passed,
And could not endure so vulgar a taste,
As soon as her Ladyship called to be dressed,
Cried, 'Madam, why surely my master's possessed;
Sir Arthur the malster! how fine will it sound?
I'd rather the Bawn were sunk underground.
But madam, I guessed there would never come good,
When I saw him so often with Darby and Wood.

And now my dream's out; for I was a-dreamed
50   That I saw a huge rat: O dear, how I screamed!
And after, methought, I had lost my new shoes;
And, Molly, she said, I should hear some ill news.

    'Dear madam, had you but the spirit to tease,
You might have a barrack whenever you please:
And, madam, I always believed you so stout,
That for twenty denials you would not give out.
If I had a husband like him, I purtest,
Till he gave me my will, I would give him no rest:
And rather than come in the same pair of sheets
60   With such a cross man, I would lie in the streets.
But, madam, I beg you contrive and invent,
And worry him out, till he gives his consent.

    'Dear madam, whene'er of a barrack I think,
An I were to be hanged, I can't sleep a wink:
For, if a new crotchet comes into my brain,
I can't get it out, though I'd never so fain.
I fancy already a barrack contrived
At Hamilton's Bawn, and the troop is arrived.
Of this, to be sure, Sir Arthur has warning,
70   And waits on the Captain betimes the next morning.

    'Now, see when they meet, how their honours behave;
"Noble Captain, your servant" – "Sir Arthur, your slave";
"You honour me much" – "The honour is mine" –
"'Twas a sad rainy night" – "But the morning is fine" –
"Pray, how does my Lady?" – "My wife's at your service."
"I think I have seen her picture by Jervas."
"Good morrow, good Captain" – "I'll wait on you down" –
"You shan't stir a foot" – "You'll think me a clown" –
"For all the world, Captain, not half an inch farther" –
80   "You must be obeyed – your servant, Sir Arthur;
My humble respects to my Lady unknown" –
"I hope you will use my house as your own."'

'Go, bring me my smock, and leave off your prate,
Thou hast certainly gotten a cup in thy pate.'
'Pray, madam, be quiet; what was it I said?
You had like to have put it quite out of my head.

'Next day, to be sure, the Captain will come,
At the head of his troop, with trumpet and drum:
Now, madam, observe, how he marches in state:
90 The man with the kettle-drum enters the gate;
Dub, dub, adub, dub. The trumpeters follow,
Tantara, tantara, while all the boys holler.
See, now comes the Captain all daubed in gold lace:
O lor'! the sweet gentleman! look in his face;
And see how he rides like a lord of the land,
With the fine flaming sword that he holds in his hand;
And his horse, the dear *creter,* it prances and rears,
With ribbons in knots, at its tail and its ears:
At last comes the troop, by the word of command
100 Drawn up in our court; when the Captain cries, "Stand."
Your Ladyship lifts up the sash to be seen,
(For sure, I had dizened you out like a Queen);
The Captain, to show he is proud of the favour,
Looks up to your window, and cocks up his beaver.
(His beaver is cocked; pray, madam, mark that,
For, a Captain of Horse never takes off his hat;
Because he has never a hand that is idle;
For, the right holds the sword, and the left holds the bridle),
Then flourishes thrice his sword in the air,
110 As a compliment due to a lady so fair;
How I tremble to think of the blood it hath spilt!
Then he lowers down the point, and kisses the hilt.
Your Ladyship smiles, and thus you begin;
"Pray, Captain, be pleased to light, and walk in":
The Captain salutes you with congee profound;
And your Ladyship curchies half way to the ground.

'"Kit, run to your master, and bid him come to us.
I'm sure he'll be proud of the honour you do us;
And, Captain, you'll do us the favour to stay,
120 And take a short dinner here with us today:

You're heartily welcome: but as for good cheer,
You come in the very worst time of the year;
If I had expected so worthy a guest –"
"Lord! madam! your Ladyship sure is in jest;
You banter me, madam, the kingdom must grant –"
"You officers, Captain, are so complaisant."'

'Hist, huzzy, I think I hear somebody coming –'
'No, madam; 'tis only Sir Arthur a-humming.

'To shorten my tale, (for I hate a long story,)
130   The Captain at dinner appears in his glory;
The Dean and the Doctor have humbled their pride,
For the Captain's entreated to sit by your side;
And, because he's their betters, you carve for him first,
The parsons, for envy, are ready to burst:
The servants amazed, are scarce ever able,
To keep off their eyes, as they wait at the table;
And Molly and I have thrust in our nose,
To peep at the Captain, in all his fine clothes:
Dear madam, be sure he's a fine-spoken man,
140   Do but hear on the clergy how glib his tongue ran;
"And madam," says he, "if such dinners you give,
You'll never want parsons as long as you live;
I ne'er knew a parson without a good nose,
But the devil's as welcome wherever he goes:
God damn me, they bid us reform and repent,
But, zounds, by their looks, they never keep Lent:
Mister Curate, for all your grave looks, I'm afraid,
You cast a sheep's eye on her ladyship's maid;
I wish she would lend you her pretty white hand,
150   In mending your cassock, and smoothing your band":
(For the Dean was so shabby and looked like a ninny,
That the Captain supposed he was curate to Jenny).
"Whenever you see a cassock and gown,
A hundred to one, but it covers a clown;
Observe how a parson comes into a room,
God damn me, he hobbles as bad as my groom;
A *scholar*, when just from his college broke loose,
Can hardly tell how to cry boo to a goose;

Your Noveds, and Blutraks, and Omurs and stuff,
160   By God they don't signify this pinch of snuff.
To give a young gentleman right education,
The army's the only good school in this nation;
My schoolmaster called me a dunce and a fool,
But at cuffs I was always the cock of the school;
I never could take to my book for the blood o' me,
And the puppy confessed, he expected no good o' me.
He caught me one morning coquetting his wife,
But he mauled me, I ne'er was so mauled in my life;
So I took to the road, and what's very odd,
170   The first man I robbed was a parson, by God.
Now madam, you'll think it a strange thing to say,
But, the sight of a book makes me sick to this day."

    'Never since I was born did I hear so much wit,
And, madam, I laughed till I thought I should split.
So, then you looked scornful, and sniffed at the Dean,
As, who should say, "Now, am I skinny and lean?"
But he durst not so much as once open his lips,
And, the Doctor was plaguily down in the hyps.'

    Thus merciless Hannah ran on in her talk,
180   Till she heard the Dean call, 'Will your Ladyship walk?'
Her Ladyship answers, 'I'm just coming down';
Then, turning to Hannah, and forcing a frown,
Although it was plain, in her heart she was glad,
Cried, 'Huzzy, why sure the wench is gone mad:
How could these chimeras get into your brains? –
Come hither, and take this old gown for your pains.
But the Dean, if this secret should come to his ears,
Will never have done with his gibes and his jeers:
For your life, not a word of the matter, I charge ye:
190   Give me but a barrack, a fig for the clergy.'

A Libel on the Reverend Dr Delany and His Excellency John, Lord Carteret

TO DR DELANY, OCCASIONED BY HIS EPISTLE TO
HIS EXCELLENCY JOHN, LORD CARTERET

Deluded mortals, whom the great
Choose for companions *tête à tête*,
Who at their dinners, *en famille*,
Get leave to sit whene'er you will;
Then, boasting tell us where you dined,
And, how his Lordship was so kind;
How many pleasant things he spoke,
And, how you laughed at every joke:
Swear, he's a most facetious man,
That you and he are cup and can.
You travel with a heavy load,
And quite mistake preferment's road.

    Suppose my Lord and you alone;
Hint the least interest of your own;
His visage drops, he knits his brow,
He cannot talk of business now:
Or, mention but a vacant post,
He'll turn it off with, 'Name your toast.'
Nor could the nicest artist paint,
A countenance with more constraint.

    For, as their appetites to quench,
Lords keep a pimp to bring a wench;
So, men of wit are but a kind
Of pandars to a vicious mind;
Who proper objects must provide
To gratify their lust of pride,
When wearied with intrigues of state,
They find an idle hour to prate.
Then, should you dare to ask a place,
You forfeit all your patron's grace,

And disappoint the sole design,
For which he summoned you to dine.

Thus, Congreve spent, in writing plays,
And one poor office, half his days;
While Montagu, who claimed the station
To be Maecenas of the nation,
For poets open table kept,
But ne'er considered where they slept;
Himself as rich as fifty Jews,
40   Was easy, though they wanted shoes;
And crazy Congreve scarce could spare
A shilling to discharge his chair,
Till prudence taught him to appeal
From Paean's fire to party zeal;
Not owing to his happy vein
The fortunes of his latter scene,
Took proper principles to thrive;
And so might every dunce alive.

Thus, Steele who owned what others writ,
50   And flourished by imputed wit,
From perils of a hundred gaols,
Withdrew to starve, and die in Wales.

Thus Gay, the hare with many friends,
Twice seven long years the court attends,
Who, under tales conveying truth,
To virtue formed a princely youth,
Who paid his courtship with the crowd,
As far as modest pride allowed,
Rejects a servile usher's place,
60   And leaves St James's in disgrace.

Thus Addison by lords caressed,
Was left in foreign lands distressed,
Forgot at home, became for hire,
A travelling tutor to a squire.
But, wisely left the muses' hill;
To business shaped the poet's quill,

Let all his barren laurels fade;
Took up himself the courtier's trade:
And grown a minister of state,
70   Saw poets at his levee wait.

Hail! happy Pope, whose generous mind,
Detesting all the statesman kind!
Contemning courts, at courts unseen,
Refused the visits of a queen;
A soul with every virtue fraught
By sages, priests, or poets taught:
Whose filial piety excels
Whatever Grecian story tells:
A genius for all stations fit,
80   Whose meanest talent is his wit:
His heart too great, though fortune little,
To lick a rascal statesman's spittle;
Appealing to the nation's taste,
Above the reach of want is placed:
By Homer dead was taught to thrive,
Which Homer never could alive:
And, sits aloft on Pindus' head,
Despising slaves that cringe for bread.

True politicians only pay
90   For solid work, but not for play;
Nor ever choose to work with tools
Forged up in colleges and schools.
Consider how much more is due
To all their journeymen, than you.
At table you can Horace quote;
They at a pinch can bribe a vote:
You show your skill in Grecian story,
But, they can manage Whig and Tory:
You, as a critic, are so curious
100   To find a verse in Virgil spurious;
But, they can smoke the deep designs,
When Bolingbroke with Pulteney dines.

Besides; your patron may upbraid ye,
That you have got a place already.
An office for your talents fit,
To flatter, carve, and show your wit;
To snuff the lights, and stir the fire,
And get a dinner for your hire.
What claim have you to place, or pension?
110 He overpays in condescension.

But, reverend Doctor, you, we know,
Could never condescend so low;
The Viceroy, whom you now attend,
Would, if he durst, be more your friend;
Nor will *in you* those gifts despise,
By which himself was taught to rise:
When he has virtue to retire,
He'll grieve he did not raise you higher,
And place you in a better station,
120 Although it might have *pleased* the nation.

This may be true – submitting still
To Walpole's more than royal will.
And what condition can be worse?
He comes to drain a beggar's purse:
He comes to tie our chains on faster,
And show us, England is our master:
Caressing knaves and dunces wooing,
To make them work their own undoing.
What has he else to bait his traps,
130 Or bring his vermin in, but scraps?
The offals of a church distressed,
A hungry vicarage at best;
Or, some remote inferior post,
With forty pounds a year at most.

But, here again you interpose;
Your favourite Lord is none of those,
Who owe their virtue to their stations,
And characters to dedications:
For, keep him in, or turn him out,
140 His learning none will call in doubt:

His learning, though a poet said it,
Before a play, would lose no credit:
Nor Pope would dare deny him wit,
Although to praise it Philips writ.
I own, he hates an action base,
His virtues battling with his place;
Nor wants a nice discerning spirit,
Betwixt a true and spurious merit:
Can sometimes drop a voter's claim,
150 And give up party to his fame.
I do the most that friendship can;
I hate the Viceroy, love the man.

But, you, who till your fortune's made
Must be a *sweetener* by your trade,
Should swear he never meant us ill;
We suffer sore against his will;
That, if we could but see his heart,
He would have chose a milder part;
We rather should lament his case
160 Who must obey, or lose his place.

Since this reflection slipped your pen,
Insert it when you write again:
And, to illustrate it, produce
This simile for his excuse.

'So, to destroy a guilty land,
An angel sent by heaven's command,
While he obeys almighty will,
Perhaps, may feel compassion still;
And wish the task had been assigned
170 To spirits of less gentle kind.'

But I, in politics grown old,
Whose thoughts are of a different mould,
Who, from my soul, sincerely hate
Both kings and ministers of state:
Who look on courts with stricter eyes,
To see the seeds of vice arise,

Can lend you an allusion fitter,
Though flattering knaves may call it bitter:
Which, if you durst but give it place,
180 Would show you many a statesman's face.
Fresh from the tripod of Apollo,
I had it in the words that follow.
(Take notice, to avoid offence
I here except his Excellence.)

   'So, to effect his monarch's ends,
From hell a Viceroy devil ascends,
His budget with corruptions crammed,
The contributions of the damned;
Which with unsparing hand, he strews
190 Through courts and senates as he goes;
And then at Belzebub's Black Hall,
Complains his budget was too small.'

   Your simile may better shine
In verse; but there is truth in mine.
For, no imaginable things
Can differ more than God and kings.
And statesmen, by ten thousand odds
Are angels, just as kings are gods.

Death and Daphne

TO AN AGREEABLE YOUNG LADY, BUT EXTREMELY LEAN

Death went upon a solemn day,
At Pluto's hall, his court to pay:
The phantom, having humbly kissed
His grisly monarch's sooty fist,
Presented him the weekly bills
Of doctors, fevers, plagues, and pills.
Pluto observing, since the Peace,
The burial article decrease;
And, vexed to see affairs miscarry,
10 Declared in council, Death must marry:

Vowed, he no longer could support
Old bachelors about his court:
The interest of his realm had need
That Death should get a numerous breed;
Young Deathlings, who, by practice made
Proficients in their father's trade,
With colonies might stock around
His large dominions underground.

    A consult of coquettes below
20   Was called, to rig him out a beau:
From her own head, Megaera takes
A periwig of twisted snakes;
Which in the nicest fashion curled,
Like toupees of this upper world;
(With flour of sulphur powdered well,
That graceful on his shoulders fell)
An adder of the sable kind,
In line direct, hung down behind.
The owl, the raven, and the bat,
30   Clubbed for a feather to his hat;
His coat, an usurer's velvet pall,
Bequeathed to Pluto, corpse and all.
But, loath his person to expose
Bare, like a carcass picked by crows,
A lawyer o'er his hands and face,
Stuck artfully a parchment case.
No new-fluxed rake showed fairer skin;
Not Phyllis after lying-in.
With snuff was filled his ebon box,
40   Of shin-bones rotted by the pox.
Nine spirits of blaspheming fops,
With aconite anoint his chops:
And give him words of dreadful sounds,
'God damn his blood', and 'Blood and wounds.'

    Thus furnished out, he sent his train
To take a house in Warwick Lane;
The Faculty, his humble friends,
A complimental message sends:

Their president, in scarlet gown,
50 Harangued, and welcomed him to town.

But, Death had business to dispatch:
His mind was running on his match.
And, hearing much of Daphne's fame,
His Majesty of terrors came,
Fine as a colonel of the Guards,
To visit where he sat at cards:
She, as he came into the room,
Thought him Adonis in his bloom.
And now her heart with pleasure jumps,
60 She scarce remembers what is trumps.
For, such a shape of skin and bone
Was never seen, except her own:
Charmed with his eyes and chin and snout,
Her pocket-glass drew slily out;
And, grew enamoured with her phiz,
As just the counterpart of his.
She darted many a private glance,
And freely made the first advance:
Was of her beauty grown so vain,
70 She doubted not to win the swain.
Nothing she thought could sooner gain him,
Than with her wit to entertain him.
She asked about her friends below;
This meagre fop, that battered beau:
Whether some late departed toasts
Had got gallants among the ghosts?
If Chloe were a sharper still,
As great as ever, at quadrille?
(The ladies there must needs be rooks,
80 For, cards we know, are Pluto's books.)
If Florimel had found her love
For whom she hanged herself above?
How oft a week was kept a ball
By Proserpine, at Pluto's hall?
She fancied, those Elysian shades
The sweetest place for masquerades:

How pleasant on the banks of Styx,
To troll it in a coach and six!

What pride a female heart inflames!
90   How endless are ambition's aims!
Cease haughty nymph; the fates decree
Death must not be a spouse for thee:
For, when by chance the meagre shade
Upon thy hand his finger laid;
Thy hand as dry and cold as lead,
His matrimonial spirit fled;
He felt about his heart a damp,
That quite extinguished Cupid's lamp:
Away the frighted spectre scuds,
100   And leaves my Lady in the suds.

An Excellent New Ballad

OR THE TRUE ENGLISH DEAN TO BE HANGED FOR A RAPE

I

Our brethren of England, who love us so dear,
    And in all they do for us so kindly do mean,
A blessing upon them, have sent us this year,
    For the good of our church a true English Dean.
A holier priest ne'er was wrapped up in crape,
The worst you can say, he committed a rape.

II

In his journey to Dublin, he lighted at Chester,
    And there he grew fond of another man's wife,
Burst into her chamber, and would have caressed her,
10   But she valued her honour much more than her life.
She bustled and struggled, and made her escape,
To a room full of guests for fear of a rape.

III

The Dean he pursued to recover his game,
    And now to attack her again he prepares,

But the company stood in defence of the dame,
   They cudgelled and cuffed him, and kicked him
      downstairs.
His Deanship was now in a damnable scrape,
And this was no time for committing a rape.

IV

To Dublin he comes, to the bagnio he goes,
   And orders the landlord to bring him a whore;
No scruple came on him his gown to expose,
   'Twas what all his life he had practised before.
He had made himself drunk with the juice of the grape,
And got a good clap, but committed no rape.

V

The Dean, and his landlord, a jolly comrade,
   Resolved for a fortnight to swim in delight;
For why, they had both been brought up to the trade
   Of drinking all day, and of whoring all night.
His landlord was ready his Deanship to ape
In every debauch, but committing a rape.

VI

This Protestant zealot, this English divine
   In church and in state was of principles sound;
Was truer than Steele to the Hanover line,
   And grieved that a Tory should live above ground.
Shall a subject so loyal be hanged by the nape,
For no other crime but committing a rape?

VII

By old popish canons, as wise men have penned 'em,
   Each priest had a concubine, *jure ecclesiae*;
Who'd be Dean of Ferns without a *commendam*?
   And precedents we can produce, if it please ye:
Then, why should the Dean, when whores are so cheap,
Be put to the peril, and toil of a rape?

VIII

If fortune should please but to take such a crotchet,
   (To thee I apply great Smedley's successor)

To give thee lawn-sleeves, a mitre and rochet,
　　Whom wouldst thou resemble? I leave thee a guesser;
But I only behold thee in Atherton's shape,
For sodomy hanged, as thou for a rape.

IX

Ah! dost thou not envy the brave Colonel Chartres,
50　　Condemned for thy crime, at three score and ten?
To hang him all England would lend him their garters;
　　Yet he lives, and is ready to ravish again,
Then throttle thyself with an ell of strong tape,
For thou hast not a groat to atone for a rape.

X

The Dean he was vexed that his whores were so willing,
　　He longed for a girl that would struggle and squall;
He ravished her fairly, and saved a good shilling;
　　But, here was to pay the devil and all.
His trouble and sorrows now come in a heap,
60　　And hanged he must be for committing a rape.

XI

If maidens are ravished, it is their own choice,
　　Why are they so wilful to struggle with men?
If they would but lie quiet, and stifle their voice,
　　No devil or Dean could ravish 'em then,
Nor would there be need of a strong hempen cape,
Tied round the Dean's neck, for committing a rape.

XII

Our church and our state dear England maintains,
　　For which all true Protestant hearts should be glad;
She sends us our bishops and judges and deans,
70　　And better would give us, if better she had;
But, Lord how the rabble will stare and will gape,
When the good English Dean is hanged up for a rape.

The Lady's Dressing Room

Five hours (and who can do it less in?)
By haughty Celia spent in dressing;
The goddess from her chamber issues;
Arrayed in lace, brocade and tissues:
Strephon, who found the room was void,
And Betty otherwise employed,
Stole in, and took a strict survey,
Of all the litter as it lay:
Whereof, to make the matter clear,
An *inventory* follows here.

And first, a dirty smock appeared,
Beneath the armpits well besmeared;
Strephon, the rogue, displayed it wide,
And turned it round on every side.
In such a case few words are best,
And Strephon bids us guess the rest;
But swears how damnably the men lie;
In calling Celia sweet and cleanly.

Now listen while he next produces,
The various combs for various uses,
Filled up with dirt so closely fixed,
No brush could force a way betwixt;
A paste of composition rare,
Sweat, dandruff, powder, lead and hair,
A forehead cloth with oil upon't
To smooth the wrinkles on her front;
Here alum flower to stop the steams,
Exhaled from sour unsavoury streams;
There night-gloves made of Tripsy's hide,
Bequeathed by Tripsy when she died;
With puppy water, beauty's help,
Distilled from Tripsy's darling whelp.
Here gallipots and vials placed,
Some filled with washes, some with paste;

Some with pomatum, paints and slops,
And ointments good for scabby chops.
Hard by a filthy basin stands,
Fouled with the scouring of her hands;
The basin takes whatever comes,
40   The scrapings of her teeth and gums,
A nasty compound of all hues,
For here she spits, and here she spews.

But oh! it turned poor Strephon's bowels,
When he beheld and smelt the towels;
Begummed, bemattered, and beslimed;
With dirt, and sweat, and ear-wax grimed.
No object Strephon's eye escapes,
Here, petticoats in frowzy heaps;
Nor be the handkerchiefs forgot,
50   All varnished o'er with snuff and snot.
The stockings why should I expose,
Stained with the moisture of her toes;
Or greasy coifs and pinners reeking,
Which Celia slept at least a week in?
A pair of tweezers next he found
To pluck her brows in arches round,
Or hairs that sink the forehead low,
Or on her chin like bristles grow.

The virtues we must not let pass,
60   Of Celia's magnifying glass;
When frighted Strephon cast his eye on't,
It showed the visage of a giant:
A glass that can to sight disclose
The smallest worm in Celia's nose,
And faithfully direct her nail
To squeeze it out from head to tail;
For catch it nicely by the head,
It must come out alive or dead.

Why, Strephon, will you tell the rest?
70   And must you needs describe the chest?

That careless wench! no creature warn her
To move it out from yonder corner,
But leave it standing full in sight,
For you to exercise your spite!
In vain the workman showed his wit
With rings and hinges counterfeit
To make it seem in this disguise,
A cabinet to vulgar eyes;
Which Strephon ventured to look in,
80   Resolved to go through *thick and thin*;
He lifts the lid: there need no more,
He smelt it all the time before.

    As, from within Pandora's box,
When Epimetheus oped the locks,
A sudden universal crew
Of human evils upward flew;
He still was comforted to find
That hope at last remained behind.

    So, Strephon, lifting up the lid,
90   To view what in the chest was hid,
The vapours flew from out the vent,
But Strephon cautious never meant
The bottom of the pan to grope,
And foul his hands in search of hope.

    O! ne'er may such a vile machine
Be once in Celia's chamber seen!
O! may she better learn to keep
'Those secrets of the hoary deep'.

    As mutton cutlets, prime of meat,
100 Which though with art you salt and beat,
As laws of cookery require,
And roast them at the clearest fire;
If from adown the hopeful chops
The fat upon a cinder drops,
To stinking smoke it turns the flame
Poisoning the flesh from whence it came;

And up exhales a greasy stench,
For which you curse the careless wench:
So things which must not be expressed,
110   When *plumped* into the reeking chest,
Send up an excremental smell
To taint the parts from which they fell:
The petticoats and gown perfume,
And waft a stink round every room.

Thus finishing his grand survey,
The swain disgusted slunk away,
Repeating in his amorous fits,
'Oh! Celia, Celia, Celia shits!'

But Vengeance, goddess never sleeping,
120   Soon punished Strephon for his peeping.
His foul imagination links
Each dame he sees with all her stinks:
And, if unsavoury odours fly,
Conceives a lady standing by:
All women his description fits,
And both ideas jump like wits,
By vicious fancy coupled fast,
And still appearing in contrast.

I pity wretched Strephon, blind
130   To all the charms of womankind;
Should I the queen of love refuse,
Because she rose from stinking ooze?
To him that looks behind the scene,
Statira's but some pocky quean.

When Celia in her glory shows,
If Strephon would but stop his nose,
Who now so impiously blasphemes
Her ointments, daubs, and paints and creams;
Her washes, slops, and every clout,
140   With which she makes so foul a rout;
He soon would learn to think like me,
And bless his ravished eye to see

Such order from confusion sprung,
Such gaudy *tulips* raised from *dung*.

A Beautiful Young Nymph Going to Bed

WRITTEN FOR THE HONOUR OF THE FAIR SEX

Corinna, pride of Drury Lane,
For whom no shepherd sighs in vain;
Never did Covent Garden boast
So bright a battered, strolling toast;
No drunken rake to pick her up,
No cellar where on tick to sup;
Returning at the midnight hour;
Four storeys climbing to her bower;
Then, seated on a three-legged chair,
Takes off her artificial hair:
Now, picking out a crystal eye,
She wipes it clean, and lays it by.
Her eyebrows from a mouse's hide,
Stuck on with art on either side,
Pulls off with care, and first displays 'em,
Then in a play-book smoothly lays 'em.
Now dexterously her plumpers draws,
That serve to fill her hollow jaws.
Untwists a wire; and from her gums
A set of teeth completely comes.
Pulls out the rags contrived to prop
Her flabby dugs, and down they drop.
Proceeding on, the lovely goddess
Unlaces next her steel-ribbed bodice;
Which by the operator's skill,
Press down the lumps, the hollows fill.
Up goes her hand, and off she slips
The bolsters that supply her hips.
With gentlest touch, she next explores
Her shankers, issues, running sores;

Effects of many a sad disaster,
And then to each applies a plaster.
But must, before she goes to bed,
Rub off the daubs of white and red.
And smooth the furrows in her front,
With greasy paper stuck upon't.
She takes a bolus e'er she sleeps;
And then between two blankets creeps.
With pains of love tormented lies;
40   Or if she chance to close her eyes,
Of Bridewell and the compter dreams,
And feels the lash, and faintly screams.
Or, by a faithless bully drawn,
At some hedge-tavern lies in pawn.
Or to Jamaica seems transported,
Alone, and by no planter courted;
Or, near Fleet Ditch's oozy brinks,
Surrounded with a hundred stinks,
Belated, seems on watch to lie,
50   And snap some cully passing by;
Or, struck with fear, her fancy runs
On watchmen, constables and duns,
From whom she meets with frequent rubs;
But, never from religious clubs;
Whose favour she is sure to find,
Because she pays them all in kind.

    Corinna wakes. A dreadful sight!
Behold the ruins of the night!
A wicked rat her plaster stole,
60   Half ate, and dragged it to his hole.
The crystal eye, alas, was missed;
And Puss had on her plumpers pissed.
A pigeon picked her issue-peas,
And Shock her tresses filled with fleas.

    The nymph, though in this mangled plight,
Must every morn her limbs unite.
But how shall I describe her arts
To re-collect the scattered parts?

Or show the anguish, toil, and pain,
70   Of gathering up herself again?
The bashful muse will never bear
In such a scene to interfere.
Corinna in the morning dizened,
Who sees, will spew; who smells, be poisoned.

Strephon and Chloe

Of Chloe all the town has rung;
By every size of poet sung:
So beautiful a nymph appears
But once in twenty thousand years:
By nature formed with nicest care,
And, faultless to a single hair.
Her graceful mien, her shape, and face,
Confessed her of no mortal race:
And then, so nice, and so genteel;
10   Such cleanliness from head to heel:
No humours gross, or frowzy steams,
No noisome whiffs, or sweaty streams,
Before, behind, above, below,
Could from her taintless body flow.
Would so discreetly things dispose,
None ever saw her pluck a rose.
Her dearest comrades never caught her
Squat on her hams, to make maid's water.
You'd swear, that so divine a creature
20   Felt no necessities of nature.
In summer had she walked the town,
Her armpits would not stain her gown:
At country dances, not a nose
Could in the dog-days smell her toes.
Her milk-white hands, both palms and backs,
Like ivory dry, and soft as wax.
Her hands, the softest ever felt,
Though cold would burn, though dry would melt.

Dear Venus, hide this wondrous maid,
30 Nor let her loose to spoil your trade.
While she engrosseth every swain,
You but o'er half the world can reign.
Think what a case all men are now in,
What ogling, sighing, toasting, vowing!
What powdered wigs! What flames and darts!
What hampers full of bleeding hearts!
What sword-knots! What poetic strains!
What billet-doux, and clouded canes!

But, Strephon sighed so loud and strong,
40 He blew a settlement along:
And, bravely drove his rivals down
With coach and six, and house in town.
The bashful nymph no more withstands,
Because her dear papa commands.
The charming couple now unites;
Proceed we to the marriage rites.

Imprimis, at the temple porch
Stood Hymen with a flaming torch.
The smiling Cyprian goddess brings
50 Her infant loves with purple wings;
And pigeons billing, sparrows treading,
Fair emblems of a fruitful wedding.
The muses next in order follow,
Conducted by the squire, Apollo:
Then Mercury with silver tongue,
And Hebe, goddess ever young.
Behold the bridegroom and his bride,
Walk hand in hand, and side by side;
She by the tender Graces dressed,
60 But, he by Mars, in scarlet vest.
The nymph was covered with her *flammeum*,
And Phoebus sung the epithalamium.
And, last to make the matter sure,
Dame Juno brought a priest demure.
Luna was absent on pretence
Her time was not till nine months hence.

The rites performed, the parson paid,
In state returned the grand parade;
With loud huzzas from all the boys,
70   That now the pair must *crown their joys*.

But, still the hardest part remains.
Strephon had long perplexed his brains,
How with so high a nymph he might
Demean himself the wedding-night:
For, as he viewed his person round,
Mere mortal flesh was all he found:
His hand, his neck, his mouth, and feet
Were duly washed to keep 'em sweet;
(With other parts that shall be nameless,
80   The ladies else might think me shameless).
The weather and his love were hot;
And should he struggle; I know what –
Why let it go, if I must tell it –
He'll sweat, and then the nymph will smell it.
While she a goddess dyed in grain
Was unsusceptible of stain:
And, Venus-like, her fragrant skin
Exhaled ambrosia from within:
Can such a deity endure
90   A mortal human touch impure?
How did the humbled swain detest
His prickled beard, and hairy breast!
His nightcap bordered round with lace
Could give no softness to his face.

Yet, if the goddess could be kind,
What endless raptures must he find!
And goddesses have now and then
Come down to visit mortal men:
To visit and to court them too:
100   A certain goddess, God knows who,
(As in a book he heard it read)
Took Colonel Peleus to her bed.
But, what if he should lose his life
By venturing *on* his heavenly wife?

For, Strephon could remember well,
That, once he heard a schoolboy tell,
How Semele of mortal race,
By thunder died in Jove's embrace;
And what if daring Strephon dies
110 By lightning shot from Chloe's eyes?

While these reflections filled his head,
The bride was put in form to bed;
He followed, stripped, and in he crept,
But, awfully his distance kept.

Now, ponder well, ye parents dear;
Forbid your daughters guzzling beer;
And make them every afternoon
Forbear their tea, or drink it soon;
That, e'er to bed they venture up,
120 They may discharge it every sup;
If not, they must in evil plight
Be often forced to rise at night;
Keep them to wholesome food confined,
Nor let them waste what causes wind;
('Tis this the sage of Samos means,
Forbidding his disciples beans)
O, think what evils must ensue;
Miss Moll the jade will burn it blue:
And when she once has got the art,
130 She cannot help it for her heart;
But, out it flies, even when she meets
Her bridegroom in the wedding-sheets.
Carminative and diuretic,
Will damp all passions sympathetic;
And, love such niceties requires,
One blast will put out all his fires.
Since husbands get behind the scene,
The wife should study to be clean;
Nor give the smallest room to guess
140 The time when wants of nature press;
But, after marriage, practise more
Decorum than she did before;

To keep her spouse deluded still,
And make him fancy what she will.

In bed we left the married pair;
'Tis time to show how things went there.
Strephon, who often had been told,
That fortune still assists the bold,
Resolved to make his first attack:
But, Chloe drove him fiercely back.
How could a nymph so chaste as Chloe,
With constitution cold and snowy,
Permit a brutish man to touch her;
Even lambs by instinct fly the butcher.
Resistance on the wedding night
Is what our maidens claim by right:
And, Chloe, 'tis by all agreed,
Was maid in thought, and word, and deed.
Yet some assign a different reason;
That Strephon chose no proper season.

Say, fair ones, must I make a pause?
Or freely tell the secret cause.

Twelve cups of tea (with grief I speak)
Had now constrained the nymph to leak.
This point must needs be settled first:
The bride must either void or burst.
Then, see the dire effect of pease,
Think what can give the colic ease.
The nymph oppressed before, behind,
As ships are tossed by waves and wind,
Steals out her hand by nature led,
And brings a vessel into bed:
Fair utensil, as smooth and white
As Chloe's skin, almost as bright.

Strephon who heard the foaming rill
As from a mossy cliff distil;
Cried out, 'Ye gods, what sound is this?
Can Chloe, heavenly Chloe piss?'

But when he smelt a noisome steam
180   Which oft attends that lukewarm stream;
(Salerno both together joins
As sovereign medicines for the loins)
And, though contrived, we may suppose
To slip his ears, yet struck his nose:
He found her, while the scent increased,
As *mortal* as himself at least.
But, soon with like occasions pressed,
He boldly sent his hand in quest
(Inspired with courage from his bride),
190   To reach the pot on t'other side.
And as he filled the reeking vase,
Let fly a rouser in her face.

The little Cupids hovering round,
(As pictures prove) with garlands crowned,
Abashed at what they saw and heard,
Flew off, nor ever more appeared.

Adieu to ravishing delights,
High raptures, and romantic flights;
To goddesses so heavenly sweet,
200   Expiring shepherds at their feet;
To silver meads, and shady bowers,
Dressed up with amaranthine flowers.

How great a change! how quickly made!
They learn to call a spade, a spade.
They soon from all constraints are freed;
Can see each other *do their need*.
On box of cedar sits the wife,
And makes it warm for 'dearest life'.
And, by the beastly way of thinking,
210   Find great society in stinking.
Now Strephon daily entertains
His Chloe in the homeliest strains;
And, Chloe more experienced grown,
With interest pays him back his own.
No maid at court is less ashamed,
Howe'er for selling bargains famed,

Than she, to name her parts behind,
Or when abed, to let out wind.

Fair Decency, celestial maid,
220 Descend from heaven to Beauty's aid;
Though Beauty must beget Desire,
'Tis thou must fan the lover's fire;
For, Beauty, like supreme Dominion,
Is best supported by Opinion;
If Decency brings no supplies,
Opinion falls, and Beauty dies.

To see some radiant nymph appear
In all her glittering birthday gear,
You think some goddess from the sky
230 Descended, ready cut and dry:
But, e'er you sell yourself to laughter,
Consider well what may come after;
For fine ideas vanish fast,
While all the gross and filthy last.

O Strephon, e'er that fatal day
When Chloe stole your heart away,
Had you but through a cranny spied
On house of ease your future bride,
In all the postures of her face,
240 Which nature gives in such a case;
Distortions, groanings, strainings, heavings;
'Twere better you had licked her leavings,
Than from experience find too late
Your goddess grown a filthy mate.
Your fancy then had always dwelt
On what you saw, and what you smelt;
Would still the same ideas give ye,
As when you spied her on the privy.
And, spite of Chloe's charms divine,
250 Your heart had been as whole as mine.

Authorities both old and recent
Direct that women must be decent;

And, from the spouse each blemish hide
More than from all the world beside.

Unjustly all our nymphs complain,
Their empire holds so short a reign;
Is after marriage lost so soon,
It hardly holds the honeymoon:
For, if they keep not what they caught,
260   It is entirely their own fault.
They take possession of the crown,
And then throw all their weapons down;
Though by the politician's scheme
Whoe'er arrives at power supreme,
Those arts by which at first they gain it,
They still must practise to attain it.

What various ways our females take,
To pass for wits before a rake!
And in the fruitless search pursue
270   All other methods but the true.

Some try to learn polite behaviour,
By reading books against their Saviour;
Some call it witty to reflect
On every natural defect;
Some show they never want explaining,
To comprehend a double meaning.
But, sure a telltale out of school
Is, of all wits, the greatest fool;
Whose rank imagination fills
280   Her heart, and from her lips distils;
You'd think she uttered from behind,
Or at her mouth was breaking wind.

Why is a handsome wife adored
By every coxcomb, but her lord?
From yonder puppet-man inquire,
Who wisely hides his wood and wire:
Shows Sheba's queen completely dressed,
And Solomon in royal vest;

But, view them littered on the floor,
290   Or strung on pegs behind the door;
Punch is exactly of a piece
With Lorraine's Duke, and Prince of Greece.

    A prudent builder should forecast
How long the stuff is like to last;
And, carefully observe the ground,
To build on some foundation sound;
What house, when its materials crumble,
Must not inevitably tumble?
What edifice can long endure,
300   Raised on a basis unsecure?
Rash mortals, e'er you take a wife,
Contrive your pile to last for life;
Since beauty scarce endures a day,
And youth so swiftly glides away;
Why will you make yourself a bubble
To build on sand with hay and stubble?

    On sense and wit your passion found,
By decency cemented round;
Let prudence with good nature strive,
310   To keep esteem and love alive.
Then come old age whene'er it will,
Your friendship shall continue still:
And thus a mutual gentle fire,
Shall never but with life expire.

Cassinus and Peter

A TRAGICAL ELEGY

Two college sophs of Cambridge growth,
Both special wits, and lovers both,
Conferring as they used to meet,
On love and books in rapture sweet;

(Muse, find me names to fix my metre,
Cassinus this, and t'other Peter)
Friend Peter to Cassinus goes,
To chat a while, and warm his nose:
But, such a sight was never seen,
10 The lad lay swallowed up in spleen;
He seems as just crept out of bed;
One greasy stocking round his head,
The t'other he sat down to darn
With threads of different coloured yarn.
His breeches torn exposing wide
A ragged shirt, and tawny hide.
Scorched were his shins, his legs were bare,
But, well embrowned with dirt and hair.
A rug was o'er his shoulders thrown;
20 A rug; for night-gown had he none.
His jordan stood in manner fitting
Between his legs, to spew or spit in.
His ancient pipe in sable dyed,
And half unsmoked, lay by his side.

Him thus accoutred, Peter found,
With eyes in smoke and weeping drowned:
The leavings of his last night's pot
On embers placed, to drink it hot.

'Why, Cassy, thou wilt doze thy pate:
30 What makes thee lie abed so late?
The finch, the linnet, and the thrush,
Their matins chant in every bush:
And I have heard thee oft salute
Aurora with thy early flute.
Heaven send thou has not got the hyps.
How? not a word come from thy lips?'

Then gave him some familiar thumps,
A college joke to cure the dumps.

The swain at last, with grief oppressed,
40 Cried, 'Celia!' thrice, and sighed the rest.

'Dear Cassy, though to ask I dread,
Yet ask I must. Is Celia dead?'

'How happy I, were that the worst!
But I was fated to be cursed.'

'Come, tell us, has she played the whore?'

'Oh Peter, would it were no more!'

'Why, plague confound her sandy locks:
Say, has the small or greater pox
Sunk down her nose, or seamed her face?
50 Be easy, 'tis a common case.'

'Oh Peter! beauty's but a varnish,
Which time and accidents will tarnish:
But, Celia has contrived to blast
Those beauties that might ever last.
Nor can imagination guess,
Nor eloquence divine express,
How that ungrateful charming maid,
My purest passion has betrayed.
Conceive the most envenomed dart,
60 To pierce an injured lover's heart.'

'Why, hang her, though she seemed so coy,
I know she loves the barber's boy.'

'Friend Peter, this I could excuse;
For, every nymph has leave to choose;
Nor, have I reason to complain:
She loves a more deserving swain.
But, oh! how ill thou hast divined
A crime that shocks all humankind;
A deed unknown to female race,
70 At which the sun should hide his face.
Advice in vain you would apply –
Then, leave me to despair and die.
Yet, kind Arcadians, on my urn
These elegies and sonnets burn,
And on the marble grave these rhymes,
A monument to after-times:

"Here Cassy lies, by Celia slain,
And dying, never told his pain."

   'Vain empty world farewell. But hark,
80 The loud Cerberian triple bark.
And there – behold Alecto stand,
A whip of scorpions in her hand.
Lo, Charon from his leaky wherry,
Beckoning to waft me o'er the ferry.
I come, I come – Medusa, see,
Her serpents hiss direct at me.
Begone; unhand me, hellish fry;
Avaunt – ye cannot say 'twas I.'

   'Dear Cassy, thou must purge and bleed;
90 I fear thou wilt be mad indeed.
But now, by friendship's sacred laws,
I here conjure thee, tell the cause;
And Celia's horrid fact relate;
Thy friend would gladly share thy fate.'

   'To force it out my heart must rend;
Yet, when conjured by such a friend –
Think, Peter, how my soul is racked.
These eyes, these eyes beheld the fact.
Now, bend thine ear; since out it must:
100 But, when thou seest me laid in dust,
The secret thou shalt ne'er impart;
Not to the nymph that keeps thy heart;
(How would her virgin soul bemoan
A crime to all her sex unknown!)
Nor whisper to the tattling reeds,
The blackest of all female deeds.
Nor blab it on the lonely rocks,
Where Echo sits, and listening, mocks.
Nor let the zephyr's treacherous gale
110 Through Cambridge waft the direful tale.
Nor to the chattering feathered race,
Discover Celia's foul disgrace.

But, if you fail, my spectre dread
Attending nightly round your bed:
And yet, I dare confide in you;
So, take my secret, and adieu.

   'Nor, wonder how I lost my wits;
Oh! Celia, Celia, Celia shits.'

To Mr Gay

ON HIS BEING STEWARD TO THE DUKE OF QUEENSBERRY

How could you, Gay, disgrace the muses' train,
To serve a tasteless court twelve years in vain?
Fain would I think, our female friend sincere,
Till Bob, the poet's foe, possessed her ear.
Did female virtue e'er so high ascend,
To lose an inch of favour for a friend?

   Say, had the court no better place to choose
For thee, than make a dry nurse of thy muse?
How cheaply had thy liberty been sold,
To squire a royal girl of two years old!
In leading strings her infant steps to guide;
Or, with her go-cart amble side by side.

   But princely Douglas, and his glorious dame,
Advanced thy fortune, and preserved thy fame.
Nor, will your nobler gifts be misapplied,
When o'er your patron's treasure you preside,
The world shall own, his choice was wise and just,
For, sons of Phoebus never break their trust.

   Not love of beauty less the heart inflames
Of guardian eunuchs to the sultan dames,
Their passions not more impotent and cold,
Than those of poets to the lust of gold.
With Paean's purest fire his favourites glow;
The dregs will serve to ripen ore below;

His meanest work: for, had he thought it fit,
That, wealth should be the appanage of wit,
The god of light could ne'er have so *blind*,
To deal it to the worst of humankind.

But let me now, for I can do it well,
30   Your conduct in this new employ foretell.

And first: to make my observation right,
I place a STATESMAN full before my sight.
A bloated minister in all his gear,
With shameless visage, and perfidious leer,
Two rows of teeth arm each devouring jaw;
And, ostrich-like, his all-digesting maw.
My fancy drags this monster into view,
To show the world his chief reverse in you.
Of loud unmeaning sounds, a rapid flood
40   Rolls from his mouth in plenteous streams of mud;
With these, the court and senate-house he plies,
Made up of noise, and impudence and lies.

Now, let me show how Bob and you agree.
You serve a potent prince, as well as he.
The ducal coffers, trusted to your charge,
Your honest care may fill; perhaps enlarge.
His vassals easy, and the owner blessed;
They pay a trifle, and enjoy the rest.
Not so a nation's revenues are paid:
50   The servant's faults are on the master laid.
The people with a sigh their taxes bring;
And cursing Bob, forget to bless the King.

Next, hearken Gay, to what thy charge requires,
With servants, tenants, and the neighbouring squires.
Let all domestics feel your gentle sway;
Nor bribe, insult, nor flatter, nor betray,
Let due reward to merit be allowed;
Nor with your kindred half the palace crowd.
Nor, think yourself secure in doing wrong,
60   By telling noses with a party strong.

Be rich; but of your wealth make no parade;
At least, before your master's debts are paid.
Nor, in a palace built with charge immense,
Presume to treat him at his own expense.
Each farmer in the neighbourhood can count
To what your lawful perquisites amount.
The tenants poor, the hardness of the times,
Are ill excuses for a servant's crimes:
With interest, and a premium paid beside,
70 The master's pressing wants must be supplied;
With hasty zeal, behold, the steward come,
By his own credit to advance the sum;
Who, while the unrighteous Mammon is his friend,
May well conclude his power will never end.
A faithful treasurer! What could he do more?
He lends my Lord, what was my Lord's before.

The law so strictly guards the monarch's health,
That no physician dares prescribe by stealth:
The council sit; approve the doctor's skill;
80 And give advice before he gives the pill.
But, the state empiric acts a safer part;
And while he poisons, wins the royal heart.

But, how can I describe the ravenous breed?
Then, let me now by negatives proceed.

Suppose your lord a trusty servant send,
On weighty business, to some neighbouring friend:
Presume not, Gay, unless you serve a drone,
To countermand his orders by your own.

Should some imperious neighbour sink the boats,
90 And drain the fish-ponds; while your master doats;
Shall he upon the ducal rights entrench,
Because he bribed you with a brace of tench?

Nor, from your lord his bad condition hide;
To feed his luxury, or soothe his pride.
Nor, at an under rate his timber sell;
And with an oath, assure him, 'all is well.'

Or swear it rotten; and with humble airs,
Request it of him to complete your stairs.
Nor, when a mortgage lies on half his lands,
100 Come with a purse of guineas in your hands.

    Have Peter Waters always in your mind;
That rogue of genuine ministerial kind
Can half the peerage by his arts bewitch;
Starve twenty lords to make one scoundrel rich:
And when he gravely has undone a score,
Is humbly prayed to ruin twenty more.

    A dexterous steward, when his tricks are found,
Hush-money sends to all the neighbours round:
His master, unsuspicious of his pranks,
110 Pays all the cost, and gives the villain thanks.
And, should a friend attempt to set him right,
His Lordship would impute it all to spite:
Would love his favourite better than before;
And trust his honesty just so much more.
Thus realms, and families, with equal fate,
Are sunk by premier ministers of state.

    Some, when an heir succeeds, go boldly on,
And, as they robbed the father, rob the son.
A knave, who deep embroils his lord's affairs,
120 Will soon grow necessary to his heirs.
His policy consists in setting traps,
In finding ways and means, and stopping gaps:
He knows a thousand tricks, whene'er he please,
Though not to cure, yet palliate each disease.
In either case, an equal chance is run:
For, keep, or turn him out, my Lord's undone.
You want a hand to clear a filthy sink;
No cleanly workman can endure the stink.
A strong dilemma in a desperate case!
130 To act with infamy, or quit the place.

A bungler thus, who scarce the nail can hit,
With driving wrong, will make the panel split:
Nor, dares an abler workman undertake
To drive a second, lest the whole should break.

In every court the parallel will hold;
And kings, like private folks, are bought and sold:
The ruling rogue, who dreads to be cashiered,
Contrives, as he is hated, to be feared:
Confounds accounts, perplexes all affairs;
140   For, vengeance more embroils, than skill repairs.
So, robbers (and their ends are just the same)
To scape inquiries, leave the house in flame.

I knew a brazen minister of state,
Who bore for twice ten years the public hate.
In every mouth the question most in vogue
Was, 'When will they turn out this odious rogue?'
A juncture happened in his highest pride:
While he went robbing on, old Master died.
We thought, there now remained no room to doubt:
150   'His work is done, the minister must out.'
The court invited more than one, or two;
'Will you, Sir Spencer? or will *you*, or *you*?'
But not a soul his office durst accept:
The subtle knave had all the plunder swept.
And, such was then the temper of the times,
He owed his preservation to his crimes.
The candidates observed his dirty paws,
Nor found it difficult to guess the cause:
But when they smelt such foul corruptions round him;
160   Away they fled, and left him as they found him.

Thus, when a greedy sloven once has thrown
His snot into the mess; 'tis all his own.

Verses on the Death of Dr Swift, D.S.P.D.

OCCASIONED BY READING A MAXIM IN ROCHEFOUCAULD

Dans l'adversité de nos meilleurs amis nous trouvons quelque chose, qui ne nous deplaist pas.

In the adversity of our best friends, we find something that doth not displease us.

As Rochefoucauld his maxims drew
From nature, I believe 'em true:
They argue no corrupted mind
In him; the fault is in mankind.

This maxim more than all the rest
Is thought too base for human breast;
'In all distresses of our friends
We first consult our private ends,
While nature kindly bent to ease us,
10   Points out some circumstance to please us.'

If this perhaps your patience move
Let reason and experience prove.

We all behold with envious eyes,
Our equal raised above our size;
Who would not at a crowded show,
Stand high himself, keep others low?
I love my friend as well as you,
But would not have him stop my view;
Then let me have the higher post;
20   I ask but for an inch at most.

If in a battle you should find,
One, whom you love of all mankind,
Had some heroic action done,
A champion killed, or trophy won;
Rather than thus be overtopped,
Would you not wish his laurels cropped?

Dear honest Ned is in the gout,
Lies racked with pain, and you without:
How patiently you hear him groan!
How glad the case is not your own!

What poet would not grieve to see,
His brethren write as well as he?
But rather than they should excel,
He'd wish his rivals all in hell.

Her end when Emulation misses,
She turns to envy, stings and hisses:
The strongest friendship yields to pride,
Unless the odds be on our side.

Vain humankind! Fantastic race!
Thy various follies, who can trace?
Self-love, ambition, envy, pride,
Their empire in our hearts divide:
Give others riches, power, and station,
'Tis all on me a usurpation.
I have no title to aspire;
Yet, when you sink, I seem the higher.
In Pope, I cannot read a line,
But with a sigh, I wish it mine:
When he can in one couplet fix
More sense than I can do in six:
It gives me such a jealous fit,
I cry, 'Pox take him, and his wit.'

Why must I be outdone by Gay,
In my own humorous biting way?

Arbuthnot is no more my friend,
Who dares to irony pretend;
Which I was born to introduce,
Refined it first, and showed its use.

St John, as well as Pulteney knows,
That I had some repute for prose;
And till they drove me out of date,
Could maul a minister of state:

If they have mortified my pride,
And made me throw my pen aside;
If with such talents heaven hath blest 'em,
Have I not reason to detest 'em?

To all my foes, dear fortune, send
Thy gifts, but never to my friend:
I tamely can endure the first,
70   But, this with envy makes me burst.

Thus much may serve by way of proem,
Proceed we therefore to our poem.

The time is not remote, when I
Must by the course of nature die:
When I foresee my special friends,
Will try to find their private ends:
Though it is hardly understood,
Which way my death can do them good;
Yet, thus methinks, I hear 'em speak;
80   'See, how the Dean begins to break:
Poor gentleman, he droops apace,
You plainly find it in his face:
That old vertigo in his head,
Will never leave him, till he's dead:
Besides, his memory decays,
He recollects not what he says;
He cannot call his friends to mind;
Forgets the place where last he dined:
Plies you with stories o'er and o'er,
90   He told them fifty times before.
How does he fancy we can sit,
To hear his out-of-fashioned wit?
But he takes up with younger folks,
Who for his wine will bear his jokes:
Faith, he must make his stories shorter,
Or change his comrades once a quarter:
In half the time, he talks them round;
There must another set be found.

'For poetry, he's past his prime,
100 He takes an hour to find a rhyme:
His fire is out, his wit decayed,
His fancy sunk, his muse a jade.
I'd have him throw away his pen;
But there's no talking to some men.'

And, then their tenderness appears,
By adding largely to my years:
'He's older than he would be reckoned,
And well remembers Charles the Second.

'He hardly drinks a pint of wine;
110 And that, I doubt, is no good sign.
His stomach too begins to fail:
Last year we thought him strong and hale;
But now, he's quite another thing;
I wish he may hold out till spring.'

Then hug themselves, and reason thus;
'It is not yet so bad with us.'

In such a case they talk in tropes,
And, by their fears express their hopes:
Some great misfortune to portend,
120 No enemy can match a friend;
With all the kindness they profess,
The merit of a lucky guess,
(When daily 'Howd'y's' come of course,
And servants answer: 'Worse and worse')
Would please 'em better than to tell,
That, God be praised, the Dean is well.
Then he who prophesied the best,
Approves his foresight to the rest:
'You know, I always feared the worst,
130 And often told you so at first':
He'd rather choose that I should die,
Than his prediction prove a lie.
No one foretells I shall recover;
But, all agree, to give me over.

Yet should some neighbour feel a pain,
Just in the parts, where I complain;
How many a message would he send?
What hearty prayers that I should mend?
Enquire what regimen I kept;
140 What gave me ease, and how I slept?
And more lament, when I was dead,
Than all the snivellers round my bed.

My good companions, never fear,
For though you may mistake a year;
Though your prognostics run too fast,
They must be verified at last.

Behold the fatal day arrive!
'How is the Dean?' 'He's just alive.'
Now the departing prayer is read:
150 He hardly breathes. The Dean is dead.
Before the passing-bell begun,
The news through half the town has run.
O, may we all for death prepare!
'What has he left? And who's his heir?
I know no more than what the news is,
'Tis all bequeathed to public uses.
To public use! A perfect whim!
What had the public done for him?
Mere envy, avarice, and pride!
160 He gave it all. – But first he died.
And had the Dean, in all the nation,
No worthy friend, no poor relation?
So ready to do strangers good,
Forgetting his own flesh and blood?'

Now Grub Street wits are all employed;
With elegies, the town is cloyed:
Some paragraph in every paper,
To curse the Dean, or bless the Drapier.

The doctors tender of their fame,
170 Wisely on me lay all the blame:

'We must confess his case was nice;
But he would never take advice;
Had he been ruled, for aught appears,
He might have lived these twenty years:
For when we opened him we found,
That all his vital parts were sound.'

From Dublin soon to London spread,
'Tis told at court, the Dean is dead.

Kind Lady Suffolk in the spleen,
180 Runs laughing up to tell the Queen.
The Queen, so gracious, mild, and good,
Cries, 'Is he gone? 'Tis time he should.
He's dead you say, why let him rot;
I'm glad the medals were forgot.
I promised them, I own; but when?
I only was a princess then;
But now as consort of the King,
You know 'tis quite a different thing.'

Now, Chartres at Sir Robert's levee,
190 Tells, with a sneer, the tidings heavy:
'Why, is he dead without his shoes?'
(Cries Bob) 'I'm sorry for the news;
Oh, were the wretch but living still,
And in his place my good friend Will;
Or had a mitre on his head
Provided Bolingbroke were dead.'

Now Curll his shop from rubbish drains;
Three genuine tomes of Swift's remains.
And then to make them pass the glibber,
200 Revised by Tibbalds, Moore, and Cibber.
He'll treat me as he does my betters.
Publish my will, my life, my letters.
Revive the libels born to die;
Which Pope must bear, as well as I.

Here shift the scene, to represent
How those I love, my death lament.

Poor Pope will grieve a month; and Gay
A week; and Arbuthnot a day.

St John himself will scarce forbear,
210   To bite his pen, and drop a tear.
The rest will give a shrug and cry
'I'm sorry; but we all must die.'
Indifference clad in wisdom's guise,
All fortitude of mind supplies:
For how can stony bowels melt,
In those who never pity felt;
When *we* are lashed, *they* kiss the rod;
Resigning to the will of God.

The fools, my juniors by a year,
220   Are tortured with suspense and fear.
Who wisely thought my age a screen,
When death approached, to stand between:
The screen removed, their hearts are trembling,
They mourn for me without dissembling.

My female friends, whose tender hearts
Have better learnt to act their parts,
Receive the news in doleful dumps,
'The Dean is dead, (*and what is trumps?*)
Then Lord have mercy on his soul.
230   (*Ladies, I'll venture for the vole.*)
Six deans they say must bear the pall.
(*I wish I knew which king to call.*)'
'Madam, your husband will attend
The funeral of so good a friend.'
'No madam, 'tis a shocking sight,
And he's engaged tomorrow night!
My Lady Club would take it ill,
If he should fail her at quadrille.
He loved the Dean. (*I lead a heart.*)
240   But dearest friends, they say, must part.
His time was come, he ran his race;
We hope he's in a better place.'

Why do we grieve that friends should die?
No loss more easy to supply.
One year is past; a different scene;
No further mention of the Dean;
Who now, alas, no more is missed,
Than if he never did exist.
Where's now this favourite of Apollo?
250 Departed; and his works must follow:
Must undergo the common fate;
His kind of wit is out of date.
Some country squire to Lintot goes,
Inquires for Swift in verse and prose:
Says Lintot, 'I have heard the name:
He died a year ago.' The same.
He searcheth all his shop in vain;
'Sir, you may find them in Duck Lane:
I sent them with a load of books,
260 Last Monday to the pastry-cook's.
To fancy they could live a year!
I find you're but a stranger here.
The Dean was famous in his time;
And had a kind of knack at rhyme:
His way of writing now is past;
The town hath got a better taste:
I keep no antiquated stuff;
But, spick and span I have enough.
Pray, do but give me leave to show 'em;
270 Here's Colley Cibber's birthday poem.
This ode you never yet have seen,
By Stephen Duck, upon the Queen.
Then, here's a letter finely penned,
Against the *Craftsman* and his friend;
It clearly shows that all reflection
On ministers, is disaffection.
Next, here's Sir Robert's vindication,
And Mr Henley's last oration:
The hawkers have not got 'em yet,
280 Your honour please to buy a set?

    'Here's Woolston's tracts, the twelfth edition;
'Tis read by every politician:
The country members, when in town,
To all their boroughs send them down:
You never met a thing so smart;
The courtiers have them all by heart:
Those maids of honour (who can read)
Are taught to use them for their creed.
The reverend author's good intention,
290 Hath been rewarded with a pension:
He doth an honour to his gown,
By bravely running priestcraft down:
He shows, as sure as God's in Gloucester,
That Jesus was a grand impostor:
That all his miracles were cheats,
Performed as jugglers do their feats:
The church had never such a writer:
A shame he hath not got a mitre!'

    Suppose me dead; and then suppose
300 A club assembled at the Rose;
Where from discourse of this, and that,
I grow the subject of their chat:
And, while they toss my name about,
With favour some, and some without;
One quite indifferent in the cause,
My character impartial draws:

    'The Dean, if we believe report,
Was never ill received at court:
As for his works in verse and prose,
310 I own myself no judge of those:
Nor, can I tell what critics thought 'em;
But, this I know, all people bought 'em;
As with a moral view designed
To cure the vices of mankind:
His vein, ironically grave,
Exposed the fool, and lashed the knave:

To steal a hint was never known,
But what he writ was all his own.

    'He never thought an honour done him,
320 Because a duke was proud to own him:
Would rather slip aside, and choose
To talk with wits in dirty shoes:
Despised the fools with stars and garters,
So often seen caressing Chartres:
He never courted men in station,
Nor persons had in admiration;
Of no man's greatness was afraid,
Because he sought for no man's aid.
Though trusted long in great affairs,
330 He gave himself no haughty airs:
Without regarding private ends,
Spent all his credit for his friends:
And only chose the wise and good;
No flatterers; no allies in blood;
But succoured virtue in distress,
And seldom failed of good success;
As numbers in their hearts must own,
Who, but for him, had been unknown.

    'With princes kept a due decorum,
340 But never stood in awe before 'em:
And to her Majesty, God bless her,
Would speak as free as to her dresser,
She thought it his particular whim,
Nor took it ill as come from him.
He followed David's lesson just,
"In princes never put thy trust."
And, would you make him truly sour;
Provoke him with a slave in power:
The Irish senate, if you named,
350 With what impatience he declaimed!
Fair LIBERTY was all his cry;
For her he stood prepared to die;
For her he boldly stood alone;
For her he oft exposed his own.

Two kingdoms, just as factions led,
Had set a price upon his head;
But, not a traitor could be found,
To sell him for six hundred pound.

'Had he but spared his tongue and pen,
360   He might have rose like other men:
But, power was never in his thought;
And, wealth he valued not a groat:
Ingratitude he often found,
And pitied those who meant the wound:
But, kept the tenor of his mind,
To merit well of humankind:
Nor made a sacrifice of those
Who still were true, to please his foes.
He laboured many a fruitless hour
370   To reconcile his friends in power;
Saw mischief by a fraction brewing,
While they pursued each other's ruin.
But, finding vain was all his care,
He left the court in mere despair.

'And, oh! how short are human schemes!
Here ended all our golden dreams.
What St John's skill in state affairs,
What Ormonde's valour, Oxford's cares,
To save their sinking country lent,
380   Was all destroyed by one event.
Too soon that precious life was ended,
On which alone, our weal depended.
When up a dangerous faction starts,
With wrath and vengeance in their hearts:
By solemn league and covenant bound,
To ruin, slaughter and confound;
To turn religion to a fable,
And make the government a Babel:
Pervert the law, disgrace the gown,
390   Corrupt the senate, rob the crown;
To sacrifice old England's glory,
And make her infamous in story.

When such a tempest shook the land,
How could unguarded virtue stand?

'With horror, grief, despair the Dean
Beheld the dire destructive scene:
His friends in exile, or the Tower,
Himself within the frown of power;
Pursued by base envenomed pens,
400 Far to the land of slaves and fens;
A servile race in folly nursed,
Who truckle most, when treated worst.

'By innocence and resolution,
He bore continual persecution;
While numbers to preferment rose;
Whose merits were, to be his foes.
When, *ev'n his own familiar friends*
Intent upon their private ends,
Like renegadoes now he feels,
410 *Against him lifting up their heels.*

'The Dean did by his pen defeat
An infamous destructive cheat.
Taught fools their interest to know;
And gave them arms to ward the blow.
Envy hath owned it was his doing,
To save that helpless land from ruin,
While they who at the steerage stood,
And reaped the profit, sought his blood.

'To save them from their evil fate,
420 In him was held a crime of state.
A wicked monster on the bench,
Whose fury blood could never quench;
As vile and profligate a villain,
As modern Scroggs, or old Tresilian;
Who long all justice had discarded,
Nor feared he God, nor man regarded;
Vowed on the Dean his rage to vent,
And make him of his zeal repent;

But heaven his innocence defends,
430   The grateful people stand his friends:
Not strains of law, nor judges' frown,
Nor topics brought to please the crown,
Nor witness hired, nor jury picked,
Prevail to bring him in convict.

'In exile with a steady heart,
He spent his life's declining part;
Where folly, pride, and faction sway,
Remote from St John, Pope, and Gay.

'His friendship there to few confined,
440   Were always of the middling kind:
No fools of rank, a mongrel breed,
Who fain would pass for lords indeed:
Where titles give no right or power,
And peerage is a withered flower,
He would have held it a disgrace,
If such a wretch had known his face.
On rural squires, that kingdom's bane,
He vented oft his wrath in vain:
Biennial squires, to market brought;
450   Who sell their souls and votes for naught;
The nation stripped, go joyful back,
To rob the church, their tenants rack,
Go snacks with thieves and rapparees,
And keep the peace, to pick up fees:
In every job to have a share,
A gaol or barrack to repair;
And turn the tax for public roads
Commodious to their own abodes.

'Perhaps I may allow the Dean
460   Had too much satire in his vein;
And seemed determined not to starve it,
Because no age could more deserve it.
Yet, malice never was his aim;
He lashed the vice but spared the name.

No individual could resent,
Where thousands equally were meant.
His satire points at no defect,
But what all mortals may correct;
For he abhorred that senseless tribe,
470 Who call it humour when they jibe:
He spared a hump or crooked nose,
Whose owners set not up for beaux.
True genuine dullness moved his pity,
Unless it offered to be witty.
Those, who their ignorance confessed,
He ne'er offended with a jest;
But laughed to hear an idiot quote,
A verse from Horace, learnt by rote.

'He knew an hundred pleasant stories,
480 With all the turns of Whigs and Tories:
Was cheerful to his dying day,
And friends would let him have his way.

'He gave the little wealth he had,
To build a house for fools and mad:
And showed by one satiric touch,
No nation wanted it so much:
That kingdom he hath left his debtor,
I wish it soon may have a better.'

On the Day of Judgement

With a whirl of thought oppressed,
I sink from reverie to rest.
An horrid vision seized my head,
I saw the graves give up their dead,
Jove, armed with terrors, burst the skies,
And thunder roars, and lightning flies!
Amazed, confused, its fate unknown,
The world stands trembling at his throne.

  While each pale sinner hangs his head,
10 Jove, nodding, shook the heavens, and said,
  'Offending race of humankind,
  By nature, reason, learning, blind;
  You who through frailty stepped aside,
  And you who never fell – *through pride*;
  You who in different sects have shammed,
  And come to see each other damned;
  (So some folks told you, but they knew
  No more of Jove's designs than you)
  The world's mad business now is o'er,
20 And I resent these pranks no more.
  I to such blockheads set my wit!
  I damn such fools! – Go, go you're bit.'

On Poetry: a Rhapsody

  All human race would fain be wits,
  And millions miss, for one that hits.
  Young's universal passion, pride,
  Was never known to spread so wide.
  Say Britain, could you ever boast,
  Three poets in an age at most?
  Our chilling climate hardly bears
  A sprig of bays in fifty years:
  While every fool his claim alleges,
10 As if it grew in common hedges.
  What reason can there be assigned
  For this perverseness in the mind?
  Brutes find out where their talents lie:
  A bear will not attempt to fly:
  A foundered horse will oft debate,
  Before he tries a five-barred gate:
  A dog by instinct turns aside,
  Who sees the ditch too deep and wide.
  But man we find the only creature,
20 Who, led by folly, combats nature;

Who, when she loudly cries, 'Forbear',
With obstinacy fixes there;
And, where his genius least inclines,
Absurdly bends his whole designs.

Not empire to the rising sun,
By valour, conduct, fortune won;
Nor highest wisdom in debates
For framing laws to govern states;
Nor skill in sciences profound,
30 So large to grasp the circle round;
Such heavenly influence require,
As how to strike the muses' lyre.

Not beggar's brat, on bulk begot;
Not bastard of a pedlar Scot;
Not boy brought up to cleaning shoes,
The spawn of Bridewell, or the stews;
Not infants dropped, the spurious pledges
Of gypsies littering under hedges,
Are so disqualified by fate
40 To rise in church, or law, or state,
As he, whom Phoebus in his ire
Hath *blasted* with poetic fire.

What hope of custom in the fair,
While not a soul demands your ware?
Where you have nothing to produce
For private life, or public use?
Court, city, country want you not;
You cannot bribe, betray, or plot.
For poets, law makes no provision:
50 The wealthy have you in derision.
Of state affairs you cannot smatter,
Are awkward when you try to flatter.
Your portion, taking Britain round,
Was just one annual hundred pound.
Now not so much as in remainder
Since Cibber brought in an attainder;
For ever fixed by right divine,
(A monarch's right) on Grub Street line.

Poor starveling bard, how small thy gains!
60   How unproportioned to thy pains!
And here a simile comes pat in:
Though chickens take a month to fatten,
The guests in less than half an hour
Will more than half a score devour.
So, after toiling twenty days,
To earn a stock of pence and praise,
Thy labours, grown the critic's prey,
Are swallowed o'er a dish of tea;
Gone, to be never heard of more,
70   Gone, where the chickens went before.

How shall a new attempter learn
Of different spirits to discern,
And how distinguish, which is which,
The poet's vein, or scribbling itch?
Then hear an old experienced sinner
Instructing thus a young beginner.

Consult yourself, and if you find
A powerful impulse urge your mind,
Impartial judge within your breast
80   What subject you can manage best;
Whether your genius most inclines
To satire, praise, or humorous lines;
To elegies in mournful tone,
Or prologue 'sent from hand unknown'.
Then rising with Aurora's light,
The muse invoked, sit down to write;
Blot out, correct, insert, refine,
Enlarge, diminish, interline.
Be mindful, when invention fails,
90   To scratch your head, and bite your nails.

Your poem finished: next your care
Is needful, to transcribe it fair.
In modern wit all printed trash is
Set off with numerous breaks – and dashes –
To statesmen would you give a wipe,
You print it in *italic type.*

When letters are in vulgar shapes,
'Tis ten to one the wit escapes;
But when in CAPITALS expressed,
100 The dullest reader smokes a jest.
Or else perhaps he may invent
A better than the poet meant,
As learnéd commentators view
In Homer more than Homer knew.

Your poem in its modish dress,
Correctly fitted for the press,
Convey by penny post to Lintot,
But let no friend alive look into't.
If Lintot thinks 'twill quit the cost,
110 You need not fear your labour lost:
And, how agreeably surprised
Are you to see it advertised!
The hawker shows you one in print,
As fresh as farthings from the mint:
The product of your toil and sweating;
A bastard of your own begetting.

Be sure at Will's the following day,
Lie snug, to hear what critics say.
And if you find the general vogue
120 Pronounces you a stupid rogue;
Damns all your thoughts as low and little,
Sit still, and swallow down your spittle.
Be silent as a politician,
For, talking may beget suspicion:
Or praise the judgement of the town,
And help yourself to run it down.
Give up a fond paternal pride,
Nor argue on the weaker side;
For, poems read without a name
130 We justly praise, or justly blame:
And critics have no partial views,
Except they know whom they abuse.
And since you ne'er provoked their spite,
Depend upon't their judgement's right:

But if you blab, you are undone;
Consider what a risk you run.
You lose your credit all at once;
The town will mark you for a dunce:
The vilest doggerel Grub Street sends,
140 Will pass for yours with foes and friends.
And you must bear the whole disgrace,
Till some fresh blockhead takes your place.

Your secret kept, your poem sunk,
And sent in quires to line a trunk;
If still you be disposed to rhyme,
Go try your hand a second time.
Again you fail, yet safe's the word,
Take courage and attempt a third.
But first with care employ your thoughts,
150 Where critics marked your former faults.
The trivial turns, the borrowed wit,
The similes that nothing fit;
The cant which every fool repeats,
Town-jests, and coffee-house conceits;
Descriptions tedious, flat and dry,
And introduced the Lord knows why;
Or where you find your fury set
Against the harmless alphabet;
On A's and B's your malice vent,
160 While readers wonder whom you meant.
A public, or a private robber;
A statesman, or a South Sea jobber.
A prelate who no God believes;
A parliament, or den of thieves.
A house of peers, or gaming crew,
A griping monarch, or a Jew.
A pickpurse, at the bar, or bench;
A duchess, or a suburb wench.
Or oft when epithets you link,
170 In gaping lines to fill a chink;
Like stepping stones to save a stride,
In streets where kennels are too wide:

Or like a heel-piece to support
A cripple with one foot too short:
Or like a bridge that joins a marish
To moorlands of a different parish.
So have I seen ill-coupled hounds,
Drag different ways in miry grounds.
So geographes in Afric maps
180 With savage pictures fill their gaps;
And o'er unhabitable downs
Place elephants for want of towns.

But though you miss your third essay,
You need not throw your pen away.
Lay now aside all thoughts of fame,
To spring more profitable game.
From party merit seek support;
The vilest verse thrives best at court.
And may you ever have the luck
190 To rhyme almost as well as Duck;
And, though you never learned to scan verse,
Come out with some lampoon on D'Anvers.
A pamphlet in Sir Bob's defence
Will never fail to bring in pence;
Nor be concerned about the sale,
He pays his workmen on the nail.

Display the blessings of the nation,
And praise the whole administration,
Extol the bench of bishops round,
200 Who at them rail bid God confound:
To bishop-haters answer thus
(The only logic used by us),
What though they don't believe in Christ,
Deny them Protestants – thou liest.

A prince the moment he is crowned,
Inherits every virtue round,
As emblems of the sovereign power,
Like *other* baubles of the Tower.
Is generous, valiant, just and wise,
210 And so continues till he dies.

His humble senate this professes,
In all their speeches, votes, addresses.
But once you fix him in a tomb,
His virtues fade, his vices bloom;
And each perfection wrong imputed
Is fully at his death confuted.
His panegyrics then are ceased,
He's grown a tyrant, dunce and beast.
The loads of poems in his praise,
220   Ascending make one funeral blaze.
As soon as you can hear his knell,
This god on earth turns devil in hell.
And lo, his ministers of state,
Transformed to imps, his levees wait:
Where, in the scenes of endless woe,
They ply their former arts below:
And as they sail in Charon's boat,
Contrive to bribe the judge's vote.
To Cerberus they give a sop,
230   His triple-barking mouth to stop:
Or in the ivory gate of dreams,
Project Excise and South Sea schemes:
Or hire their party pamphleteers,
To set Elysium by the ears.

Then poet, if you mean to thrive,
Employ your muse on kings alive;
With prudence gathering up a cluster
Of all the virtues you can muster:
Which formed into a garland sweet,
240   Lay humbly at your monarch's feet;
Who, as the odours reach his throne,
Will smile, and think 'em all his own:
For law and gospel both determine
All virtues lodge in royal ermine.
(I mean the oracles of both
Who shall depose it upon oath.)
Your garland in the following reign,
Change but the names, will do again.

But if you think this trade too base,
250 (Which seldom is the dunce's case)
Put on the critic's brow, and sit
At Will's, the puny judge of wit.
A nod, a shrug, a scornful smile,
With caution used, may serve awhile.
Proceed no further in your part,
Before you learn the terms of art:
(For you can never be too far gone,
In all our modern critics' jargon).
Then talk with more authentic face,
260 Of 'unities, in time and place'.
Get scraps of Horace from your friends,
And have them at your fingers' ends.
Learn Aristotle's rules by rote,
And at all hazards boldly quote:
Judicious Rymer oft review:
Wise Dennis, and profound Bossu.
Read all the prefaces of Dryden,
For these our critics much confide in,
(Though merely writ at first for filling
270 To raise the volume's price, a shilling).

A forward critic often dupes us
With sham quotations *Peri Hupsous*:
And if we have not read Longinus,
Will magisterially outshine us.
Then, lest with Greek he overrun ye,
Procure the book for love or money,
Translated from Boileau's translation,
And quote quotation on quotation.

At Will's you hear a poem read,
280 Where Battus from the table head,
Reclining on his elbow-chair,
Gives judgement with decisive air.
To him the tribe of circling wits,
As to an oracle submits.
He gives directions to the town,
To cry it up, or run it down,

(Like courtiers, when they send a note,
Instructing members how to vote).
He sets a stamp of bad and good,
290   Though not a word be understood.
Your lesson learnt, you'll be secure
To get the name of connoisseur.
And when your merits once are known,
Procure disciples of your own.

For poets (you can never want 'em,
Spread through Augusta Trinobantum)
Computing by their pecks of coals,
Amount to just nine thousand souls.
These o'er their proper districts govern,
300   Of wit and humour, judges sovereign.
In every street a city bard
Rules, like an alderman his ward.
His indisputed rights extend
Through all the lane, from end to end.
The neighbours round admire his shrewdness,
For songs of loyalty and lewdness.
Outdone by none in rhyming well,
Although he never learnt to spell.

Two bordering wits contend for glory;
310   And one is Whig, and one is Tory.
And this, for epics claims the bays,
And that, for elegaic lays.
Some famed for numbers soft and smooth,
By lovers spoke in Punch's booth.
And some as justly fame extols
For lofty lines in Smithfield drolls.
Bavius in Wapping gains renown,
And Maevius reigns o'er Kentish Town:
Tigellius placed in Phoebus' car,
320   From Ludgate shines to Temple Bar.
Harmonious Cibber entertains
The court with annual birthday strains;
Whence Gay was banished in disgrace,
Where Pope will never show his face;

Where Young must torture his invention,
To flatter knaves, or lose his pension.

But these are not a thousandth part
Of jobbers in the poet's art,
Attending each his proper station,
330   And all in due subordination;
Through every alley to be found,
In garrets high, or underground:
And when they join their pericranies,
Out skips a book of miscellanies.

Hobbes clearly proves that every creature
Lives in a state of war by nature.
The greater for the smaller watch,
But meddle seldom with their match.
A whale of moderate size will draw
340   A shoal of herrings down his maw.
A fox with geese his belly crams;
A wolf destroys a thousand lambs.
But search among the rhyming race,
The *brave* are worried by the *base*.
If, on Parnassus' top you sit,
You rarely bite, are always bit:
Each poet of inferior size
On you shall rail and criticize;
And strive to tear you limb from limb,
350   While others do as much for him.
The vermin only tease and pinch
Their foes superior by an inch.
So, naturalists observe, a flea
Hath smaller fleas that on him prey,
And these have smaller yet to bite 'em,
And so proceed *ad infinitum*:
Thus every poet in his kind,
Is bit by him that comes behind;
Who, though too little to be seen,
360   Can tease, and gall, and give the spleen;
Call dunces, fools, and sons of whores,
Lay Grub Street at each other's doors:

Extol the Greek and Roman masters,
And curse our modern poetasters.
Complain, as many an ancient bard did,
How genius is no more rewarded;
How wrong a taste prevails among us;
How much our ancestors outsung us;
Can personate an awkward scorn
370   For those who are not poets born:
And all their brother dunces lash,
Who crowd the press with hourly trash.

    O, Grub Street! how I do bemoan thee,
Whose graceless children scorn to own thee!
This filial piety forgot,
Deny their country like a Scot:
Though by their idiom and grimace
They soon betray their native place:
Yet *thou* hast greater cause to be
380   Ashamed of them, than they of thee.
Degenerate from their ancient brood,
Since first the court allowed them food.

    Remains a difficulty still,
To purchase fame by writing ill:
From Flecknoe down to Howard's time,
How few have reached the low sublime!
For when our high-born Howard died,
Blackmore alone his place supplied:
And lest a chasm should intervene,
390   When death had finished Blackmore's reign,
The leaden crown devolved to thee,
Great poet of the *Hollow Tree*.
But, oh, how unsecure thy throne!
Ten thousand bards thy rights disown:
They plot to turn in factious zeal,
Duncenia to a common-weal;
And with rebellious arms pretend
And equal privilege to *descend*.

In bulk there are not more degrees,
400 From elephants to mites in cheese,
Than what a curious eye may trace
In creatures of the rhyming race.
From bad to worse, and worse they fall,
But, who can reach to worst of all?
For, though in nature depth and height
Are equally held infinite,
In poetry the height we know;
'Tis only infinite below.
For instance: when you rashly think,
410 No rhymer can like Welsted sink:
His merits balanced you shall find,
The laureate leaves him far behind.
Concanen, more aspiring bard,
Climbs downwards, deeper by a yard:
Smart Jemmy Moor with vigour drops,
The rest pursue as thick as hops:
With heads to points the gulf they enter,
Linked perpendicular to the centre:
And as their heels elated rise,
420 Their heads attempt the nether skies.

O, what indignity and shame
To prostitute the muse's name,
By flattering kings whom heaven designed
The plagues and scourges of mankind.
Bred up in ignorance and sloth,
And every vice that nurses both.

Perhaps you say Augustus shines
Immortal made in Virgil's lines,
And Horace brought the tuneful choir
430 To sing his virtues on the lyre,
Without reproach of flattery; true,
Because their praises were his due.
For in those ages kings we find,
Were animals of humankind,
But now go search all Europe round,
Among the savage monsters crowned,

With vice polluting every throne
(I mean all kings except our own)
In vain you make the strictest view
440 To find a king in all the crew
With whom a footman out of place
Would not conceive a high disgrace,
A burning shame, a crying sin,
To take his morning's cup of gin.
Thus all are destined to obey
Some beast of burden or of prey.
'Tis sung Prometheus forming man
Through all the brutal species ran,
Each proper quality to find
450 Adapted to a human mind;
A mingled mass of good and bad,
The worst and best that could be had;
Then from a clay of mixture base,
He shaped a king to rule the race,
Endowed with gifts from every brute,
Which best the regal nature suit.
Thus think on kings, the name denotes
Hogs, asses, wolves, baboons and goats,
To represent in figure just
460 Sloth, folly, rapine, mischief, lust.
O! were they all but Nebuchadnezzars,
What herds of kings would turn to grazers.

    Fair Britain, in thy monarch blessed,
Whose virtues bear the strictest test;
Whom never faction can bespatter,
Nor minister nor poet flatter.
What justice in rewarding merit!
What magnanimity of spirit!
How well his public thrift is shown!
470 All coffers full except his own.
What lineaments divine we trace
Through all his figure, mien, and face;
Though peace with olive bind his hands,
Confessed the conquering hero stands.

Hydaspes, Indus, and the Ganges,
Dread from his hand impending changes.
From him the Tartar, and Chinese,
Short by the knees intreat for peace.
The consort of his throne and bed,
480 A perfect goddess born and bred.
Appointed sovereign judge to sit
On learning, eloquence and wit.
Our eldest hope, divine Iulus,
(Late, very late, O, may he rule us).
What early manhood has he shown,
Before his downy beard was grown!
Then think, what wonders will be done
By going on as he begun;
An heir for Britain to secure
490 As long as sun and moon endure.

The remnant of the royal blood,
Comes pouring on me like a flood.
Bright goddesses, in number five;
Duke William, sweetest prince alive.

Now sing the minister of state,
Who shines alone, without a mate.
Observe with what majestic port
This Atlas stands to prop the court:
Intent the public debts to pay,
500 Like prudent Fabius by delay.
Thou great vicegerent of the King,
Thy praises every muse shall sing:
In all affairs thou sole director,
Of wit and learning chief protector;
Though small the time thou hast to spare,
The church is thy peculiar care.
Of pious prelates what a stock
You choose to rule the sable flock.
You raise the honour of the peerage,
510 Proud to attend you at the steerage.
You dignify the noble race,
Content yourself with humbler place,

Now learning, valour, virtue, sense,
To titles give the sole pretence.
St George beheld thee with delight,
Vouchsafe to be an azure knight,
When on thy breast and sides Herculean,
He fixed the star and string cerulean.

Say, poet, in what other nation,
520   Shone ever such a constellation.
Attend ye Popes, and Youngs, and Gays,
And tune your harps, and strow your bays.
Your panegyrics here provide,
You cannot err on flattery's side.
Above the stars exalt your style,
You still are low ten thousand mile.
On Lewis all his bards bestowed,
Of incense many a thousand load;
But Europe mortified his pride,
530   And swore the fawning rascals lied:
Yet what the world refused to Lewis,
Applied to George exactly true is:
Exactly true! Invidious poet!
'Tis fifty thousand times below it.

Translate me now some lines, if you can,
From Virgil, Martial, Ovid, Lucan;
They could all power in heaven divide,
And do no wrong to either side:
They teach you how to split a hair,
540   Give George and Jove an equal share.
Yet, why should we be laced so straight;
I'll give my monarch butter-weight.
And reason good; for many a year
Jove never intermeddled here:
Nor, though his priests be duly paid,
Did ever we desire his aid:
We now can better do without him,
Since Woolston gave us arms to rout him.

* * * * * * * * *Caetera desiderantur* * * * * * * * *

To a Lady

WHO DESIRED THE AUTHOR TO WRITE SOME
VERSES UPON HER IN THE HEROIC STYLE

After venting all my spite,
Tell me, what have I to write?
Every error I could find
Through the mazes of your mind,
Have my busy muse employed
Till the company is cloyed.
Are you positive and fretful
Heedless, ignorant, forgetful?
These, and twenty follies more,
10   I have often told before.

    Hearken what my Lady says,
'Have I nothing then to praise?
Ill befits you to be witty,
When a fault should move your pity.
If you think me too conceited,
Or to passion quickly heated:
If my wandering head be less
Set on reading than on dress;
If I always seem so dull t'ye;
20   I can solve the difficulty.

    'You would teach me to be wise;
Truth and honour how to prize;
How to shine in conversation,
And with credit fill my station:
How to relish notions high:
How to live, and how to die.

    'But it was decreed by fate,
Mr Dean, you come too late;
Well I know, you can discern,
30   I am now too old to learn:
Follies, from my youth instilled,
Have my soul entirely filled:

In my head and heart they centre;
Nor will let your lessons enter.

'Bred a fondling and an heiress;
Dressed like any Lady Mayoress;
Cockered by the servants round,
Was too good to touch the ground,
Thought the life of every lady
40   Should be one continual play-day:
Balls, and masquerades, and shows,
Visits, plays, and powdered beaux.

'Thus you have my case at large;
And may now perform your charge.
Those materials I have furnished,
When by you refined and burnished,
Must, that all the world may know 'em,
Be reduced into a poem.
But, I beg, suspend a while
50   That same paltry, burlesque style;
Drop for once your constant rule,
Turning all to ridicule:
Teaching others how to ape ye;
Court nor parliament can 'scape ye;
Treat the public and your friends
Both alike, while neither mends.

'Sing my praise in strain sublime;
Treat not me with doggerel rhyme.
'Tis but just, you should produce
60   With each fault, each fault's excuse:
Not to publish every trifle,
And my few perfections stifle.
With some gifts at least endow me,
Which my very foes allow me.
Am I spiteful, proud, unjust?
Did I ever break my trust?

Which, of all our *modern* dames,
Censures less, or less defames?
In good manners am I faulty?
70 Can you call me rude or haughty?
Did I e'er my mite withhold
From the impotent and old?
When did ever I omit
Due regard for men of wit?
When have I esteem expressed
For a coxcomb gaily dressed?
Do I, like the female tribe,
Think it wit to fleer and gibe?
Who, with less designing ends,
80 Kindlier entertains their friends?
With good words and countenance sprightly,
Strive to treat them all politely?

'Think not cards my chief diversion:
'Tis a wrong unjust aspersion:
Never knew I any good in 'em,
But to doze my head like laudanum:
We by play, as men by drinking,
Pass our nights to drive out thinking.
From my ailments give me leisure,
90 I shall read and think with pleasure:
Conversations learn to relish,
And with books my mind embellish.'

Now, methinks, I hear you cry:
'Mr Dean, you must reply.'

Madam, I allow 'tis true:
All these praises are your due.
You, like some acute philosopher,
Every fault have drawn a gloss over;
Placing in the strongest light
100 All your virtues to my sight.

Though you lead a blameless life,
Live an humble, prudent wife;
Answer all domestic ends,
What is this to us your friends?
Though your children by a nod
Stand in awe without a rod:
Though by your obliging sway
Servants love you, and obey;
Though you treat us with a smile;
110 Clear your looks, and smooth your style;
Load our plates from every dish;
This is not the thing we wish.
Colonel – may be your debtor;
We expect employment better.
You must learn, if you would gain us,
With good sense to entertain us.

Scholars, when good sense describing,
Call it tasting and imbibing:
Metaphoric meat and drink
120 Is to understand and think:
We may *carve* for others thus;
And let others carve for us.
To discourse and to attend,
Is, to *help* yourself and friend.
Conversation is but *carving*;
Carve for all, yourself is starving:
Give no more to every guest,
Than he's able to digest:
Give him always of the prime;
130 And but little at a time.
Carve to all but just enough:
Let them neither starve, nor stuff:
And that you may have your due,
Let your neighbours carve for you.
This comparison will hold,
Could it well in rhyme be told,
How conversing, listening, thinking,
Justly may resemble drinking;

For a friend a glass you fill,
140   What is this but to instil?

    To conclude this long essay,
Pardon, if I disobey;
Nor, against my natural vein,
Treat you in heroic strain.
I, as all the parish knows,
Hardly can be grave in prose:
Still to lash, and lashing smile,
Ill befits a lofty style.
From the planet of my birth,
150   I encounter vice with mirth.
Wicked ministers of state
I can easier scorn than hate:
And, I find it answers right;
Scorn torments them more than spite.
All the vices of a court
Do but serve to make me sport.
Were I in some foreign realm,
Which all vices overwhelm;
Should a monkey wear a crown,
160   Must I tremble at his frown?
Could I not, through all his ermine,
Spy the strutting, chattering vermin?
Safely write a smart lampoon,
To expose the brisk baboon?

    When my muse officious ventures
On the nation's representers:
Teaching by what golden rules,
Into knaves they turn their fools:
How the helm is ruled by Walpole,
170   At whose oars, like slaves, they all pull:
Let the vessel split on shelves;
With the freight enrich themselves:
Safe within my little wherry,
All their madness makes me merry:
Like the watermen of Thames,
I row by, and call them names.

Like the ever-laughing sage,
In a jest I spend my rage.
(Though it must be understood,
180   I would hang them if I could):
If I can but fill my niche,
I attempt no higher pitch.
Leave to D'Anvers and his mate,
Maxims wise to rule the state.
Pulteney deep, accomplished St Johns,
Scourge the villains with a vengeance:
Let me, though the smell be noisome,
Strip their bums; let Caleb hoise 'em;
Then apply Alecto's whip,
190   Till they wriggle, howl, and skip.

'Deuce is in you, Mr Dean:
What can all this passion mean?
Mention courts, you'll ne'er be quiet;
On corruptions running riot.
End, as it befits your station:
Come to use, and application:
Nor, with senates keep a fuss.'
I submit, and answer thus.

If the machinations brewing
200   To complete the public ruin,
Never once could have the power
To affect me half an hour;
(Sooner would I write in buskins,
Mournful elegies on Blueskins)
If I laugh at Whig and Tory;
I conclude *a fortiori*,
All your eloquence will scarce
Drive me from my favourite farce.
This I must insist on. For, as
210   It is well observed by Horace,
Ridicule has greater power
To reform the world, than sour.
Horses thus, let jockeys judge else,
Switches better guide than cudgels.

Bastings heavy, dry, obtuse,
Only dullness can produce;
While a little gentle jerking
Sets the spirits all a-working.

Thus, I find it by experiment,
220 Scolding moves you less than merriment.
I may storm and rage in vain;
It but stupefies your brain.
But with raillery to nettle,
Sets your thoughts upon their mettle:
Gives imagination scope;
Never lets your mind elope:
Drives out brangling and contention,
Brings in reason and invention.
For your sake as well as mine,
230 I the lofty style decline.
I should make a figure scurvy,
And your head turn topsyturvy.

I, who love to have a fling,
Both at senate house and king;
That they might some better way tread,
To avoid the public hatred;
Thought no method more commodious,
Than to show their vices odious:
Which I chose to make appear,
240 Not by anger, but a sneer:
As my method of reforming
Is by laughing, not by storming,
(For my friends have always thought
Tenderness my greatest fault)
Would you have me change my style?
On your faults no longer smile
But, to patch up all your quarrels,
Quote you texts from Plutarch's *Morals*;
Or from Solomon produce
250 Maxims teaching wisdom's use.

If I treat you like a crowned head,
You have cheap enough compounded;
Can you put in higher claims,
Than the owners of St James'?
You are not so great a grievance,
As the hirelings of St Stephen's.
You are of a lower class
Than my friend Sir Robert Brass.
None of these have mercy found,
260   I have laughed and lashed them round.

Have you seen a rocket fly?
You could swear it pierced the sky:
It but reached the middle air,
Bursting into pieces there:
Thousand sparkles falling down,
Light on many a coxcomb's crown:
See, what mirth the sport creates;
Singes hair, but breaks no pates.
Thus, should I attempt to climb,
270   Treat you in a style sublime,
Such a rocket is my muse;
Should I lofty numbers choose,
E'er I reached Parnassus' top,
I should burst, and bursting drop.
All my fire would fall in scraps;
Give your head some gentle raps;
Only make it smart a while;
Then, could I forbear to smile,
When I found the tingling pain,
280   Entering warm your frigid brain:
Make you able upon sight
To decide of wrong and right;
Talk with sense whate'er you please on;
Learn to relish truth and reason.

Thus we both should gain our prize:
I to laugh, and you grow wise.

A Character, Panegyric, and Description of the Legion Club

As I stroll the city, oft I
Spy a building large and lofty,
Not a bow-shot from the College,
Half a globe from sense and knowledge.
By the prudent architect
Placed against the church direct;
Making good my grandam's jest,
Near the church – you know the rest.

    Tell us, what this pile contains?
10 Many a head that holds no brains.
These demoniacs let me dub
With the name of 'Legion Club'.
Such assemblies, you might swear,
Meet when butchers bait a bear;
Such a noise, and such haranguing,
When a brother thief is hanging.
Such a rout and such a rabble
Run to hear jack-pudding gabble;
Such a crowd their ordure throws
20 On a far less villain's nose.

    Could I from the building's top
Hear the rattling thunder drop,
While the devil upon the roof,
If the devil be thunder-proof,
Should with poker fiery red
Crack the stones, and melt the lead;
Drive them down on every skull,
While the den of thieves is full,
Quite destroy that harpie's nest,
30 How might then our isle be blessed?
For divines allow, that God
Sometimes makes the devil his rod:
And the gospel will inform us,
He can punish sins enormous.

Yet should Swift endow the schools
For his lunatics and fools,
With a rood or two of land,
I allow the pile may stand.
You perhaps will ask me, why so?
40   But it is with this proviso,
Since the House is like to last,
Let a royal grant be passed,
That the club have right to dwell
Each within his proper cell;
With a passage left to creep in,
And a hole above for peeping.

Let them, when they once get in
Sell the nation for a pin;
While they sit a-picking straws
50   Let them rave of making laws;
While they never hold their tongue,
Let them dabble in their dung;
Let them form a grand committee,
How to plague and starve the city;
Let them stare and storm and frown,
When they see a clergy-gown.
Let them, 'ere they crack a louse,
Call for the orders of the House;
Let them with their gosling quills,
60   Scribble senseless heads of bills;
We may, while they strain their throats,
Wipe our arses with their votes.

Let Sir Tom, that rampant ass,
Stuff his guts with flax and grass;
But before the priest he fleeces
Tear the bible all to pieces.
At the parsons, Tom, halloo boy,
Worthy offspring of a shoe-boy,
Footman, traitor, vile seducer,
70   Perjured rebel, bribed accuser;
Lay the paltry privilege aside,
Sprung from papists and a regicide;

Fall a-working like a mole,
Raise the dirt about your hole.

Come, assist me, muse obedient,
Let us try some new expedient;
Shift the scene for half an hour,
Time and place are in thy power.
Thither, gentle muse, conduct me,
I shall ask, and thou instruct me.

See, the muse unbars the gate;
Hark, the monkeys, how they prate!

All ye gods, who rule the soul;
Styx, through hell whose waters roll!
Let me be allowed to tell
What I heard in yonder hell.

Near the door an entrance gapes,
Crowded round with antic shapes;
Poverty, and Grief, and Care,
Causeless Joy, and true Despair;
Discord periwigged with snakes,
See the dreadful strides she takes.

By this odious crew beset,
I began to rage and fret,
And resolved to break their pates,
Ere we entered at the gates;
Had not Clio in the nick,
Whispered me, 'Let down your stick';
'What,' said I, 'is this the madhouse?'
'These,' she answered, 'are but shadows,
Phantoms, bodiless and vain,
Empty visions of the brain.'

In the porch Briareus stands,
Shows a bribe in all his hands:
Briareus the secretary,
But we mortals call him Carey.
When the rogues their country fleece,
They may hope for pence apiece.

Clio, who had been so wise
110 To put on a fool's disguise,
To bespeak some approbation,
And be thought a near relation;
When she saw three hundred brutes,
All involved in wild disputes;
Roaring till their lungs were spent,
'Privilege of parliament',
Now a new misfortune feels,
Dreading to be laid by the heels.
Never durst a muse before
120 Enter that infernal door;
Clio stifled with the smell,
Into spleen and vapours fell;
By the Stygian steams that flew,
From the dire infectious crew.
Not the stench of Lake Avernus,
Could have more offended her nose;
Had she flown but o'er the top,
She would feel her pinions drop,
And by exhalations dire,
130 Though a goddess, must expire.
In a fright she crept away,
Bravely I resolved to stay.

When I saw the keeper frown,
Tipping him with half a crown;
'Now,' said I, 'we are alone,
Name your heroes, one by one.

'Who is that hell-featured bawler,
Is it Satan? No, 'tis Waller.
In what figure can a bard dress
140 Jack, the grandson of Sir Hardress?
Honest keeper, drive him further,
In his looks are hell and murther;
See the scowling visage drop,
Just as when he's murdered Throp.

'Keeper, show me where to fix
On the puppy pair of Dicks;
By their lantern jaws and leathern,
You might swear they both are brethren:
Dick Fitz-Baker, Dick the player,
150 Old acquaintance, are you there?
Dear companions hug and kiss,
Toast old Glorious in your piss.
Tie them, keeper, in a tether,
Let them stare and stink together;
Both are apt to be unruly,
Lash them daily, lash them duly,
Though 'tis hopeless to reclaim them,
Scorpion rods perhaps may tame them.

'Keeper, yon old dotard smoke,
160 Sweetly snoring in his cloak.
Who is he? 'Tis humdrum Wynne,
Half encompassed by his kin:
There observe the tribe of Bingham,
For he never fails to bring 'em;
While he sleeps the whole debate,
They submissive round him wait;
Yet would gladly see the hunks
In his grave, and search his trunks.
See they gently twitch his coat,
170 Just to yawn, and give his vote;
Always firm in his vocation,
For the court against the nation.

'Those are Allens, Jack and Bob,
First in every wicked job,
Son and brother to a queer,
Brainsick brute, they call a peer.
We must give them better quarter,
For their ancestor trod mortar;
And at Howth to boast his fame,
180 On a chimney cut his name.

'There sit Clements, Dilkes, and Harrison,
How they swagger from their garrison.
Such a triplet could you tell
Where to find on this side hell?
Harrison, and Dilkes, and Clements,
Souse them in their own excrements.
Every mischief in their hearts,
If they fail 'tis want of parts.

'Bless us, Morgan! Art thou there, man?
190   Bless mine eyes! Art thou the chairman?
Chairman to yon damned committee!
Yet I look on thee with pity.
Dreadful sight! What, learned Morgan,
Metamorphosed to a gorgon!
For thy horrid looks, I own,
Half convert me to a stone.
Hast thou been so long at school,
Now to turn a factious tool!
Alma Mater was thy mother,
200   Every young divine thy brother.
Thou a disobedient varlet,
Treat thy mother like a harlot!
Thou, ungrateful to thy teachers,
Who are all grown reverend preachers!
Morgan! Would it not surprise one?
Turn thy nourishment to poison!
When you walk among your books,
They reproach you with their looks;
Bind them fast, or from the shelves
210   They'll come down to right themselves:
Homer, Plutarch, Virgil, Flaccus,
All in arms prepare to back us:
Soon repent, or put to slaughter
Every Greek and Roman author.
While you in your faction's phrase
Send the clergy all to graze;
And to make your project pass,
Leave them not a blade of grass.

'How I want thee, humorous Hogart!
220 Thou I hear, a pleasant rogue art;
Were but you and I acquainted,
Every monster should be painted;
You should try your graving tools
On this odious group of fools;
Draw the beasts as I describe 'em,
Form their features, while I gibe them;
Draw them like, for I assure you,
You will need no caricatura;
Draw them so that we may trace
230 All the soul in every face.
Keeper, I must now retire,
You have done what I desire:
But I feel my spirits spent,
With the noise, the sight, the scent.'

 'Pray be patient, you shall find
Half the best are still behind:
You have hardly seen a score,
I can show two hundred more.'
'Keeper, I have seen enough,'
240 Taking then a pinch of snuff;
I concluded, looking round 'em,
May their god, the devil confound 'em.

Notes

The following abbreviations are used in the notes:

Corr   *The Correspondence of Jonathan Swift*, ed. H. Williams, 5 vols. (1963–5)

Ehrenpreis   Irvin Ehrenpreis, *Swift: The Man, His Works, and the Age*, 3 vols. (1962–83)

JTS   *Journal to Stella*, ed. H. Williams, 2 vols. (1948)

OED   *Oxford English Dictionary*

Poems   *The Poems of Jonathan Swift*, ed. H. Williams, 3 vols. (1958)

Prose Works   *The Prose Works of Jonathan Swift*, ed. H. Davis et al., 14 vols. (1939–68)

VERSES WROTE IN A LADY'S IVORY TABLE-BOOK

The exact date of composition is not known; dates between 1698 and 1706 were given in early editions, with the former the more likely. First published in the *Miscellanies* of 1711 and reprinted in Faulkner's 1735 collection, which provides the basis for the text here.

A table-book was generally no more than a notebook, but with the addition of 'ivory' it seems to come close to the meaning recorded in *OED* from the nineteenth century, 'an ornamental book for a drawing-room table'. 'Far an el breath' (l. 10) is a crude attempt to say 'to cure bad breath'. At l. 19 the meaning is 'with the aid of a rag and some spit'.

The poem is an exercise in Swift's favourite vein of misapplied cliché. Pope may have remembered its collection of bills and billets-doux, cosmetics and compliments, when he explored the world of Belinda in *The Rape of the Lock*.

THE HUMBLE PETITION OF FRANCES HARRIS

Written *c.* 1701 and first published in a clandestine manner in 1709; later collected in the 1711 *Miscellanies* and in Faulkner's 1735 edition, the basis of the text here. There is no proper title in early editions and the one used here has been abstracted from the heading. This heading parodies the form of petitions to those in authority.

'Lady Betty' in l. 1 is Lady Elizabeth Germain (1680–1769), a lifelong friend of Swift. Her father, the second Earl of Berkeley, was one of the Lord Justices of Ireland; Swift served as his chaplain at the beginning of the century. The many corruptions of language in Mrs Harris's effusion include some distorted names, notably 'Dromedary' (l. 28) for the Earl of Drogheda, a minor politician who became caretaker Lord Justice in early 1701 'Cunning-man' (l. 48) refers to a fortune-teller; to 'cast a nativity' (l. 53) was to make a prediction with the use of a horoscope.

The best discussion of the technique of this poem will be found in Ehrenpreis, II, 32–3. The garrulity of Mrs Harris is conveyed in the over-long lines, possibly based on Tudor 'fourteeners' (though they often run to sixteen syllables in this case), and in her racy language, which employs dialect, vulgarisms and proverbs (esp. ll. 38–45).

THE DESCRIPTION OF A SALAMANDER

First published in the *Miscellanies* of 1711, and reprinted in the Faulkner edition of 1735, the basis of the text here. Probably written *c.* 1705. Ehrenpreis, II, 162–5 is the best guide.

John, Baron Cutts (1661–1707) had earned a high reputation for bravery at the Siege of Namur in 1695; as well as acquiring the nickname 'the salamander' for his resistance under fire, he was celebrated by Isaac Watts as 'the hardy soldier'. It is not altogether clear why Swift hated him so much. Line 19 refers to the French general, the Vicomte de Turenne, and the Dutch admiral, Tromp. The women in l. 62 were courtesans of the time.

Swift draws on Pliny's *Natural History* for his account of the lizard-like amphibian (ll. 29–36, 47–56). However, he is interested in the mythical attributes of the salamander rather more than its literal qualities.

BAUCIS AND PHILEMON

First published in 1709; the original date of composition is not known, but the poem was revised around 1708 at the behest of Joseph Addison. It is said that Addison encouraged Swift to 'blot out four score [lines], add four score, and alter four score'. The original draft indeed differs quite considerably from the published version. The text here is based on Faulkner's 1735 printing.

The source of the story, freely adapted, is Ovid's *Metamorphoses*, Book VIII. Swift is aware of Dryden's translation (1700), and also of an earlier adaptation, Matthew Prior's *The Ladle* (1704). The opening here is particularly close to Prior's first lines. The fullest account of the poem will be found in Eric Rothstein, 'Jonathan Swift as Jupiter: "Baucis and Philemon"', *The Augustan Milieu* (1970), pp. 205–24.

There is a strong folk, or folksy, element in the writing: ll. 94–6 list ballads regularly printed in chap-book form and widely familiar to the common people. At l. 40 the candles 'burning blue' were an omen of death, thought to indicate the presence of the Devil or of ghosts. At l. 143 the full sense is 'go down', i.e. prove good enough. Some of the language, for example 'fetch a walk' (l. 154), is deliberately archaic or provincial.

A DESCRIPTION OF THE MORNING

First published in no. 9 of the new periodical *The Tatler* (30 April 1709), run by Richard Steele, who was still a good friend of Swift at this stage. It subsequently appeared in the major collections of Swift's work, becoming one of his best-known poems, and the text found in Faulkner's 1735 edition has been used as the basis for the version printed here. It helped to introduce a new vein of poetry generally called the 'town eclogue', that is a work which applies the convential attributes of pastoral poetry (a remote, idyllic, balmy landscape, peopled by innocent primitives) to the modern urban scene, with its squalor, commerce, rush and tension. In addition Swift borrows the classical sense of a description as a carefully organized review of a given subject, itemizing the main features in order to produce a coherent view of the whole. This aspect is treated in Roger Savage, 'Swift's Fallen City', in *The World of Jonathan Swift*, ed. B. Vickers (1968), pp. 171–94. For a general account, see Ehrenpreis, II, 248–50.

There may be a recollection of Jaques's speech in *As You Like It*, II.vii.146–8, in the last line. Otherwise the main poetic device is the introduction of 'low' elements such as 'Brickdust' (tanned by heavy outdoor labour) or 'duns' (bailiffs collecting debts) within the highminded framework of a classical description.

THE VIRTUES OF SID HAMET THE MAGICIAN'S ROD

Published in October 1710, a few days after Swift had completed the poem, which he started on 26 September (*JTS* I, 30). Reprinted several times before its appearance in Faulkner's 1735 edition, the basis of the text here.

Swift gave Stella news of its reception on 14 October: 'My lampoon is cried up to the skies; but nobody suspects me for it, except Sir Andrew Fountaine: at least they say nothing of it to me. Did I not tell you of a great man who received me very coldly? That's he; but say nothing; 'twas only a little revenge.' Stella's response can be gauged from an entry on 14 December: 'What you say of *Sid Hamet* is well enough; that an enemy should like it, and a friend not; and that telling the author would make both change their opinions' (*JTS* I, 59, 127–9).

The 'great man' was Sidney Godolphin (1645–1712), who had received Swift 'with a great deal of coldness' on 8 September. Just one month earlier Godolphin had been dismissed by Queen Anne from the post of Lord Treasurer. For his revenge Swift adapted a periodical essay published on 28 August and 8 September in a short-lived paper called *The Visions of Sir Heister Ryley*. This had attacked the fashionable religious prophets under the guise of a French charlatan named James Aymar, the possessor of a magic wand. See Pat Rogers, 'The Origins of Swift's Poem on "Sid Hamet"', *Modern Philology*, LXXIX (1982), 304–8.

The overall aim of the poem is to portray Godolphin as a trickster, in the manner of Aymar, who had now lost his supposed powers with his removal from the office of Lord Treasurer. Now that he is exposed, there will be retribution in store ('rod in piss', l. 86, is a coarse variant of 'rod in pickle', proverbial for punishment in reserve).

Swift's poem works through a succession of puns and allusions, based on the rod in Scripture and mythology. These include the rod of Moses and Aaron; the witch's broomstick; the dowsing rod; the wand of Mercury (l. 35); the sceptre of Achilles in *Iliad*, Book I; the golden bough of myth; and the staff of the Lord Treasurer, which Godolphin had been forced to break on his dismissal. There is also a flurry of proverbs at ll. 81–6. Sid Hamet's name is taken from that of the supposed narrator of *Don Quixote*, as well as alluding to Godolphin's Christian name. At l. 76 the reference is to a shop selling 'toys' (fancy gifts) in Fleet Street, kept by Mather, who was described in *The Tatler* as 'the first that brought toys into fashion, and baubles to perfection'.

At l. 83, Swift refers to Godolphin's fondness for horse-racing by mentioning a riding whip. Newmarket was just achieving pre-eminence as a racecourse and Godolphin was a regular attender. It was Godolphin's son, the second earl, who a few years later imported the Godolphin Barb, one of the three Arabian stallions who are the progenitors of all thoroughbred British bloodstock to the present day.

A DESCRIPTION OF A CITY SHOWER

Written within a matter of days before it appeared in no. 238 of *The Tatler* (run by Swift's friend at the time, Richard Steele), on 17 October 1710. It is a longer and more complex successor to 'A Description of the Morning'. The main technique involves applying the pastoral properties of a classical *descriptio* to a squalid urban scene. There are specific echoes of Virgil's *Georgics* and *Aeneid*, principally felt through the medium of Dryden's translation (1697). In turn the poem was the source of many ideas in John Gay's *Trivia* (1716).

The final verse paragraph has a definite location on the northern edge of the city of London. The 'torrents' emerge from waterways feeding into the notorious Fleet Ditch, a major artery of the city and its principal sewer. 'Daggled' at l. 33 means 'bespattered'; to 'cheapen goods' (l. 34) is to bargain or haggle; 'kennels' (l. 53) were open gutters running down the middle of the streets. The deliberately inflated mock-heroic language includes words such as 'devoted' (l. 32), which retains its etymological sense of 'doomed'. The last three lines embody a conscious thrust at the popular triplet rhymes, which Swift regarded as belonging to 'the licentious manner of modern poets' (note to Faulkner's edition of 1735).

AN EXCELLENT NEW SONG

Composed at the instigation of Robert Harley on 6 December 1711 and published as a broadsheet the same day (*JTS* II, 430). On the previous day Swift had told Stella that Lord Nottingham, 'a famous Tory and speech-maker, is gone over to the Whig side; they [say] . . . "It is Dismal (so they call him from his looks) will save England at last."' The text here is based on the first edition.

Daniel Finch, second Earl of Nottingham (1647–1730) had long been prominent in English politics. He led the High Church campaign to ban 'occasional conformity', that is the practice by which dissenters satisfied the legal requirements for public office. At the juncture when Swift wrote this poem, Nottingham had just agreed to trade his support of Whig foreign policy, involving opposition to the Tory peace terms, in exchange for Whig co-operation on the issue of occasional conformity. Nottingham's real speech was delivered to Parliament a day later, on 7 December.

The poem satirizes Nottingham personally: his gloomy appearance, his garrulity, his tergiversations and shifting alliances. But it is directed more widely against the desire among the Whigs to prolong the War of the Spanish Succession, their refusal to make a 'peace without Spain' (l. 12), that is without ousting French influence in Spain, and their support for high taxation on landowners.

Swift constructs his refrain around a pun: 'not in game', meaning out of office. Cf. also the submerged pun in 'altered my note' (l. 39), an old expression for changing one's mind; and the play on Nottingham's family name Finch at l. 8. At line 4 *vi et armis* is a legal tag meaning 'with physical violence'. At l. 6 Swift refers to the diplomatic mission made by his friend Matthew Prior, poet and man of affairs, who had gone to Paris in secret to negotiate the terms of a treaty to end the long-lasting War of the Spanish Succession. 'Hoppy' (l. 9) was probably a minor politician, Edward Hopkins, later an Irish placeman. Line 15 refers to the palatial mansion of the Duke and Duchess of Marlborough recently erected at Blenheim, always a sore point with the Tories.

CADENUS AND VANESSA

Swift's longest poem was first published in 1726, three years after the death of Vanessa. Its composition cannot be dated with certainty, but the traditional ascription, 1712–13, has most to commend it. The text here is based on Faulkner's 1735 edition, with the addition of ll. 562–9 from an earlier printing.

Swift probably met Esther Vanhomrigh (c. 1688–1723) in London around 1708. When he moved to Dublin in 1714, she followed him. Many highly coloured stories have been told of their subsequent stormy relations, none of which can be firmly authenticated. Swift invented the name Vanessa by taking syllables from Esther's first and last names. Cadenus is simply an anagram of Decanus, or Dean. The fullest account is Sybil Le Brocquy, *Cadenus* (1962).

The setting of the poem is the Court of Love, presided over by Venus. Swift transforms the traditional topos by investing it with modern courtroom protocol and jargon, for example ll. 72, 107 (legal authorities), 121–2, 847–9.

Much of the extensive commentary on the poem is absorbed by the question of autobiographical reference and reliability. It is clear that some 'historical' details are presented in what might be called straight terms, but there seem also to be many departures from the true record of the friendship between Swift and Vanessa. Some are joking, some possibly proceed from a kind of wish-fulfilment. Many allusions to Ovid and Virgil have been discovered, some more convincing than others; there are also echoes of *The Rape of the Lock*, which first appeared in its shorter form in 1712.

HORACE, EPISTLE VII, BOOK I: IMITATED AND ADDRESSED TO THE EARL OF OXFORD

After his installation as Dean of St Patrick's, Swift returned to England in September 1713. This imitation was quickly composed after he reached London, and was published on 23 October. The basis for this text is the reprint in Faulkner's edition of 1735.

Swift follows only the second half of the poem by Horace, which is addressed to *his* noble patron, Maecenas. Pope later wrote an imitation 'in the manner of Dr Swift' (1738), which corresponds to the first half of the original. Detailed parallels with the text of Horace are indicated in footnotes added to early editions; however, Swift strays farther from his 'control' text than Pope generally does, whilst the events appear to be largely imaginary.

Robert Harley (1661–1724), created Earl of Oxford and made Lord Treasurer in 1711, was the head of a divided Tory government between 1710 and 1714. He was subsequently disgraced and sent to the Tower of London, but escaped impeachment. Swift was particularly close to him whilst Harley held office. The two men joined with Pope (another ally of Harley), Arbuthnot, Gay and Parnell to form the Scriblerus Club, a convivial group whose literary hoaxes and parodies underlay many great works of Augustan satire, including *Gulliver's Travels* and *The Dunciad*. Wharton (l. 36) is Thomas, Earl Wharton (1648-1715), a Whig magnate and former Lord Lieutenant of Ireland, who was cordially hated by Swift. Erasmus Lewis (1670-1754), mentioned at l. 16, was a civil servant who enjoyed a long friendship with Swift; it was he who introduced Swift to Harley. At l. 111 the reference is to Isaiah Parvisol, Swift's steward.

THE AUTHOR UPON HIMSELF

This poem, written probably around July 1714, first appeared in print in Faulkner's 1735 edition. When the volume of poems in Faulkner's set was reconstructed just prior to publication, this was one of the poems which was quite heavily censored. The text here is based on the version which was used in the published volume, but blanks have been filled in by reference to the uncancelled state of the poem.

Swift attacks several of his strongest adversaries, and sets out the reasons which, he believed, lay behind his failure to be appointed to a bishopric. The 'dangerous treatise' (l. 48) was *A Tale of a Tub*, which was widely regarded as irreligious and almost certainly did work against Swift's prospects for advancement in the Church. Those opposed to his preferment are mentioned in the first two lines: an influential figure at court, the Duchess of Somerset; the rigidly orthodox Archbishop of York, John Sharp; and Queen Anne herself. 'St John' at l. 34 was glossed in the first edition 'Then Secretary of State, now Lord Bolingbroke, the most universal genius in Europe'. In 1714 Henry St John, Viscount Bolingbroke (1678-1751) had been a leading figure in the Tory ministry and a boon companion of Swift. In 1735 he was a major focus of the opposition to Walpole, as well as a philosopher and writer whose theories had made some contribution to Pope's *Essay on Man*. 'Finch' (l. 37) is the Earl of Nottingham: see note to 'An Excellent New Song', p. 200. At l. 18, Child's and Truby's were glossed 'A coffee-house and tavern near St Paul's much frequented by the clergy'. At ll. 53-4 Swift drags up an old scandal, the murder of Thomas Thynne, husband of Elizabeth Percy (later Duchess of Somerset), by a rival for her favours, Count Philipp von Königsmark. The story is revived to assist in Swift's campaign against the Duchess, one of his most inveterate enemies.

The last line originally carried a footnote, 'The author retired to a friend in Berkshire, ten weeks before the Queen died; and never saw the ministry after.' In fact Swift spent the summer of 1714 near Wantage, before the death of the Queen on 1 August and the collapse of the ministry. The rest of his life involved his 'retirement' to Ireland; acquaintance with Bolingbroke was renewed only in 1726, when Swift was arranging for the publication of *Gulliver's Travels*. Ehrenpreis, II, 728-63, provides the best background to the poem.

HORACE, LIB. 2, SAT. 6

Swift was working on this poem at the time of Queen Anne's death on 1 August 1714 (*Corr* II, 99, 114). However, the item did not appear in print until the Pope-Swift *Miscellanies* of 1728, after which it appeared in Faulkner's edition of 1735. Matters became more complex in 1738, when a London edition appeared, with an interpolation between ll. 8 and 9 of the present text, and a further 89 lines added at the end. It is generally agreed that the latter section is wholly by Pope. Opinions differ on the former: Harold Williams attributed it to Swift (*Poems* I, 197–8), but the evidence is not conclusive. I have excluded the lines from the text printed here, which is based on Faulkner, since Pope is at least as likely to be the author.

The imitation follows quite closely Horace's famous satire *Hoc erat in votis*, a favourite work in eighteenth-century England. Early editions placed the Latin text opposite the imitation, as was done by Pope in his versions of Horace. Line 29 refers to the insignia of the Order of the Garter and its Scottish equivalent, the Thistle. At l. 74 the reference is Thomas Parnell (1679–1718), an Irish poet and member of the Scriblerus Club, whose poems were posthumously edited by Pope in 1722.

MARY THE COOK-MAID'S LETTER TO DR SHERIDAN

This was one of a number of high-spirited exchanges in verse between Swift and his friend Sheridan around October 1718. It was first published in 1732, but the text here is based on the reprint in Faulkner's 1735 edition.

Thomas Sheridan (1687–1738) was a clergyman who kept a school in Dublin. He often entertained Swift and Stella at his homes in Dublin and in Co. Cavan (see p. 208). Swift had a high regard for his learning and literary taste, and enjoyed the poetic contests in which he and Sheridan took part. Sheridan's son Thomas became an actor and writer on rhetoric, and wrote a biography of Swift in 1784; and his grandson was Richard Brinsley Sheridan, the dramatist.

The vigorous language attributed to the cook makes use of 'Irish' inflections ('parsonable', l. 10) and proverbs which Swift was already collecting for his anthology *Polite Conversation* (ll. 7, 9, 19, 23, 32). The *devil/civil* rhyme (ll. 23–4) was a favourite with Swift and indicates the pronunciation of the former word.

STELLA'S BIRTHDAY [1719]

The first of a group of about a dozen poems addressed to Swift's friend, and according to some stories clandestine wife, Hester Johnson (1681–1728). Six of the poems are specifically linked to Stella's birthday, which was 13 March. Not all the poems are included in this selection.

Swift had met Hester, whom he rechristened Stella, whilst serving Sir William Temple at Moor Park, Surrey, from the year 1689. Around 1701 she moved to Ireland with her companion Rebecca Dingley, and together they were the recipients of the famous *Journal to Stella* (1710–13). Stella lived in Dublin until her death. The best treatment is Sybil Le Brocquy, *Swift's Most Valuable Friend* (1964).

There is some licence in Swift's handling of dates. He first met Stella when she was about eight (not sixteen, as l. 5); and in 1719 she was thirty-eight, not thirty-four. The poem was not published until 1728.

THE PROGRESS OF BEAUTY

First published in 1728; written *c.* 1719–20. One of three 'progress' poems written around this time. The word did not then imply improvement, but rather, the simple course of things: hence its use in negative contexts, such as the progress of error, or *The Rake's Progress*.

Swift takes familiar amatory conventions and systematically debases them. The normally idealizing parallel of a live woman with the moon goddess Diana is brought down to earth, literally, by persistent reference to bodily decay, mostly attributable to venereal disease (see especially ll. 109–16). Mercury was the main specific used in the case of syphilis. The allusions to the sky are filled out when the poet introduces Partridge and Gadbury, two astrologers, and John Flamsteed, the first Astronomer Royal. Another linguistic strand reveals Swift's long-lasting debt to *The Rape of the Lock*: ll. 61–4 echo a prominent theme in Pope's poem.

TO STELLA, WHO COLLECTED AND TRANSCRIBED HIS POEMS

First published in the Pope–Swift *Miscellanies* of 1728 and reprinted in Faulkner's edition of 1735 (the basis for the present text), where it was stated to have been 'written in the year 1720'. It may date from a few years later. Prior to its publication Swift had asked Thomas Sheridan to make a copy of the poem and send it to Twickenham, where Swift was then staying with Pope on his final visit to England (*Corr* III, 221–2).

As usual in the poems to Stella, there are few verbal complexities or recondite allusions. Line 50 refers to the infamous publisher Edmund Curll (1683–1747), a raker-up of the unconsidered trifles of Swift as of other distinguished writers; Maevius (l. 71) is the type of a feeble poetaster, drawn from Virgil; crambo (l. 74) is a contest to find ingenious rhymes; whilst ll. 121–6 refer to the resentment felt by Ajax when the armour of Achilles was bestowed on Odysseus and not on him.

UPON THE SOUTH SEA PROJECT

Swift sent the manuscript of this poem, later popular and much reprinted, to his friend Charles Ford on 15 December 1720, and it was published in the following January. Most early editions carry the title 'The Bubble', but the title used here, which was adopted in Faulkner's edition of 1735, may be more authentic. On 28 February 1721 the poet Matthew Prior wrote to Swift, 'I am tired with politics and lost in the South Sea: the roaring of the waves and the madness of the people were justly put together' [in Isaiah 5:30] (*Corr* II, 378). This clearly picks up on the imagery in Swift's poem.

The South Sea Bubble had burst in the late summer of 1720. Ostensibly set up to trade in the Pacific, the South Sea Company was in effect a device for capitalizing the national debt in order to turn government borrowing into a tradable stock. The price of shares rose to implausible heights in the first half of 1720, and at midsummer stock nominally valued at £100 was standing at £1000. The fall was sudden and dramatic, and beggared not only investors but also the holders of government annuities. For a full account see John Carswell, *The South Sea Bubble* (1960).

Swift employs a number of sustained conceits, most of them literalizing phrases like 'his credit sunk' (l. 55) or 'dipped over head and ears in debt' (l. 24). There are several proverbial usages (for example ll. 24, 115, 185). Even more prominent are the biblical echoes: of Exodus at ll. 37, 213–16; of Psalm 107 at ll. 157–60; and of the Magnificat and the identical psalm at ll. 217–20, which form a compressed litany. The Latin quotation at the end is from Virgil, *Aeneid*, I, 118–19: 'And here and there above the waves were seen/Arms, pictures, precious goods, and floating men' (tr. Dryden). The fullest description of the poem's rhetorical workings will be found in Pat Rogers, *Yearbook of English Studies*, XVIII (1988), 41–50.

STELLA'S BIRTHDAY [1721]

The original publication in the *Miscellanies* of 1728 gave the date 1720, but a transcript which Stella herself made recorded the year as 1720/21, indicating March 1721 by modern usage. Stella was forty that month.

The text is based chiefly on Faulkner (1735), but with ll. 35–6 added from the transcript.

THE PART OF A SUMMER

The poem refers to a period Swift spent at a country house in Co. Westmeath, forty miles from Dublin, between June and October 1721. The exact date of composition is not known, but the poem first appeared in print in Dublin some time before October 1722, when Swift mentions a reply which had been published in Dublin (*Corr* II, 426). The item was reprinted in Faulkner's 1735 edition, which is the basis for the text here.

Swift's host was George Rochfort (*c.* 1682–1730), an Irish MP. George's wife, formerly Lady Betty Moore, was present, along with his father, a retired judge, Rev. Daniel Jackson, Thomas Sheridan and Patrick Delany. According to one story, Swift, tired of the rural delights and the company, abruptly left without warning to return to Dublin.

The poem, which in early editions bore the title *The Journal*, is the subject of an extensive analysis by Aubrey Williams in *Literary Theory and Structure*, ed. F. Brady et al. (1973), pp. 227–43. This reading sees the poem as embodying 'Swift's dispute with Lucretius'. Most of the references are domestic and intelligible. Lines 95–104 move out to the Great Northern War involving Czar Peter the Great and Charles XII of Sweden, as reported by the Tory newsletter of Richard Pue. 'Nim' is George's brother John Rochfort, known as Nimrod because of his passion for hunting.

THE PROGRESS OF MARRIAGE

Composed according to Swift's autograph, now in the Forster collection, in January 1722, but not published until 1765. The text here is based on the autograph. The poem is founded on real events involving John Pratt, who had died on 5 December 1721. Pratt was a former provost of Trinity College, Dublin, and then Dean of Down. He married the daughter of the Earl of Abercorn about a year before his death. She was many years his junior. Swift had known him since their undergraduate days; he had generally got along well with this worldly and prosperous clergyman, though he found Pratt's social ambitions absurd.

Lines 108–20 refer to the myth of the river god Achelous, who possessed a horn broken by Hercules; the story is told in Ovid's *Metamorphoses*, Book IX. The verbal play surrounds the idea of a cuckold's horn. The poem refers to the new popularity of Bath as a health resort and leisure centre; James II's queen, Mary of Modena, had visited the Cross Bath, close to the Roman Baths, and had subsequently conceived (see ll. 137–8). '*Aetatis suae*' (l. 1) means 'at the age of'. Betty (l. 41) is the generic name for a maidservant: cf. *The Rape of the Lock*, I, 148.

A SATIRICAL ELEGY ON THE DEATH OF A LATE FAMOUS GENERAL

Swift had been bitterly hostile towards the Duke of Marlborough for more than a decade when the great Duke died on 16 June 1722. The poem was probably written soon afterwards, in response to the spate of laudatory obituary notices in the press, not to mention a lavish state funeral. However, publication was delayed until 1764.

Marlborough, who was seventy-two, had suffered from senile dementia for several years. It is a grisly coincidence that Swift was to end his days in the same condition, and Samuel Johnson would link the fates of the two men: 'From Marlborough's eyes the streams of dotage flow,/And Swift expires a driveller and a show' (*The Vanity of Human Wishes*, ll. 317–18). Swift sustains the old Tory line that Marlborough had prosecuted a bloody and unnecessary war (that of the Spanish Succession), prolonging it to line the pockets of contractors and moneylenders, and causing a heavy toll in human lives. Swift also attacks Marlborough's notorious miserliness, his enjoyment of Blenheim Palace as a gift from the nation, and the cloudy nature of his origins and early years. This hostile view is strongly affected by party considerations, and a much more favourable view of Marlborough is possible.

UPON THE HORRID PLOT DISCOVERED BY HARLEQUIN THE BISHOP OF ROCHESTER'S FRENCH DOG

First published by Faulkner in 1735; written in late 1722 or early 1723. The poem concerns the arrest of Swift's friend Francis Atterbury, Bishop of Rochester, in August 1722 on suspicion of complicity in a Jacobite plot. In May 1723, Atterbury (1662–1732) was tried before his peers in the House of Lords in a show trial designed to expose the threat of Jacobite invasion; he had certainly been in contact with the Pretender's court and was probably guilty in a technical sense. He was exiled for the remainder of his life. Pope, who was called at the trial as a character witness, maintained links with Atterbury by correspondence in after-years.

Harlequin was the name of a small spotted dog belonging to Atterbury's wife; it was through references to the dog that a primitive code in Atterbury's intercepted correspondence could be broken. 'Discovered' thus means revealed or exposed. Several other suspected Jacobites (Plunket, Skean, Neyno and Mason) are alluded to in the text. For the background see Edward Rosenheim jr, 'Swift and the Atterbury Case', in *The Augustan Milieu* (1970), pp. 174–204.

The most prominent verbal device is the inclusion of a string of proverbial usages involving dogs (ll. 15, 28, 30, 32, 36, 40, 58, 60, 72). These combine to suggest the meaning 'the real dirty dogs in this affair are Walpole and others who incriminated Atterbury'. For a full analysis of this technique, see Pat Rogers, *Eighteenth Century Encounters* (1985), pp. 29–40. Many of these expressions were also used satirically in Swift's *Polite Conversation*.

STELLA'S BIRTHDAY [1723]

When reissued in Faulkner's 1735 edition, following initial publication in the 1728 *Miscellanies*, it was stated that the poem was written 'about the year 1722'. This almost certainly indicates 1722/3, i.e. 1723 by modern usage. The text here is based on Faulkner.

Most of the names refer to friends, such as Charles Ford (see below), and domestic servants, including the housekeeper Mrs Brent. 'Rebecca' (l. 60) is Stella's companion Rebecca Dingley (c. 1665–1743). 'Eusden' (l. 30) is the hapless Poet Laureate Laurence Eusden (1688–1730), a frequent butt of the Scriblerus wits. Line 22 contains the Latinized form of a proverb better known in English, 'Once a year Apollo laughs'.

TO CHARLES FORD, ESQ. ON HIS BIRTHDAY

First published in 1762, from what seems to be a later version; Swift's original fair copy survives and is dated 31 January 1723. This may be a way of relating the poem to Ford's forty-first birthday on that date, and the draft could have been completed later since ll. 27–50 seem to refer to the Atterbury affair, which came to a head in the summer of 1723 (see note to 'Upon the Horrid Plot . . .'). The text is based on the fair copy, which was sent to Ford at at unknown date.

Charles Ford (1682–1741) was one of Swift's most trusted friends and most regular correspondents. He was Irish by birth and had an estate at Woodpark, Co. Meath, where both Swift and Stella stayed, but he spent most of his life in London. Swift uses the opportunity to urge Ford to return to Ireland, where Swift's feelings of exile were growing more acute. The poem is stuffed with Opposition rhetoric, a mode of language nakedly hostile to Walpole and the entire Hanoverian regime. 'Vice' and 'virtue' (ll. 41–2) are code words for the ministry and the Opposition. Lines 51–6 should be compared with a passage in Swift's letter to John Gay on 8 January 1723 (Corr II, 442): 'I was three years reconciling myself to the scene and business to which fortune hath condemned me, and stupidity was what I had recourse to. Besides, what a figure should I make in London while my friends are in poverty, exile, distress, or imprisonment, and my enemies with rods of iron.' Line 80 refers to clergymen friends of Swift who exchanged light verses with him.

PETHOX THE GREAT

First published in 1728; according to Faulkner's edition, written in 1723.

The poem is a kind of extended riddle. Its title is an anagram of 'the pox', i.e. syphilis. There is a good deal of play with the standard expressions connected with venereal disease, as at l. 20, which hints at expressions such as 'French disease', and l. 21, alluding to the ancient name of Naples, hence 'Neapolitan disease'. There is a hidden pun in l. 37: the bird of Pallas was the owl, emblem of Athens and of Minerva or Pallas; bubo is Latin for owl, but also the name for a swelling in the groin – a typical piece of submerged wit on Swift's part. Similarly, at l. 86, Hermes is Mercury, and this suggests the most widely used cure for syphilis. 'Pontific' (l. 94) is defined by OED as pontiff-like, but there seems to be a pun on the bridge of the nose, where the disease would make its depredations.

TO STELLA. WRITTEN ON THE DAY OF HER BIRTH

First published in 1765 by Deane Swift; this text is based on Faulkner's edition of the same year. Composed in March 1724, at a time when Swift was suffering from a complication of maladies, reported in his letters (*Corr* III, 2–9). As the poem indicates, Stella's own health had begun its long course of decline.

PROMETHEUS

First published in a Dublin broadside version around November 1724, and reprinted in London soon afterwards. The text here is based on Faulkner's 1735 collection.

One of several poems written at the height of the crisis surrounding the Irish coinage. Swift had used the opportunity to step forward as the 'Drapier', uniting broad sections of the public against the Irish establishment, which imposed the economic and political policy of the English government. William Wood (1671–1730) was an ironmaster and projector (i.e. speculative entrepreneur) from the English Midlands, who had been granted a patent to produce new halfpenny coins for Ireland. It was believed that he had gained the patent through bribery of officials close to Walpole, and that his coins were both inferior in quality and unneeded. Swift attacks him not so much for his personal defects as for his symbolic role as an English carpet-bagger and his symptomatic place in the world ruled by Walpole.

Much of the language of the poem eddies around metal: the iron on which Wood had built his fortune, the brass used in the coinage and the 'brazen' qualities of Walpole (one of whose nicknames was Robert Brass). The rhetoric suggests that the new Prometheus, Wood, deserves a different punishment from that of his forebear (ll. 53–6): only hanging is good enough (l. 72). But ultimately we must read 'Walpole' for 'Wood'.

STELLA'S BIRTHDAY [1725]

First included in the 1728 *Miscellanies* and then taken into Faulkner's 1735 edition, the basis for this text. Both sources give the date 1724, which means 1725 in modern usage. However, the ages fit the year 1724, a fact which may be explained by the eighteenth-century habit of celebrating, for example, a fiftieth birthday on the date of entering the fiftieth year.

The opening couplet uses a proverbial expression, still common when Jane Austen exploits it in *Emma*, but now rarely heard. It is one of the shop-soiled conversational gambits Swift introduces into *Polite Conversation* (*Prose Works* IV, 145). In the last line Swift alludes to his own increasing problems with deafness, which caused him great concern in 1725 (*Corr* III, 60).

A RECEIPT TO RESTORE STELLA'S YOUTH

Another of the poems addressed to Stella: see p. 203. Written in the spring or summer of 1725 and first published in Faulkner's edition of 1735.

Both Swift and Stella spent the summer months at Quilca, a house in Co. Cavan belonging to their friend Thomas Sheridan. Swift wrote some amusing squibs in verse on this 'country house in no very good repair' (see for example the following poem). Line 18 refers to the myth of the sorceress Medea and her magic cauldron, probably drawn most directly from Ovid, *Metamorphoses*, Book VII.

Swift's concern for Stella's health was rewarded by an apparent improvement (see *Corr* III, 89: 'Mrs Johnson is much better and walks three or four Irish miles a day over bogs and mountain'). But the decline in her condition was irreparable and she lived only another three years.

TO QUILCA

For the facts mentioned in the subtitle, see note to the preceding poem. The poem was first published in Faulkner's edition of 1735, and the text here is based on that version.

Swift wrote in a letter of 14 August 1725 that he had been 'for four months in a little obscure Irish cabin about forty miles from Dublin' (*Corr* III, 84). Swift's letters and a short prose squib he wrote about the stay at Quilca make complaints of rain, cold, a smoking chimney and collapsing furniture. 'Sheelah' in l. 7 is probably the lady's maid, 'awkward and clumsy', whom Swift describes in his satire.(*Prose Works* V, 219–21).

A PASTORAL DIALOGUE BETWEEN RICHMOND LODGE AND MARBLE HILL

Written shortly after the death of George I on 12 June 1727. It was widely expected that the new monarch, George II, would bring in sweeping changes which would lead to the dismissal of Walpole as prime minister. Among those hoping for this transformation were the mistress of the new king, Mrs Howard, and Swift himself, then on his final visit to England. In the event things went on as before and these high hopes were soon dashed.

Richmond Lodge, now demolished, stood in what has become Kew Gardens. It had been occupied by the new king and queen when they were Prince and Princess of Wales. Marble Hill stands on the left bank of the Thames some two miles away, and was close to Pope's home at Twickenham, where Swift had been staying. It was built for Mrs Howard by Roger Morris (1724–9); Pope helped to lay out the gardens. The house has now been fully restored. There are several accounts, including Marie P. G. Draper and W. A. Eden, *Marble Hill House and its Owners* (1970). Line 91 refers to the menagerie at Marble Hill and l. 93 to the fanciful 'natural' gardens at Richmond.

Henrietta Howard (*c.* 1687–1767) became a lady-in-waiting to Princess, later Queen, Caroline, and then mistress to the Prince, later George II. Through the succession of her first husband, she was Countess of Suffolk from 1731. A friend of Pope, Gay and Swift, she subsequently belonged to the Opposition to the court. Line 47 refers to Pope's closest woman friend, Martha Blount (1690–1763). 'Ancient Mirmont' (l. 64) was a French refugee who had been given a pension by the court; 'Moody' (l. 96) was a gardener. At l. 28 Swift alludes to the land tax, levied for many years at four shillings in the pound, and an object of dislike to the propertied classes.

THE FURNITURE OF A WOMAN'S MIND

Possibly not published until it appeared in Faulkner's 1735 edition, the basis of the text here. Stated by Faulkner to have been 'written in the year 1727'. There are some connections with *The Journal of a Modern Lady* (see p. 210).

'*Robustious*' (l. 48) is italicized to mark it off as a piece of fashionable jargon, duly utilized in *Polite Conversation* (*Prose Works* IV, 167). Johnson's *Dictionary* states that this was 'now only used in low language'. In l. 59 the reference is to Sarah Harding, widow of the Dublin printer John Harding; both husband and wife were involved in some risky publications on Swift's behalf.

HOLYHEAD. SEPTEMBER 25, 1727

Swift's original manuscript version survives in a small pocketbook preserved in the Forster collection (Victoria & Albert Museum); this is the basis of the text here. Not published until 1882.

Three poems accompany a short journal in prose (*Prose Works* V, 201–8), all relating to Swift's final return to Ireland in September 1727. He spent five days at Holyhead waiting for the weather to change so that he could take the ferry to Dublin. His low spirits were caused partly by a realization that he would probably never leave Ireland again (in fact, he did not), and partly by fears that he might be too late to see the mortally stricken Stella alive. In the event she survived until the following January (see ll. 23–4).

THE JOURNAL OF A MODERN LADY

First published in 1729, not long after it seems to have been written, while Swift was staying at Market Hill, near Armagh. His hostess, Lady Acheson, is certainly the lady whom Swift addresses at the start. According to one view she is also the sustained object of the poem's satire, but this is far from self-evident, although Swift did later criticize Lady Acheson as 'an absolute Dublin rake' (*Corr* IV, 92). Some commentators have seen the poem as evolving from *The Furniture of a Woman's Mind* (?1727), but the link is somewhat tenuous. As in so many of his poems Swift calls up reminiscences of *The Rape of the Lock*. There is an explicit allusion at l. 39 (compare *Rape*, I, 15–20); but many other echoes can be traced, for example at ll. 52, 74, 132–3 and 188–95. The card-games recall a scene in Swift's own *Polite Conversation*: see *Prose Works* IV, 115–16.

THE GRAND QUESTION DEBATED

A little-known but highly characteristic poem, it was written while Swift was staying with Lady Acheson at Market Hill, either on 2 September 1728 or 2 September 1729, depending on which of Swift's manuscript endorsements one chooses to trust; in my view 1729 is the likelier. First published early in 1732. A holograph copy survives, with many differences from the early printed texts. In this selection the text is based on Faulkner's edition of 1735, which is a cleaned-up version but one which Swift may have cleaned up himself. Swift refers to the publication of the work, to which he gives three confusingly different titles (apart from the one used here), in some letters he wrote during 1732: see *Corr* IV, 26–7, 31, 82–3. An elaborate story about copyright, involving the Lord Lieutenant of Ireland, does not leave it clear how far Swift was complicit with the alleged piracies in 1732.

In the subtitle, 'Bawn' means a cattlefold, standing near the house; the modern settlement of Hamilton's Bawn lies three miles north of Market Hill in Co. Armagh. In the preface, the 'certain very great person' is the Lord Lieutenant, Lord Carteret, with whom Swift maintained surprisingly good relations considering the fact that he was the English overlord appointed by Walpole's government. 'Rums' (l. 28) refers to poor country clergymen. A note in early editions identifies 'Darby and Wood' (l. 48) as 'two of Sir Arthur's managers'. Swift has considerable fun with dialect and demotic forms, such as 'purtest' (l. 57) for 'protest'. At l. 159 the Captain distorts the names of Ovid, Plutarch and Homer. 'Down in the hyps' (l. 178) refers to the 'hyps', or hypochondria, a fashionable term for depression.

A LIBEL ON THE REVEREND DR DELANY AND HIS EXCELLENCY JOHN, LORD CARTERET

Published early in 1730. On 6 February Swift warned Pope to expect 'eighteen lines relating to yourself, in the most whimsical paper that ever was writ, and which was never intended for the public' (*Corr* III, 370). The poem cannot have been written long before, since it is the second of two replies to a poem by Swift's friend Delany, which had itself appeared only a few weeks before. Delany's work is reprinted in *Poems* II, 471–4.

Patrick Delany (*c.* 1685–1768) is best remembered today as the husband of the literary lady Mary Delany. In his lifetime he was known as a prominent Irish churchman, and as the friend and later (1752) biographer of Swift. His poem contained an appeal to the Lord Lieutenant for further preferment; Swift had half-seriously suggested that Delany's straitened circumstances followed from the expenses he had incurred at Delville, his country house just north of Dublin. John Carteret, later Earl Granville, was Lord Lieutenant of Ireland from 1724 to 1730.

Swift considers the fate of several literary figures who had been well-known to him – Congreve, Steele, Gay, Addison and Pope – emphasizing the lack of support they received from such patrons as Lord Halifax ('Montagu', l. 35). He draws a contrast with the facile panegyrics of Ambrose 'Namby Pamby' Philips (l. 144). Swift thought this his best poem (*Corr* IV, 83).

DEATH AND DAPHNE

First published by Faulkner in 1735, the source of the text here. The poem is there stated to have been 'written in the year 1730'. It concerns Anne Acheson (d. 1737), the estranged wife of a baronet, whom Swift liked to 'rally' for her faults and also on account of her excessive thinness. For the circumstances in which the poem came to be written, see Lord Orrery's *Remarks* on Swift (1752), pp. 86–7.

The technique of the poem is to describe the underworld, that is, the realm of Pluto (l. 2), in terms of the fashionable life of an eighteenth-century lady. Swift alleged that Lady Acheson's poor health was 'got by cards, and laziness, and keeping ill hours' (*Corr* IV, 375), though she was probably consumptive. 'Aconite' (l. 42) is a comically abstruse word for poison; 'Warwick Lane' (l. 46) refers to the headquarters of the Royal College of Physicians ('the Faculty'). As so often, the biggest single influence on the idiom of the poem is *The Rape of the Lock*.

AN EXCELLENT NEW BALLAD

First published as a broadside in Dublin (1730), and clearly written in that year. Faulkner's edition of 1735 is the basis of the text here.

Swift described the background of the poem in a letter dated 28 August 1730:

'There is a fellow here from England, one Sawbridge, he was last term indicted for rape. The plea he intended was his being drunk when he forced the young woman; but he bought her off. He is a Dean and I name him ... because I am confident you will hear of his being a Bishop; for in short, he is just the counterpart of Chartres, that continual favourite of ministers' (*Corr* III, 405). The 'fellow' was Thomas Sawbridge (d. 1773), who had been appointed from England to be Dean of Ferns in 1728. His trial had taken place in June 1730, when he was acquitted after producing an alibi.

The method is to align Sawbridge with well-known dissolute figures from history (John Atherton, Bishop of Waterford, who had been hanged in 1640 for unnatural offences, at l. 47) and from contemporary life (Francis Chartres at l. 49). Chartres or Charteris (1675–1732) ran the gamut of roguery as a gambler, usurer, brothel habitué and possibly pimp, and corrupt politician. Earlier in 1730 he had been convicted of rape but allowed to go free, thanks to his friends in high places – such at least was the view of Pope, Hogarth, Fielding and other moral censors of the age. Once more Chartres and Sawbridge stand in for Walpole in Swift's picture of English exploitation. The inner meaning of the last stanza is that England should be convicted of raping Ireland.

'*Jure ecclesiae*' (l. 38) means 'by the law of the church'; a '*commendam*' (l. 39) is an extra perquisite in office, such as a previous benefice which could be retained along with the deanery.

THE LADY'S DRESSING ROOM

First published around July 1732; there was a flurry of issues in both London and Dublin. Later collected in Faulkner's 1735 edition, which serves as the basis of the text here. Faulkner gives the date of composition as 1730. There were a number of hostile pamphlets in reply, one of them the work of Lady Mary Wortley Montagu. Perhaps the most spirited is Miss W—'s 'The Gentleman's Study', reprinted in R. Lonsdale (ed.), *Eighteenth-Century Women Poets* (1989), pp. 130–34.

A large literature has grown up around the so-called excremental or scatological poems, of which this is the first. I. Ehrenpreis in *The Personality of Jonathan Swift* (1958), pp. 29–49, provides a useful context for the discussion of obscenity; see also J. N. Lee, *Swift and Scatological Satire* (1971).

The main technique is that of surrounding with squalor and repulsive detail the high-flown expectations of poetry and mythology. Lines 19–42 grotesquely transpose Belinda's toilet in *The Rape of the Lock*, whilst l. 98 travesties *Paradise Lost*, II, 891. At ll. 83–8 there is a brutally misplaced allusion to the myth of Pandora's box; and ll. 133–4 anticipate Hogarth's *Strolling Actresses Dressing in a Barn* (1738). The word 'jump' (l. 126) means 'agree'; the proverb 'great wits jump' is found in *Polite Conversation* (*Prose Works* IV, 159), as well as in Sterne's *Tristram Shandy*, III, ix.

A BEAUTIFUL YOUNG NYMPH GOING TO BED

The second in the group of four obscene or scatological poems; for a general commentary on this group, see above. Published with two others in the group (the two following poems in this selection) in a small volume around December 1734. Perhaps written around 1731.

The opening lines take us into a genre scene located around Covent Garden in London, then a notorious haunt of prostitutes. Bridewell (l. 41) was the house of (vigorous) correction for vagrant women, which stood on the edge of the Fleet Ditch. Much of the unpleasant detail in ll. 30-39 relates to the after-effects of venereal disease; 'plumpers' (l. 17) were padding to fill out cheeks hollowed by the loss of teeth from the same cause. 'Shock' (l. 64) was the generic name for a lap-dog: compare Pope, *The Rape of the Lock*, I, 115. Corinna is, indeed, a low-life travesty of Belinda at her toilet.

STREPHON AND CHLOE

First published along with the preceding poem and the next poem (see note to 'A Beautiful Young Nymph . . .') in 1734. Faulkner's edition of 1735 gives the date of composition as 1731, which is the only indication we have. For the collective 'scatological' poems, see note to 'The Lady's Dressing Room'.

Some links have been discerned with a pamphlet by Swift called *A Letter to a Young Lady, on her Marriage*: see *Prose Works* IX, 83-94. One feature of the idiom is the reliance on proverbs (e.g. ll. 16, 148, 204, 306), as well as stock expressions from the prayer-book and other familiar sources. Among the many allusions to classical and English poetry, those to Ovid's *Metamorphoses* and to *The Rape of the Lock* are the most numerous. One way of reading the work, suggested by Nora Crow Jaffe, is as a parodic epithalamium, or marriage song. '*Flammeum*' (l. 61) refers to a flame-coloured veil worn by Roman brides. Line 115 is a quotation from a song in *The Beggar's Opera*.

CASSINUS AND PETER

The remaining poem in the 'scatological' group, published with the two preceding items in 1734. The text here is based on its reprinted form in Faulkner's 1735 edition. There is no means of deciding the date of composition, though an allusion in ll. 1-4 to *The Dunciad*, II, 347-50, indicates that it was no earlier than 1728.

The opening lines suggest a fabliau and Swift may have remembered *The Reeve's Tale* of Chaucer. At l. 21, a 'jordan' is a chamber-pot. Lines 79-88 form a compressed parody of a favourite text for Swift, the sixth book of the *Aeneid*.

TO MR GAY

First published in Faulkner's edition of 1735. This volume was reset at a late stage apparently because some of the poems gave offence, and in the process the verses 'To Mr Gay' were extensively revised. In this selection the text is that of the uncancelled state of the 1735 edition, which surfaced in 1967.

Composition can be fixed around 1731. Swift wrote on 13 March to congratulate Gay in the mistaken belief that he had been appointed to manage the affairs of the Duke and Duchess of Queensberry. He quoted ll. 57-64 and stated that the poem was designed to prove 'that poets are the fittest persons to be treasurers and managers to great persons, from their virtue and contempt of money &c.' In a joint letter with the Duchess, Gay wrote back on 18 July to deny the story, telling Swift that the Duke had taken over the management of his own affairs 'upon the discharge of an unjust steward' (*Corr* IV, 444, 447). The Duke (1698-1778), referred to as Douglas at l. 13, and Duchess (c. 1701–77) were leading figures in the Opposition; she had been dismissed from court for supporting Gay's banned sequel to *The Beggar's Opera*, entitled *Polly*, in 1729.

The 'female friend' in l. 3 is Henrietta Howard, Countess of Suffolk, a neighbour of Pope at Twickenham and the closest friend at court of the Scriblerian group. Lines 7–12 refer to what had been considered an insulting offer to Gay in 1727, that is a post in the service of the two-year-old Princess Louisa. Lines 63–76 sustain the characterization of Walpole ('Bob') as the unjust steward by reference to his sumptuous mansion in Norfolk. There are many interesting parallels to the description of Timon's villa in Pope's 'Epistle to Burlington' (also 1731). The theme of the false steward is best understood with the help of Howard Erskine-Hill, *The Social Milieu of Alexander Pope* (1975), where the present poem is discussed on pp. 253–5. Erskine-Hill provides a full account of Peter Walter and explains the allusion at l. 101. Walter (c. 1664–1746) was a land-agent, attorney, marriage broker, accountant and much else in the financial sphere; he might be seen as an eighteenth-century management consultant. Pope and Fielding also attacked him, as a kind of lesser Walpole. The 'juncture' mentioned at l. 147 is the death of George I and succession of George II in 1727. Underlying the entire poem, though it is explicitly cited only at l. 73, is the parable of the unjust steward in Luke 16:1–13.

VERSES ON THE DEATH OF DR SWIFT, D.S.P.D.

What is now seen as the authentic version of Swift's most famous poem was published by Faulkner in 1739. There are three variant forms of the work. A version of 202 lines entitled *The Life and Genuine Character of Dr Swift* was published in London in 1733. Next, a version running to 381 lines appeared in 1739, edited by Alexander Pope and William King. This has many points of correspondence with the authentic text; it is not clear whether Pope rewrote the poem or had a different manuscript by Swift to hand. Lastly, a conflation of the two 1739 texts was published by 1756, and for long remained the standard form of the poem. The text in this selection is based on the 1739 Faulkner version of 484 lines, eked out by contemporary manuscripts which fill in a number of blanks.

It is virtually certain that the poem was written in 1731; Swift wrote to Gay, on 1 December in that year, that he had written 'near five hundred lines on a pleasant subject, only to tell what my friends and enemies will say on me after I am dead' (*Corr* III, 506). At this stage he seems to have envisaged deferring publication until after his real death (*Corr* IV, 152). There is not much sign of later revision.

Swift and Pope referred to the work as the lines 'upon Rochefoucauld's maxim'; the epigraph is taken from la Rochefoucauld's *Réflexions: ou Sentences et Maximes morales* (1665), no. xcix. D.S.P.D. stands for Dean of St Patrick's Cathedral, Dublin. There is a very wide range of contemporary allusion, mostly dealing with Swift's fortunes under Queen Anne (ll. 375 ff.); the affair of Wood's coinage, in which Swift had intervened as the Drapier (ll. 411 ff.); and more recent Irish episodes. There are also many biblical echoes, whilst ll. 319–38 in particular are close in feel and wording to Pope's *Epistle to Dr Arbuthnot* (written 1731–4, published 1735), ll. 334–59.

There is a large body of commentary on the poem. Most often critics have debated the nature of the concluding apologia (ll. 307–488). This section has been variously seen as exhibiting naïve self-satisfaction, subtle irony, stern Christian moralism and mischievous distortion of the record. The best summary of the differing approaches will be found in A. H. Scouten and R. D. Hume, 'Pope and Swift: Text and Interpretation of Swift's Verses on His Death', in *Philological Quarterly*, LII (1973), 205–31.

ON THE DAY OF JUDGEMENT

A bibliographical thicket surrounds this short poem. At least five early versions survive, and three printings in 1773–4 (the first appearance in print) differ in several respects. For details see Williams's discussion in *Poems*, II, 576–8. The most interesting early location is a letter in French from Lord Chesterfield to Voltaire, dated 27 August 1752, transmitting a copy of the poem. It is possible that Swift left two or three different versions: see S. L. Gulick, in *Papers of the Bibliographical Society of America*, LXXI (1977), 333–6. The date of composition is not known; 1731 is the most popular guess, but this is no more than conjecture.

The last word of the poem – 'bit' – means 'fooled', that is, the victim of Jove's cosmic joke.

ON POETRY: A RHAPSODY

This poem was first published in early 1734 (or possibly 31 December 1733). The likeliest date for composition in my view is 1732. Six supplementary passages, omitted from all early editions, have later been found in manuscript. In this selection these passages are incorporated into the text at ll. 165–6, 189–92, 197–204, 217–18, 427–62 and 469–70. For an argument that the lines may have been deliberately omitted by Swift, and that it does artistic violence to the text to admit them, see *Poems*, II, 639. In my judgement there is ample reason for their original exclusion in their plain-spoken and often libellous commentary on politics.

A rhapsody in the early eighteenth century implied a loose and somewhat improvisatory effusion, rather than the impassioned outburst which it became in Romantic art, especially in the field of music. Lines 353–60 draw their basic idea from Addison's paper in *The Tatler* no. 229, 26 September 1710. There is a very wide range of allusion to contemporary figures, both literary and political. Most can be identified from biographical reference books, but it should be noted that D'Anvers (l. 192) is the author of the opposition journal *The Craftsman*; Sir Bob (l. 193) is the prime minister, Robert Walpole; Iulus (l. 483) is Frederick, Prince of Wales, around whom the Opposition would shortly gather; Atlas (l. 498) is Walpole again; Lewis (l. 527) is Louis XIV; and Thomas Woolston (l. 548) is a freethinking clergyman of the type Swift most distrusted. In the wake of *The Dunciad*, Swift pays off a number of old scores, but most of the poetasters named had offended against Pope or Gay rather than against Swift himself, ensconced in Dublin. Swift's main reason for hating Grub Street would have lain in the activities of nefarious publishers who had pirated his books and attributed inauthentic productions to him, but for some reason the principal offender, Edmund Curll, is allowed to escape on this occasion.

At l. 296 Swift employs the ancient name of London, derived from the British tribe of Trinobantes, who inhabited the region where Roman London was built.

At l. 333, 'pericranies' is used for 'brains', from the Latin '*pericranium*'. '*Caetera desiderantur*' (l. 549) means 'the rest is missing'.

TO A LADY

First published in London (1734), and subsequently reprinted there. It was originally included in Faulkner's 1735 edition of the *Works*, but at a late stage this volume was reconstructed and the poem omitted. It may well be that the need to reorder the volume was occasioned by the inflammatory contents of this poem. The text here is based on the uncancelled state of Faulkner's volume, that is, the poem as it was originally intended to appear. No certainty has been reached on the date of composition. Harold Williams suggested that the first half was written around 1728–30 and the second half in 1732–3 (*Poems* II, 629). What we do know is that the poem was carried over to England in the autumn of 1733. The various agents in this process, including the poet Mary Barber and the bookseller Lawton Gilliver, found themselves in trouble with the authorities, and enough had been done to deter Faulkner from including it in the *Works* as planned.

The lady is Swift's friend Lady Acheson of Market Hill (see p. 211). Line 183 refers to Caleb D'Anvers, editor of the best-known Opposition journal, *The Craftsman*, although, as a footnote indicated, the *Craftsman* papers were 'supposed to be written by the Lord Bolingbroke and Mr Pulteney'. William Pulteney (1684–1764) helped to lead the Opposition against Walpole throughout the 1730s, but was outmanœuvred by the Pelhams in the subsequent era and became a politically impotent Earl of Bath, devoting himself to literary pursuits. At l. 149 Swift claims Jupiter as the planet presiding over his birth in order to explain his simulated joviality in the face of wrongdoing.

A CHARACTER, PANEGYRIC, AND DESCRIPTION OF THE LEGION CLUB

First published in England in 1736, but the text here is based on a more reliable version Faulkner issued in 1762. Up till then the inflammatory contents had deterred Irish publication. Swift described it to his friend Sheridan as 'a very masterly poem' on 24 April 1736; in subsequent weeks he pretended unconvincingly that the work had been falsely 'imputed' to him, and that others were making their own additions (*Corr* IV, 480, 492, 501). There is no reason to doubt that the poem as printed here is altogether the work of Swift.

The Legion Club of the title is the Irish House of Commons, which in March 1736 made itself unpopular with the clergy, not least Swift, by voting to remit certain tithes. This was seen as self-interest as the members were strongly representative of the landowning class. A splendid new Parliament House designed by Edward Lovett Pearce (the 'prudent architect' of l. 5) was under construction across College Green from Trinity College. An estimate in the early 1730s had put the cost at £40,000, but eventually the 'most beautiful, magnificent building' cost more than twice as much. See Thomas and Valerie Pakenham, *Dublin: A Traveller's Companion* (1988), pp. 182–96, for further details.

Swift chose the title remembering Luke 8:30: 'And Jesus asked him, What is thy name? And he said, Legion: because many devils were entered into him.' He may also have recalled Milton's use of 'demoniac legion' (*Apology against Smectymnuus*). The range of allusion is wide. The proverb cited at l. 8 – 'Near the church'

– continues 'and far from God'. As well as scriptural and proverbial phrases concerning the Devil, there is a sustained parody of the sixth book of Virgil's *Aeneid* at ll. 81–108 especially: see P. J. Schakel, 'Virgil and the Dean', *Studies in Philology*, LXX (1973), 427–38. The thirteen individual members attacked include men with whom Swift had tangled previously, but some, such as Mark Antony Morgan (l. 189), had been on reasonable terms with him. At ll. 219–30 Swift invokes William Hogarth, whom he did not know personally but who had come to prominence recently with his *Harlot's Progress* (1731) and *Rake's Progress* (1735); he had also used a scene based on *Gulliver's Travels* for a caricature satirizing Walpole's ministry, which would have endeared him to Swift. A 'jack-pudding' (l. 18) was a jester working with a street mountebank. 'Clio' at l. 97 is the muse of history.

Index of Titles

Author upon Himself, The   47

Baucis and Philemon   7
Beautiful Young Nymph Going to Bed, A   133

Cadenus and Vanessa   19
Cassinus and Peter   143
Character, Panegyric, and Description of the Legion Club, A   189

Death and Daphne   123
Description of a City Shower, A   15
Description of a Salamander, The   5
Description of the Morning, A   12

Excellent New Ballad, An   126
Excellent New Song, An   17

Furniture of a Woman's Mind, The   101

Grand Question Debated, The   112

Holyhead. September 25, 1727   103
Horace, Epistle VII, Book I: Imitated and Addressed to the Earl of Oxford   43
Horace, Lib. 2, Sat. 6   49
Humble Petition of Frances Harris, The   2

Journal of a Modern Lady, The   104

Lady's Dressing Room, The   129
Libel on the Reverend Dr Delany and His Excellency John, Lord Carteret, A   118

Mary the Cook-maid's Letter to Dr Sheridan   52

On Poetry: a Rhapsody   166
On the Day of Judgement   165

Part of a Summer, The   70
Pastoral Dialogue between Richmond Lodge and Marble Hill, A   97
Pethox the Great   87
Progress of Beauty, The   54

Progress of Marriage, The   74
Prometheus   91

Receipt to Restore Stella's Youth, A   95

Satirical Elegy on the Death of a Late Famous General, A   78
Stella's Birthday [1719]   54
Stella's Birthday [1721]   69
Stella's Birthday [1723]   82
Stella's Birthday [1725]   93
Strephon and Chloe   135

To a Lady   181
To Charles Ford, Esq. on His Birthday   84
To Mr Gay   147
To Quilca   97
To Stella, Who Collected and Transcribed His Poems   58
To Stella, Written on the Day of Her Birth   90

Upon the Horrid Plot Discovered by Harlequin the Bishop of Rochester's French
   Dog   79
Upon the South Sea Project   62

Verses on the Death of Dr Swift, D.S.P.D.   152
Verses Wrote in a Lady's Ivory Table-book   1
Virtues of Sid Hamet the Magician's Rod, The   13

Index of First Lines

Aetatis suae fifty-two   74
After venting all my spite   181
All human race would fain be wits   166
All travellers at first incline   69
An orator dismal of Nottinghamshire   17
A set of phrases learned by rote   101
As I stroll the city, oft I   189
As mastiff dogs in modern phrase are   5
As Rochefoucauld his maxims drew   152
As, when a beauteous nymph decays   93
As when a lofty pile is raised   58
As, when the squire and tinker, Wood   91

By an old red-pate, murdering hag pursued   47

Careful observers may foretell the hour   15
Come, be content, since out it must   84
Corinna, pride of Drury Lane   133

Death went upon a solemn day   123
Deluded mortals, whom the great   118

Five hours (and who can do it less in?)   129
From Venus born, thy beauty shows   87

Harley, the nation's great support   43
His Grace! impossible! what, dead!   78
How could you, Gay, disgrace the muses' train   147

I asked a Whig the other night   79
In ancient times, as story tells   7
In spite of Pope, in spite of Gay   97
I often wished that I had clear   49
It was a most unfriendly part   104

Let me my properties explain   97
Lo here I sit at Holyhead   103

Now hardly here and there a hackney coach   12

Of Chloe all the town has rung   135

Our brethren of England, who love us so dear   126

Peruse my leaves through every part   1

Resolved my annual verse to pay   82

Stella this day is thirty-four   54

Thalia, tell in sober lays   70
That I went to warm myself in Lady Betty's chamber, because I was cold   2
The rod was but a harmless wand   13
The Scottish hinds, too poor to house   95
The shepherds and the nymphs were seen   19
Thus spoke to my Lady, the knight full of care   112
Tormented with incessant pains   90
Two college sophs of Cambridge growth   143

Well; if ever I saw such another man since my mother bound my head   52
When first Diana leaves her bed   54
With a whirl of thought oppressed   165

Ye wise philosophers! explain   62